CHOSEN SOLDIERS

D1280508

PB
SCO

CHOSEN SOLDIERS

R. H. SCOTT

NORTH BAY PUBLIC LIBRARY
MAR 0 2016
DISCARDED

HARPER

VOYAGER
IMPULSE

An Imprint of HarperCollinsPublishers

This is a work of fiction. Names, characters, places, and incidents are products of the author's imagination or are used fictitiously and are not to be construed as real. Any resemblance to actual events, locales, organizations, or persons, living or dead, is entirely coincidental.

CHOSEN SOLDIERS. Copyright © 2016 by R. H. Scott. All rights reserved under International and Pan-American Copyright Conventions. By payment of the required fees, you have been granted the nonexclusive, nontransferable right to access and read the text of this e-book on screen. No part of this text may be reproduced, transmitted, downloaded, decompiled, reverse-engineered, or stored in or introduced into any information storage and retrieval system, in any form or by any means, whether electronic or mechanical, now known or hereafter invented, without the express written permission of HarperCollins e-books.

EPub Edition FEBRUARY 2016 ISBN: 9780062457202

Print Edition ISBN: 9780062457219

10 9 8 7 6 5 4 3 2 1

To the ones I love.
Mama Bear, Bird, Banana, Dwardle, Weezy, and Nana.

CHAPTER 1

Sloan stopped in her tracks, her standard-issue boots squeaking against the linoleum floor. The brief pause nearly caused a collision with the cadet behind her. She could feel a weight in the room, the claustrophobic air tightening around her. She ran her thumbs down the edges of her food tray and swallowed the metallic taste of despair that rolled over her tongue as she locked eyes on the empty space at Table 27 . . . the space where Tandy had eaten all of her meals for the past fourteen years. She snatched a breath with pursed lips, glancing up to the digital clock that hung above the food-processing row. It was indeed 7 a.m.

Sloan had never arrived before Tandy.

A nudge in her back from the tray of another student spurred her forward. She walked to Table 27, eyes narrowing and shoulders back. Everyone except

Tandy was there. She tried to catch Jared's eye, but he was intently speaking to Paul. *Looking away because you know I want to talk?*

Everything was normal—the smells of their breakfast plates, the bustling of early-risen students, the droning chatter of peers. Everything was normal except every day before this Tandy had filled the space on the bench opposite Paul.

And this morning she didn't.

Sloan found her own habitual spot, opposite Jared. She stared at him, feeling uncomfortable at the table, never having sat here without her best friend beside her. "When did it happen?" Her voice was quiet and tense.

Jared took a sip of his coffee, finally looking at her and holding her stare with his brilliant blue eyes. "Dawn."

Jared, as captain, had seniority over her. He would have been *there*, informed ahead of time to escort Tandy to the Order. She studied his cobalt eyes, dark blue with gilded flecks. Were these eyes the last Tandy had seen? Sloan's mind flashed with an image of Tandy, but all she could imagine was a white sheet over her slender ebony body, a clinically sterile room—a beautiful girl in a crematorium. Sloan's throat tightened. *Keep it together, Radcliffe.*

"Is that why you were out of bed so early this morning?" Her tone silenced the rest of the group—she knew how protective the table could be of their captain. She didn't care if they disapproved; he might be their captain, but she was their lieutenant.

He nodded slowly. It was clear he had anticipated her anger, and for some reason that made her angrier, wondering how he could keep something like this from her. She took a deep breath and looked around the group, but as each one of them met her stare, they quickly looked away. She wanted to hear her friends speak, to know what they knew, the extent to which they cared—but they wouldn't meet her gaze. She had trained them to fear her volatile nature. The way Jared had taught her.

"Has anyone seen Kenneth?" she pressed. No one answered. Mika moved food around aimlessly while Paul sipped his juice—all their gazes were cast downward.

Kenneth, a lieutenant on Table 93, was Tandy's boyfriend. They had not yet gotten been engaged but everyone had been certain of their betrothal. Now they would never match, never marry. Tandy would . . . never.

Erica finally spoke. "I saw him at the Infirmary before I got here. He's taking the day off." She sounded so *fine*. Sloan stared at the girl, causing Erica to look away, flicking her long hair over her shoulder and leaning into Devon, her own partner. Intimidated, but not as subordinate as Sloan would have her be. *No wonder they love Jared and still hate you. . .*

Sloan cleared her throat before speaking, pushing

the pathetic thought out of her mind. "Tie your hair back." She watched as Jared leaned past Paul to see if Erica had actually been sitting there with her hair loose. Sloan locked in on Jared.

How could he have let this happen? How could he have kept this from her?

"You could have told me."

"No, Sloan, I couldn't have. You know as well as I that these things are never announced beforehand, to avoid any spectacles . . . anything that might interrupt the scheduled proceeding."

You mean to avoid "this," she thought, hearing the rebuke in his voice.

"You should have told me. She was my . . ." Sloan began, but let her voice trail off. Tandy was her best friend. Her only friend. The only one who had ever appreciated her leadership and guidance. She grabbed for her coffee. It tasted stale and too hot. Jared leaned towards her, lowering his voice.

"To what end? To see you devastated before it happened, or worse, to see you try to intervene?"

"I could have done *something*. I could have put in an appeal. This was over that exam, wasn't it?"

"You couldn't have done anything. She failed twice. We all know the rules."

That's not the point.

The rest of the group shifted away from them, making idle conversation to disguise the fact that they were actually listening. She needed to stay calm.

She failed at that.

"*Dammit*, Jared . . ." She hated him for letting her find out this way, for feeling so ambushed. She should have known before the rest of them.

He should have told me.

Jared shot a glance over the surrounding tables. "Can we just talk about this later?"

Sloan followed his eyes over the large hall, filled with meticulously lined tables. Tables that held families of cadets, lieutenants and captains. That's what your table was. Assigned to you in childhood for the entirety of your training, those on your table were your brothers, sisters, partners and trainers. They were responsible for your life, and you theirs, but the minute someone became a liability they were culled from the family.

If the enemy ever came for the person sitting next to you, well, you were expected to throw your own body in the way. You were expected to defend them to the death . . . but if the *Order* demanded their head, you were expected to step back and let it happen.

Because the Order knows best . . . Cull the few to save the many.

Jared was right in wanting to hold off. With their senior rankings they had authority over most of the students around them, on 27 and the surrounding tables. It was important for them to set a standard of appropriate conduct. This was neither the time nor the place. She shot him a knowing look. *We are finishing this later, though.*

"Forget about it. It's nothing we can't work out in

training." She zeroed in on the group. "Paul, how is your jiujitsu coming along?"

He shrugged, answering her between bites of food. "It's okay."

"Good. I will be testing that in training today."

Paul's head dropped. "Can I just train in group for the next week and then by Monday—"

Jared cut him off. "You can fight Sloan or you can fight me—the choice is yours—but don't speak back to her again, Paul."

Paul sighed. "Sorry. I'll take Sloan."

Jared reached across the table, resting his hand on top of hers. She mouthed a silent *thank you* to him and he winked at her nonchalantly.

It was no secret that there was a fraction of students within the Academy who excelled beyond the rest. From the day they arrived they had all worked to achieve their military ranks. From seven to fifteen, you were a basic cadet, but after that, meritocracy took over. Those awarded rank had proven their superior ability, academically and martially. And while they all wore the same navy blue uniform—cargo trousers and fitted shirts—their rankings were defined by gold sleeve stripes, distinguishing captains like Jared from lieutenants like Sloan and from second lieutenants and cadets, like the rest of 27.

Sloan's hand twitched under Jared's. She loved him with her entire heart, but his touch, which usually rendered her so calm, seemed ineffective today. She could feel anger and frustration swelling through her muscles.

She was ready to fight.

Paul lunged carelessly. Sloan grabbed his wrist, twisted inward and pulled him past her. He buckled at the waist and she held his arm up behind him. He collapsed, tapping the floor for a break. She released him and stepped back.

"I feel like you haven't made any progress. How are you going to survive the war when you can't get through a simple spar?"

Paul rolled over, squeezing his arm. They trained all their lives to prepare for the war on the mainland; the one thing they knew for certain was that if you couldn't fight in *here*, you had no chance of surviving *out there*.

"You could take it easy on him, Sloan," Mika piped up.

Sloan spun on the girl, shooting her a warning glance. "Concentrate on your own training."

Sloan was close to the others on her table but they didn't understand. They drifted through the Academy, perhaps trying harder than some, but never truly pushing themselves to keep up with Sloan and Jared. This lackluster approach to Academy life was why Tandy was gone.

Why so many of them were gone. The Order removed the weak.

"Get back to work, Mika," Jared called over, lending Sloan his authority—not that she should need it after all these years. Still, the others naturally fell in line when Jared asked.

Sloan snaked circles around Paul, letting him recover. They were in the training hall, a massive combat arena with synthetic polymer floors. In the corner was a fight simulator with three-dimensional holographic assault courses; rows of hand-to-hand weapons donned the walls; and on the periphery were viewer stands, to sit and watch fights take place.

For the sake of solidarity, most students were allowed to train in their own groups without interruption, especially if their group had a captain. At times they were mixed in with other tables by trainers, the combat experts who answered to their general, Walt Stone. She glanced over to Stone as he marched through the hall, overseeing spars and barking orders.

Jared was training Devon and Erica simultaneously, easily deflecting their assaults. As they strained for breath, he effortlessly called out orders. He was an incredible fighter and a good teacher, managing to direct complex sequences and explain intricate moves. He caught her watchful gaze and offered her a smile. She hated that even when she was this angry, she couldn't ignore that disarming smile. Just as she turned away from him he called out her name—but it was too late.

Sloan fell to her knee, resting one hand on the floor to regain her balance. Her skin felt alight; a fire was burning between her jaw and eye. Paul had punched her.

He sucker punched you. . .

She shook her head and blinked away a stinging tear. She wanted to grab her face, to rush to Jared, but acting like a victim was how you lost. Sloan was no victim. She quickly focused her thoughts, thankful that even as her gaze blurred, she managed to catch Paul's foot flying towards her—he was still attacking her.

Finally, getting the fight she had longed for.

The sensation she felt was instantaneous. It was animalistic—her basic nature springing forth. A calm reserve overcame her entire body. Any thoughts, any feelings, dissipated as her tunnel vision kicked in. A steady breath filled her with a blind commitment to one singular goal—winning.

She deflected his next kick, pivoted on her knee and jumped up. She spun around, ready, but Paul was already pinned in a headlock, being choked down. She first thought it had been Jared, rushing in to defend her, but it wasn't him. It took her a moment to recognize Elijah Daniels, the captain from Table 82. The captain she had never spoken to. Why was *he* intervening in *her* fight? *He has no right . . .* She grabbed Elijah's wrist and twisted it counterclockwise, freeing Paul.

Elijah shot her a confused look and it took all her might to not lay into him too.

Does it look like I need your help?

Defending her in front of so many students made her look weak. He knew that. They *all* knew that. He began to step in her way and she viciously shoved him back. As he stumbled away, she caught sight of his eyes. It was the first time she had noticed that his were the brightest green she had ever seen. A hunter's green, a verdant shade found in the forest, in the rivers of the woods. A shade of green that could momentarily distract her from her rage . . . but only momentarily. She tore away from him and descended on Paul.

Ignoring Paul's surrendering hands, she landed a roundhouse kick against the side of his head, flipping him onto his back. He leaped to his feet—which would have impressed her ten minutes ago—only for her to connect a series of punches to his neck and face. When he intuitively put his arms out, she grabbed his wrist, twisted it outward, curved it into his body and flipped his heavy frame over her. She held on to his wrist as he lay on his stomach, kneeling on his back, outstretching his arm high up behind him. Without hesitation, she shoved it unnaturally downward, towards the space parallel his bloodied face. The cracking of his shoulder rippled through her, startling her enough to free him.

Suddenly, Sloan was in someone's arms, being hauled away from her fight. Without thinking, she elbowed back at whoever held her, connecting with a jaw.

"*Dammit!*" a voice yelled.

It was Elijah Daniels. *Again.*

She spun around but before she could say anything to him, Jared appeared, standing in front of her. He faced off with Elijah.

"Back off, Daniels." His voice was a low commanding growl.

At his words Sloan realized the entire auditorium had gone silent, and a group of students had circled to watch her fight. General Stone stood there, amongst the students, staring at her with wide-eyed shock. She glanced over their stunned expressions, over Stone's stern face, to Paul, who was writhing on the ground. She could taste blood on her lip and remembered how she had lost her temper in the first place. Elijah was the first to leave, weaving past Jared and disappearing into the crowd.

Jared spun around and stared at her with a surprised look in his eyes. His shock subsided as he slowly regarded her injured face. He brought his hand up and gently cupped her cheek. He didn't care that they were in front of a crowd. He didn't care that they were in front of the general. Jared and Sloan had many things in common—tunnel vision amongst them. He only saw her.

She rested her hand against his, lowering it slowly. *I'm okay, I promise.*

General Stone stepped forward, gesturing to two cadets and pointing to Paul. "You two, get him to the Infirmary." The students hesitantly approached, warily watching Sloan. As soon as they reached Paul they heaved him up, ignoring his cry of pain as they backed away from her quickly. Sloan could see Paul's red hair was matted in blood, a crimson stain over his skin and shirt. She knew she had lost her temper too easily, but her face throbbed, her skin prickled uneasily . . . .

He deserved it.

Stone took another step forward. "The rest of you, hit the showers and get ready for classes."

Jared remained in front of her, shielding her from Stone's anger. "General, are *we* excused?"

"You are, Dawson," Stone said, looking straight past him to see Sloan. Jared hesitated before slowly walking away, waiting with the rest of 27. The general looked her up and down. "Save the rage for this month's Fight Night, Lieutenant."

Sloan stood up straight and nodded. "Yes, sir."

"You're excused," he said. "The *both* of you." He had obviously known Jared would be waiting for her behind his back. Without saying another word, Stone walked away from them, heading to the back of the hall where his office was. She was embarrassed for losing her temper, for turning training into an actual fight. Losing Tandy, and Paul's cowardly attack, had set her off. Embarrassed for losing control—but not apologetic.

Why should I be sorry? I am what they made me to be. I did what I was trained to do. She repeated her silent mantra as she turned to leave.

She wanted to head straight to Jared, straight for the door, but the others on 27 blocked her path.

Sloan looked at the wall Erica, Mika, Will and Devon made. Crossed arms and horrified expressions.

"What?" Sloan barked. She could feel blood pulsating from her lip and near her eye. She ran her hand over her face, wiping it away.

"You're angry that Tandy is dead so you break Paul's shoulder?" Erica accused.

Hearing the truth spoken aloud for the first time, that her best friend was dead, overwhelmed Sloan. She could feel her heart pounding, a drumming of blood pulsating through her limbs, her fingers twitching anxiously at her side. She had only ever been close to one other student who had been Dismissed—Luke Maxwell. He hadn't been on her table, but they had formed a friendship nonetheless. She could remember Luke telling her he had been requested to go before the Order. She could hear the conviction in his voice when he spoke his last words to her. *"If they kill me, don't let it kill you."*

Sloan pushed the memory away, regarding Erica with a stern expression. She narrowed her gaze on her subordinate. "Who the hell do you think you are? Standing here, waiting to question *me* about *my* choices."

She took an angry step towards the group. "What I am angry about is that the only people on 27 who haul ass are Jared and I. You guys barely make the cut. It's like you're waiting to be Dismissed."

They glared at her with defiance. Apparently hearing the truth out loud hurt them too. *Good,* Sloan thought, *maybe they'll realize how serious this is.*

Mika shook her head. "You can be such a bitch, Sloan."

I am what they made me to be.

"Do you think I care that I 'can be such a *bitch*'? *I* am pushing you; *I* am trying to keep you alive. Now, get the *hell* out of my way and think about the fact that you and Erica will be training with me for all of tomorrow's session and you better be *damn* well ready for it."

She could feel Jared reaching for her hand. He was going to calm her, going to speak on her behalf . . . but she didn't want to hear it. She jerked away from him and broke through the group. Shoving the door open, she rounded the corner quickly, immediately knocking into someone leaning against the wall.

It was Elijah Daniels. *Of course it's you again*, she thought angrily, regaining her footing. He turned and looked down at her expectantly, as though he had been waiting for her. His dark hair was messy—*barely regulation*—his wide jaw clenched, his broad shoulders pulled back tight. He was tall too, towering over her by several inches. Immediately—*oddly*—Sloan felt self-conscious, wiping at her bloodied face quickly, and then she felt self-conscious for feeling self-conscious. *Why do you care what he thinks of you?*

She crossed her arms, refraining from messing with her appearance. "What's your problem?"

He leaned over her with his imposing form. "What's *my* problem? What is *your* problem? I was trying to help you."

She shook her head at him, feeling her honey-blond hair stick against her bloodied forehead—her braid must have come loose. "I don't want your help. I don't *need* your help. You're not even on my table—you have no right intervening in my training."

He stood up straighter at her words, a look of reproach in his eyes. "I am a captain—I have every right to intervene in that hall. I take rank over you and the redhead."

He's pulling rank on me? It was one thing to hear it from General Stone, quite another to get a lecture from this guy.

"You may be captain, but so is Jared, and if he thought intervening was necessary, he would have."

Elijah huffed, a cynical expression playing over his face. "If your *boyfriend* cared about you having a beat-up face then he would have done something." The deliberate disgust in the way he referred to Jared confused her.

Do you even know Jared by more than reputation? she thought, knowing the jealous dislike so many of their peers had for her and her partner.

She shook her head at him. "Jared cares. He just doesn't leap at opportunities to make me look weak, and helpless, so *thanks* for that, *Captain*."

Sloan didn't know why, amidst her sarcasm, her voice sounded unnaturally doubtful. She *knew* Jared would have intervened—he had done it before.

She had been fifteen at the time, sparring with Joshua Bleak, a senior boy. Joshua had been faster, stronger, infinitely more capable than her. He had a renowned temper, but she hadn't known before their spar that Joshua had a darkness in him too. A sadist, he relished beating her and laughed as he dominated their spar. Before any trainers had even noticed their unsanctioned fight, Jared had intervened, but not before Joshua had broken her eye socket and three ribs.

The memory filled her mind. She had felt her ribs crushing underneath the strength of Joshua's hands. She had tried everything she knew and none of it worked. He had been relentless in his assaults and it had terrified her. She had screamed for Jared, knowing that wherever he was, he would come for her. And he had. Jared, at fifteen, had already become a champion fighter who could contend with senior boys. Which, it turned out, put a target on Sloan's back. She could remember waking up in the Infirmary to see Jared, watching her. *"What happened today made us both look weak, Sloan."*

His words had hurt, so surely they had been the truth.

Elijah shook his head at her. "Defending you makes you look weak? Come on, you're a seventeen-year-old girl who got decked by a guy twice your size and you broke his shoulder. No one thinks you're the weak one."

Sloan thought of Joshua Bleak again, visiting her in the Infirmary. She had woken up to find him sitting right beside her. His mere presence had set her heart monitor off, filling the room with urgent crying beeps. *"You let the entire Academy know that Jared Dawson has an Achilles' heel."* It was as if he had been echoing what Jared had already told her. He had stood and smiled at her, leaning over to brush her hair out of her face. And in that moment, all she had hoped for was that Jared would come help her again.

That day changed everything. She wouldn't be anyone's Briseis. She would never be the reason Jared got hurt, even if he was the reason she was.

Sloan struggled to hold Elijah's intense gaze. "What's your point?"

"If you were my betrothed, I wouldn't let someone mess up your face like that." Elijah slowly raised his hand, as if to touch her cheek. Suddenly, he recoiled, thinking better and letting his hand fall.

What the hell was that?

For a moment—the briefest of moments—Sloan fell for his words. There was a small part of her that had once wished she didn't always have to be the strongest, be the hardest, fastest and most vicious. A small part of her that had wished she didn't have to be the best or the bravest . . . But Jared had loved those qualities in her, and, more importantly, she had loved them too. She loved them more than she loved the idea of being cherished and protected. Being too strong was better than being any form of weak.

She narrowed her eyes on him, pushing away the thoughts of a world where she didn't always have to be the best, be the *'bitch'* she was known to be. "Well, I am *not* your betrothed. Wake up, Captain. I don't need protecting." She moved to sidestep him but he grabbed her arm, holding her near. He ducked low, bringing his mouth to her ear.

"Need protecting? No, I wouldn't say you need it, but you damn sure deserve it."

His breath trailed over her skin like smoke, leaving the taste of his words, causing her skin to quiver and her to become acutely aware of their closeness. She jerked her arm free and walked away from him, trying to shake off the feeling that being close to him had left her with. She gnawed on her lip, wondering why his words had rattled her so deeply, and the feeling didn't dissipate until she realized the truth. She had once wished for Jared to say them to her.

As soon as she got in the pod she took a deep breath. The shell-shaped elevators were large enough to fit ten people when everyone sat on the white leather sofa that curved around the wall. Since childhood, Sloan had thought that being inside the pod was what it would be like to be inside an egg. The pods traveled in all directions—upward, downward, sideways, like veins through the Academy body—and they were constantly in use. She was blissfully thankful she had this pod to herself at this particular moment. She quickly punched her living quarters' code into the keypad, and as the doors slid shut behind her, she caught her reflection in the mirrored walls.

Her blond hair was stained with the blood that streaked across her pale face. She was a mess, with a cut over her lip and one under her eye. Paul had hit her *hard*; she already had a bruise forming over her cheekbone. She sat down and cradled her head in her sore hands. She hadn't meant to lose her temper like that, to make a spectacle of her rage once again . . . She knew how they felt, 27 and the rest of them, they all hated her. They tolerated her because Jared loved her. She couldn't blame them. She was the drill sergeant they'd never asked for. Couldn't they tell that she did it all *for* them? That she had forsaken any sort of weakness to be the best, to be the chosen one, the champion who would keep them alive?

I am what they made me to be . . . It wasn't her fault. The Order and her mentors had designed her to perfection. She and Jared were their elite soldiers—they were what they were supposed to be. Why did it bother the others so much? *And why is it bothering me so much? I'm the archetype—I am what they wanted. I will keep the rest of them alive out there.*

She wasn't used to second-guessing herself . . . or feeling self-conscious. She had long ago embraced the title of martinet, forsaking any childhood delusions of protection and chivalry, of fear or weakness. If she was going to be an Academy soldier then she was going to be the best. Jared wouldn't settle for anything less and neither would she.

This was all because of Tandy. The death had rattled her too greatly, and she knew that she needed to move on, to let this go . . . And yet, it seemed an impossible task. She had experienced loss before but never of this caliber. She couldn't imagine what Kenny was feeling.

How could you survive losing the one you loved?

Sloan thought about the next Betrothal Calling—it would be soon. How could she go and watch all the pairings that would occur, or more importantly, the ones that wouldn't? Her own Betrothal Calling had been one of the greatest nights of her life—everything she had worked so hard for had been given to her that night when it was confirmed that she and Jared were truly meant to be. Tandy had deserved a moment like that.

Sloan stepped out of the shower to find Jared standing there, holding out a towel. He shook his head at her, eyeing up her face. She grabbed the towel from him and wrapped it tightly around herself. He took her hand and pulled her to him, inspecting her face closer.

"I could kill Paul for doing this to you."

"*If you were my betrothed I wouldn't let someone mess up your face like that . . .*" Sloan shook her head. *Why am I so fixated on what Elijah said?*

She pulled away from him, moving into the bedroom. He followed her closely. "I will have him running 10 k's a day for this."

Sloan glanced back at him over her shoulder. "He's got a broken shoulder, Jared."

He shrugged. "Yeah, a broken shoulder, not a broken leg."

Sloan opened her dresser drawer, pulling out a fresh uniform. "We need to get a training session in this week. I should have never been blindsided like that."

"You can take it easy for a few days; you took a big hit."

Sloan spun on him, raising her brow questioningly. "From *Paul*. I'm fine."

If I am so fine, why are my hands shaking?

"You lost your temper today, Sloan. You went full fighter-mode and you can't do that with 27."

Sloan shook her head with annoyance. "You have got to stop babying them, Jared."

He sat on the bed, letting her continue to get ready. "I'm not babying them. I just see them for what they are."

Sloan dried her body off and began to dress, knowing they needed to get to class soon.

"And what's that?"

"Students."

She pulled her trousers up, fumbling with the zip. "They are soldiers."

"No, *you're* a soldier."

She studied him hard—knowing his sentiment was meant to be a compliment. *But then why does it sound like I'm being singled out? You're the same as me.*

Being a soldier was her identity—she was the best because she worked the hardest. Being a soldier wasn't only all she knew, it was all she had been made to be, all she had ever known how to be—it was what defined her as Jared's perfect partner. If he was the best he had to be with the best.

She shook her head, clearing her mind. "Well, they need to work harder. We need more sessions with them."

Jared nodded. "I agree. I wouldn't be surprised if Paul got pulled up for Review for today's debacle."

Sloan froze. She imagined Paul going to Review— any failure to excel could land you in Review, where the Order could give you a warning or sentence you to Dismissal. She imagined Paul being Dismissed. Like Luke Maxwell had been.

Like Tandy.

"No . . . we can't lose anyone else to them."

Jared arched a brow at her. "Them?"

"I mean the Order."

"There is no *them*. It's all of us—Academy and Order—together as one."

"I know that," she answered. *You know I know that.*

He stood, nearing her. "I'm going to hop in the shower and then we need to get back to class."

"Okay." She nodded.

He smiled and stripped his shirt off. Sloan couldn't pinpoint the day Jared had changed, when his small frame had been reshaped into the body of a man—which was surprising, since she had never taken her eyes off him.

"Jared, one more thing."

He nodded, waiting.

"Why did Elijah Daniels intervene in my fight today? Do you know him?"

His face hardened under her words and she could see his fingers twitching. Jared shared her temper and she looked out for his tells as keenly as he did for hers.

What is making you so mad?

"Let me deal with that, Sloan."

"Jare—"

But he cut her off. "You're done with Elijah Daniels, okay?"

It wasn't really a question. His words were a command. She said nothing, but they both knew her silence was not a mark of subservience. Slowly, he smiled and walked past her, stepping into their bathroom.

Sloan listened to the pour of the shower and sat on the bed, trying to make sense of Jared's quick attitude change and evasiveness. What had happened between him and Elijah that she didn't know about?

As a couple, they had experienced jealousy before—she had always known that half the Academy dreamed of being paired with Jared Dawson. But Sloan had also always known, in her heart, that she was the only one for him. No one else would be able to hear the difference in his voice, the one that revealed that even when his words sounded like a request they were actually an order. No one else could calm his temper, as he alone, in turn, could calm hers. No one else could read his thoughts, could think like him, strategize like him and work as hard as him. She *was* his perfect partner—and nothing in life brought her more joy.

Sloan reached into her bedside dresser drawer and pulled out the small worn photograph that she kept in there. It had been taken on the night of her Betrothal Calling. Sloan was wearing her white dress, Tandy's bronzed arms locked around her.

Love is vulnerability.

She wouldn't be in this much pain if she hadn't loved her friend so greatly. It was odd, Sloan thought, that when they spent their entire lives training to become the perfect soldiers, they hadn't figured out how to stop loving, how to stop wanting . . . Sloan knew now that she only had one remaining weakness—only one remaining vulnerability. She needed him to be the strongest, the fastest; she needed him to be the best—to ensure he never got hurt, because if Jared got cut, Sloan bled.

He stepped back into the room, a towel wrapped around his waist. "Are you ready?"

Sloan thought about the question, tossing the photograph back into the drawer. She eyed him from head to toe. They were truly in love and it weakened them both. It's why they trained so hard . . . They were responsible for their lives because they both knew that if one of them died out there—it would kill the other.

"Yes, I'm ready."

CHAPTER 2

Sloan rolled over, her arm falling on the pillow beside her. She rubbed her tired eyes, and instantly remembered her injury. The pain helped her wake up. Jared was already gone. He was always awake first, always the first one prepared.

It had been three days since the morning of Tandy's death, since she had broken Paul's shoulder. She rolled out of bed and made her way to the bathroom. Brushing her teeth, she admired Paul's handiwork. She looked awful. The Infirmary could take care of the injury but it was an unspoken rule that you wore your bruises with pride.

She thought back to the last time she had donned such a bruise—her fight with Joshua Bleak. It had taken six months of intensive training before Sloan had felt ready to challenge him again, and her body during that time had been a giant walking bruise. Yet, it had been worth it, just for the moment when she had shoved him, publically challenging him to give it his best shot. And he had. He had broken two of her fingers, sprained her ankle and torn muscles throughout her body.

But she had won.

Because for all the pain he had once again put her through—*she* had put him in the Infirmary with three broken bones and a concussion. Jared had asked her what she had been thinking by challenging Bleak again. *"I'm letting them all know they can't hurt us."*

He had kissed her bruises, had beamed with pride. *"That's why you're my girl."*

Sloan washed her face softly, thinking about what she would say to Paul. He had been in the Infirmary since their fight, but she knew he would be at the table this morning. Ultimately, she decided she wasn't going to apologize, whether she had lost her temper or not. She would try to use their altercation as a way to motivate him and the rest of 27.

Sloan walked to the pod and waited for the doors to open. She would tell him that he did a good job of finally defending himself. The doors opened and revealed three young girls sitting on the white seat. She stepped inside and, promptly, the girls stood and saluted. When she sat, they sat.

"Morning, girls." She watched as they eyed her face, fearful and speculative.

The small brunette leaned past her friends to see Sloan better. "You're Jared Dawson's girlfriend, right?"

"I'm Lieutenant Radcliffe," she answered sternly. In

Sloan's world, she had only ever wanted one thing—Jared. To be with the best, you had to be the best. So she became that. But somewhere along the way her natural abilities and excessive training had made her more than "Jared Dawson's girlfriend"—they had made her elite, they had made her the pinnacle of Academy excellence. *They made me what I am.*

She studied the girl's reprimanded demeanor and felt a touch of compassion. She could remember being that age, when all that mattered was the want to fall in love with the boy who had a perfect smile. When nothing that really mattered seemed to matter at all.

She offered the girl a small smile. "Yes, I am betrothed to Captain Dawson."

The girl beamed back. "You are so lucky."

The redheaded girl beside her nodded, leaning into her friend. "He's so perfect . . . him and your captain, Jenna."

"Who's that? Brett Crews-Tyler?" Sloan guessed, pulled into their girlish chitchat. Brett was a friend of Jared's and it was common knowledge that he was handsome.

"No—I mean yeah, him too—but we're talking about Captain Daniels." The girl smiled.

Elijah.

Sloan practically fell out of her seat—she hadn't heard his name since the fight and she had been trying to keep it that way.

But why wouldn't they think that? she thought. *He is handsome. Not like Jared, but still, definitely handsome.*

Shaking the thought from her head, Sloan stood, knowing they neared the dining hall. "Well, ladies, hopefully you'll get betrothed to one who can fight. It's not all looks . . ."

The young cadet—Jenna—stood excitedly. "He can fight! He's *my* captain and he never loses."

Well, tell that to Jared—reigning Academy champion. . .

She smiled at the girl. It was normal to idolize your captain, the way 27 did with Jared. *Let them have their heroes . . . their crushes.* Sloan didn't think she had ever idolized Jared, though. She hadn't formed some childhood crush on him; they hadn't had a trivial exchange of uncertain feelings. She had, for as long as she could remember, a definitive understanding—an unwavering certainty—that Jared was the one true love of her life. More than body connected them, more than just shared thoughts or attraction. He breathed and air filled her lungs.

The pod came to a slow stop. "Well, I hope you girls find a great match when your Calling comes around." The doors opened and she let them rush past her into the dining hall. She watched them rush past Table 82, where Elijah Daniels sat eating breakfast. She quickly diverted her eyes up to the clock—7 a.m. on the dot. She took a deep breath and made her way to the food-processing row, where she grabbed a tray and took her place in line.

She eyed her fingers, deciding which to touch to the machine. The chrome box at the front of the meal line was a blood processor. Each morning you would offer your finger for a prick of blood. The results were rapidly processed and informed the kitchen of your vitamin and nutritional requirements, and based off that, they provided a standard meal to balance your diet.

She opted for the left middle and winced at the familiar pinch. The machine freed her hand and she waited for her results to process. She watched the head cook, John, review her printed docket.

"Low in iron, Lieutenant Radcliffe," he called to her. She shrugged indifferently as he ripped aluminum foil off a plate of food. He placed it on her tray, the docket on the side.

She moved down the line but halted as the boy before her stood, staring at her face. "That looks awful."

"Want one to match?" Her threat hurried him off. She sighed, shaking her shoulders loose. She grabbed her coffee and took a deep breath. She needed to stay calm before joining the table. She glanced down at her tray, scanning the docket. It described her through a list of attributes—Height: 5'9"; Weight: 56 kg; a series of facts, nutritional information, dietary notes . . .

Everything I am can be summed up in this docket.

She balanced her tray on one hand and crumpled up the docket, making her way to 27. Paul was back, as she expected, his arm in a sling.

Sloan took her seat opposite Jared. He looked up at her and winked, drawing out a quick smile from her.

"Morning, everyone," she ventured. Sloan did not pull off friendly very well, but they *were* her friends.

They were the people she had been closest to her whole life.

"Morning." A communal grumble.

Paul was silent. Sloan cut up her food, eyeing him up. His face was bruised but not as badly as her own. The sling was what really revealed the fact that he had taken a beating.

She took a deep breath—*here goes nothing.*

"Paul, I just wanted to say I *am* proud of you for the other day." Everyone stopped, silenced. Erica dropped her fork.

Paul stared at her warily.

"I'm being serious. I know our fight *escalated*, but you finally defended yourself, so . . . well done."

I can't chew on the left side of my mouth because you bruised me so badly but sure, well done.

Everyone waited tensely—and then he smiled. "Thanks. The doctors say that even with laser treatments the healing will take a while."

His friendly response cued everyone else to relax and she looked to Jared, who nodded approvingly.

"If Elijah Daniels hadn't stepped in to save you who knows who would have won," Paul added.

The tension returned instantly. Sloan didn't understand why he was so antagonistic, but she didn't have patience for it. "He didn't *save* me."

Paul offered her a condescending smile. "Sure."

You avoid fighting me every chance you get and now you're pretending you could've beaten me?

"He *didn't*," she insisted, rolling her fork around

with her fingers, agitation swelling. "He just post-poned the inevitable."

Paul pushed his tray away. "What's *that* supposed to mean?"

"It means whether I was there or not she would have kicked your ass." Elijah's voice startled them all. Sloan looked up to see him standing at the end of their table, staring down across 27.

"Whatever," Paul grumbled, shrinking back.

"Excuse me, Second Lieutenant?" Elijah asked softly.

"Nothing . . . *Captain* Daniels."

Sloan realized she was still staring up at him. She shot her gaze to Jared and their eyes met briefly as he calmly sipped his coffee.

Elijah leaned on their table, his hand inches away from Sloan's, staring down at Paul. "How about as soon as that shoulder heals up you fight someone your own size?"

He leaned over the table, smiling as he added, "In a *Fight Night*."

Sloan flicked her gaze between Paul and Elijah. Paul had never gone in for a Fight Night—but she couldn't remember ever seeing Elijah in one either. She looked to Jared—Fight Night was *his* domain.

Jared slowly put his coffee down, looking to Elijah. "Paul wouldn't have beaten Sloan, and he wouldn't beat you." He crossed his arms over his broad chest, smiling up to Elijah confidently. "But if you're look-ing to have someone knock you unconscious on Fight Night, you know I'm your guy."

Elijah stood up straighter. "Is that a challenge, Dawson?" Jared rose and squared off with him. His imposing form was usually enough to back someone down, but Elijah matched his size.

"You bet it is."

Sloan stared at the two of them, wondering what history they shared that she somehow didn't know about. Everyone at the Academy was either in love with Jared or disliked him with envy, in which case they were usually too intimidated to say so.

Sloan readjusted in her seat. "Just relax, guys." She smiled to Jared. "Fight Night is ages away." She watched them cautiously.

Elijah smirked, eyeing Jared up. "Yeah, it's *ages away*. Gives you plenty of time to train up, Dawson."

Jared jolted in what appeared to be a move towards Elijah, and Sloan was on her feet in an instant, but he restrained himself, regaining his composure . . . somewhat. She saw his hands curled into fists, his whole body tense.

Elijah turned to her, smiling. "I'm sorry about your face, beautiful." Before she could move he had touched her cheek.

She could feel Jared's cold stare and she recoiled from him. "Do *not* touch me."

Elijah shrugged, turning from her, fixating his stare on Jared. "See you Fight Night, Dawson." He offered a challenging smile as he turned on his heel and left them.

She looked to Jared. He was furious; staring at her like what had transpired had somehow been *her* fault.

He grabbed his tray and walked off. She followed suit, storming after him. They tossed their trays and she barely managed to get into the same pod as him. As the doors slid shut behind them, they turned on one another.

"What's the story with Daniels, Jared?" she demanded. This wasn't all some coincidence. First he intervened in her fight, made the comments he did, and now this morning . . .

He sat down, crossing his arms angrily. "You couldn't possibly understand . . . Like I said, just stay away from him."

"What are you keeping from me? You and I have never had anything to do with Daniels and now he's showing up everywhere, telling me he wouldn't have let my face get knocked in if I were his betrothed, challenging you to a Fight Night . . ." Her voice trailed off under his hardened stare.

"*What* did he say to you?"

Sloan sat down slowly . . . She hadn't told him that Elijah had spoken to her in the corridor after the fight with Paul. "Nothing really. He was just being a jerk, saying if I were his he wouldn't let me get hurt . . ."

He shook his head at her. "Well, now who's keeping secrets?"

Sloan scoffed. *Really?*

"You're acting like a child, Jare."

"Am I? Or are you, running around speaking to Daniels behind my back, acting like a slut?"

Her hand cracked across his face. She had reacted

without thinking. A fiery outline of her fingers appeared on his cheek. He raised his own hand slowly, touching the mark she had left. Sloan inched closer to him. She had never hit Jared outside of training.

He's never given you a reason to, she thought, still reeling from his words.

"I'm sorry," she whispered.

"No, I am. I'm *so* sorry. I would never call you that." He shook his head, ashamed. "Forgive me. Please." His voice was fragile, showing how much pain he was in, and not because she had hit him. Her slap didn't hurt him, not the way his words had hurt her.

He cradled his head in his hands and Sloan wrapped her arms around his wide body, pulling him to her. He leaned into her, desperate for the contact they both longed for when they were near one another. They had always possessed an indescribable ability to impact one another with their mere touch—they could calm each other, incite one another, fill the other with passion or anger. They had always existed as if they had shared the same body.

He shook his head against her softly. "The way Daniels looks at you . . . it's like he doesn't realize you belong to *me*."

And she did belong to him, just as he belonged to her. She kissed his shoulder and held his face, the mark already fading. He pulled her into his arms, kissing her hungrily, his want for her igniting her constant desire for him. The pod doors opened and they tumbled into their living quarters. She tore buttons off his shirt and he dug his fingers into her back, lowering her to the floor. She kissed his neck and he ran his hands over her hair. Jared rolled her onto her back, pinning her underneath him.

This is us, she thought. *This is how we are meant to be.*

"You're the reason I breathe, Sloan." She loved hearing those words, so much so that she couldn't admit that under the weight of Jared, she sometimes struggled to catch her own breath.

The next Fight Night was announced the following day. It would be in four weeks' time and would involve nominated pairings of junior boys and girls and senior boys and girls. In addition, Fight Night champions were guaranteed a fight if they wanted it. But any student could enter nominated pairings, as long as the Order approved the match.

"Please don't nominate yourself," Sloan urged Jared as they walked down to the outdoor circuit field.

He locked an arm around her waist. "What are you worried about? When was the last time I lost?"

The fact was, Jared had *never* lost at Fight Night; he was the reigning male champion. That wasn't the point, though. The point was that Jared had nothing to prove, nothing to request in Winnings, no reason to enter. Fight Night was like gambling. If you wanted something—anything—you could request it as your Winnings in a Fight Night. If you won, you *won*, and if you lost, the Winnings request of your opponent was granted. It wasn't just about winning a prize or a boon, though. Because while some students self-nominated, there were others who were called upon to participate in order to demonstrate their physical ability for the Order.

But Jared had all he could need; he was the Order's favorite student, the Academy's greatest male soldier. Sloan didn't understand why he would enter. *Just because of Elijah?*

"Jare, you have no reason to do this . . . you could get hurt." Despite how much they worried over one another's safety, they had an unspoken understanding that they would never back away from a challenge, never show weakness when an opportunity to show strength arose.

Then why am I asking him to back out of this?

Jared let go of her as they stepped onto the field. "Sloan, drop it."

She stared up at him, frustrated. He had never lost a fight, so what about this was bothering her so much? *If he could just tell me what was going on with Elijah. . .*

She sighed heavily before acquiescing. "*Fine.* Where are you training?"

He gestured to the far end of the field. "Archery with the juniors. You?"

She hadn't worked on her knife skills in a while. "I will be with West in weapons training."

"Alright, when I'm done I will bring 27 to you and we can work them together." He smiled, running a hand through his short dark hair. Something about the ease of his movement distracted her from her anxiety . . . his tan skin glistened under the sun, his blue eyes watched her, his easy smile formed—he was perfect; he was the best thing she had ever seen in every sense of the word.

She nodded. "Alright."

"Say hi to the major for me," he said, smiling. Of course she would say hi to West for him. The major and Jared were close, bonding over what had happened years ago with Carson West . . . but they never spoke about that. She began to set off when she heard him call her name.

"Sloan, keep an eye on that bruise. I don't want you getting hurt."

She smiled, nodding to him as he turned away.

She set off towards the opposite end of the field. She tried to silence her thoughts but she couldn't help but still feel bothered by Jared entering Fight Night. Was she afraid of him getting hurt?

No, but you know he'll rip Elijah to shreds . . . The thought surprised her. Why should she care if Daniels got hurt? She didn't even know him and he had brought this on himself.

If I just knew why they had it in for each other. Sloan wracked her mind, trying to think of anything that may have spurred this hostility between the two captains. What had she missed?

Why won't Jared just tell me? Because he hasn't been the same since Carson—he hasn't trusted anyone.

It was the truth and she knew that . . . What happened that day with Carson had changed Jared—it had been the day that defined him, and they never talked about it.

Should he talk about it—could he? He expects me to move on from Tandy's death but. . .

Sloan shook her head. She couldn't think about that now. She needed to train, to regroup and focus. Thinking about Tandy or Carson wouldn't help right now; she needed to find out what was really going on between Jared and Elijah.

She continued across the green, keeping a safe distance as she worked around training units. The field was divided into various areas of practice. Archers shot at rows of moving simulated targets against a backdrop of a chrome wall. In the simulator rings, students could test weaponry against artificial opponents—combat rings where holographic weapons could be used by the less skilled, real weapons for the more advanced.

Sloan sidestepped a group of juniors training in judo and just about knocked into General Stone, who was leading their session. She hadn't spoken to him since breaking Paul's shoulder, which marked one of the longest periods of silence between the two. Stone was not only her general and premier trainer, he was her mentor . . . He had overseen her development since her arrival at the Academy; he was the person who had shaped her into the soldier she was.

She stood next to him quietly, rocking on her heels until she thought of something to say. She wrapped her arms around herself and glanced up to him. "You have yourself a nice little army, sir."

One of Sloan's earliest memories of Stone had been when he oversaw a sparring session between her and Jared. *"Hurt him before he hurts you,"* he had advised. She had seen the opportunity to pin him and had let it pass, throwing the fight. *"You lost,"* Stone had chided. But Jared had smiled at her, holding her with his beautiful blue eyes.

"No, I didn't."

Stone kept his eyes trained on the students. "They are doing okay. The brunette is in for her first junior Fight Night."

"Fight Night . . . of course she is." Sloan sighed heavily.

"Since when was the reigning female champ not a fan of Fight Night?" It was true; Sloan had a streak of success equal to Jared's. They usually entered Fight Night to request leave from the Academy, to go camping and have time alone.

"Since Jared took it upon himself to kill Elijah Daniels," she answered candidly. She could say anything to Stone. She trusted the man with her life and he had shown time and time again that she could come to him for anything.

He glanced down at her, drawing a slow breath.

Does he already know about their intended fight? Does he know why they have it in for each other?

"You need to let them figure this one out for themselves, Radcliffe, whether you like it or not. I am sorry you're caught up in the middle of it, though."

So, he does know. Sloan quickly leaped back as a girl

was flipped onto the ground before her. "Sir, maybe you could change his mind?"

"I would never ask one of my own to shy away from a fight," he began, looking at her with his warm grey eyes. "But even if I did, neither of those boys will back out of this one."

She studied his familiar face. He knew more than he was letting on. "If you knew why they were doing this, would you tell me?"

He huffed, turning from her. "Just get to your training, Lieutenant."

Sloan hated knowing something was being kept from her. She nodded slowly, knowing he had no more to say to her, and carried on down the field. She thought about her trust in Jared. She could trust him with her life, but was aware that full disclosure—perfect honesty—was not something she could always expect. The moment in the pod had reaffirmed that knowledge. The summer before last, after Carson, was when Sloan had noticed Jared's change. He had taken her hiking in the woods; they had scaled a rock cliff that hung treacherously over the lake. Despite her reservations he had convinced her to jump, and only once she had did he choose to tell her that students had previously died attempting the same leap.

"Why would you have me risk it then?"

He had held her tightly, keeping her near him on the shore. *"Because whatever the circumstances are, you're safe when you're with me."*

She had pulled away from him. *"You could have told me before I jumped."*

But all he had done was smile at her knowingly. *"You wouldn't have done it if you knew the risks."*

She had shaken her head at him. *"I'm safer when I know the truth."*

He had let his smile fade, pulling her closer. *"That's the whole point—when you're with me, you're safe regardless of what you know."*

From that day on Sloan was keenly aware that she might never know the dangers involved when Jared asked for her trust.

As Sloan approached Major West's training session, she noticed a large circle of students had formed. She pushed her way in and saw a girl viciously attacking a bare-chested young man. The girl swung at him, a training blade tightly clenched in her fist. Sloan watched him deflect and couldn't help but think how similar his body was to Jared's. His abs contracted as he twisted his broad chest, sweat matted with grass over his taut shoulders. She followed the deep line of his spine up to his dark locks of hair, watching him spiral around . . .

It was Elijah Daniels.

Sloan felt embarrassment warm over her and immediately concentrated on his female opponent. The girl moved well, her fiery red hair flying around her wildly. She wasn't bad—definitely skilled—but Sloan couldn't help notice that she was short, which meant short arms and legs, which meant she had to risk getting physically nearer her opponent if she wanted to do any damage. In this spar it wasn't as big a deal because they both fought with holographic training blades so the only real injury risked would be bruising from the hilt—which, Sloan knew, was a very real possibility.

As the girl made forceful jabs towards Elijah, Sloan saw his moment to pin her and end the fight. When he aimlessly sidestepped instead, though, Sloan realized he was taking it easy. She glanced past them, spotting Major West. He clapped, calling the spar to an end. Elijah and the girl stopped their fight and Sloan watched as the girl hugged him affectionately.

Is she his betrothed?

West entered the circle, smiling. "If you two expect to do well in Fight Night then you need to up your game—Elijah, you passed on a moment to end the spar and, Maya, a different opponent would have used your error to their advantage."

"Yes, sir," the two answered in unison.

Sloan was sick of hearing about Fight Night. This girl who now clung to Elijah's side would be vying for Sloan's champion title?

"These two will be fighting the reigning champions?" Sloan asked, stepping into the circle. She felt like grandstanding, defensive of her championship, defensive of her relationship, angry about Fight Night and whatever Elijah Daniels was planning.

West approached her, a warm smile crossing his face. "Haven't seen you here for a few weeks, Lieutenant Radcliffe. You've been missed in the ring. You could be of some real assistance to the other seniors." These sorts of compliments were common for students like her and Jared, but it didn't stop her from standing a bit taller upon hearing them. Jared was the best and received constant worship from everyone for it; she was the best and her peers hated her for it . . . She relished commendation from her mentors.

I am what they made me to be—I earned this.

"Thank you. I've been concentrating on hand-to-hand for a while, but I'm happy to be back."

He nodded. "How's Dawson?"

"He's good. He says hi, and that he's coming by later." She offered him a small smile, and a thought crossed her mind. *Could West talk Jared out of Fight Night?*

"Sloan, meet Second Lieutenant Maya Woods and Captain Elijah Daniels," he introduced, gesturing to the girl standing beside Elijah. Sloan took a step towards them, regarding Maya's small frame and uncertain expression. She would know Sloan by reputation—the champion whose title she was competing for.

Sloan narrowed in on the girl. "So you're the senior girl coming up against me in Fight Night?"

Sloan hadn't intended to self-nominate in this quarter's fight . . . but something about the uneasy expression on Elijah's face, the look of fear in his eyes, made her do it. He seemed to care about this girl—he knew she was no match for Sloan.

West glanced down at her. "I didn't know you were self-nominating, Radcliffe."

Sloan shrugged. "I would have to beat the winner regardless to maintain my title; might as well skip the waiting."

Sloan looked from Elijah to Maya. "How long have you two been training together?"

Maya crossed her arms over her chest. "Six weeks." She answered with such a sense of pride that Sloan nearly laughed. *Six weeks of training and you think you can take me?*

Sloan shook her head, containing a smile, and pulled her shirt off, revealing her training garments. They were all standard issue; she wore the same black sports bra and cargo pants as Maya. The material was made of bound synthetic fibers, forming a body armor that couldn't be torn, burnt or slashed.

The surrounding students regarded Sloan with excitement, a flurry of whispers, realizing she was about to spar.

She stretched her arms out, limbering up. "Well, after *six whole weeks*, you should be ready to give me a go."

West took a step between them. "Give it a rest, Radcliffe. Maya just finished sparring."

But Maya stepped forward angrily, a determined look in her eye. "No, I can take her."

Sloan shrugged to West; if Maya was willing to fight, then Sloan was happy to give her a preview of how Fight Night would go. Sloan had a way of mentally categorizing students in the Academy—those who knew she had earned her mantle of champion and those who thought her reputation was an extension of Jared's success. Maya obviously fell in the latter . . . *Well, that's about to change.*

Sloan remembered watching Jared in his first senior Fight Night; he had easily dominated the spar, and then, for good measure, he had ensured his opponent ended up in the Infirmary. Sloan had asked him why he had taken it so far. *"Make an example of one to teach all the others a lesson about challenging us."*

Example time.

West shook his head at Maya. "Woods, you aren't ready to take Sloan. She is your senior champion—you need more training."

"I said I could do it. Let me fight her," Maya growled, her fists tensing at her sides. It almost amused Sloan, the way this girl assumed her own abilities rivaled Sloan's.

West nodded slowly—he knew how this would go, but there was no convincing Maya otherwise. "Fine. Daniels, step out."

Elijah slowly moved to the fringe of the circle, waiting on the periphery. *Close enough to rescue your girl if you need to,* Sloan thought, shaking her head at him.

West tossed her a training blade and cued the girls to take position. It didn't surprise Sloan that he threw her only one knife despite Maya having two—she didn't need two to win this fight.

Sloan took her stance: knife in her left hand, horizontal in front of her torso; right hand remaining open, but tense, by her face. Maya took position: arms crossing over her torso to create an X in front of her chest, knives in both hands.

West circled the girls slowly. Sloan took a deep breath . . . this was her in her element. The wind ran a cool calm over her body; she rolled her shoulders back and closed her eyes, allowing her instincts to take over.

"Fight!" West's voice was a starting pistol.

Sloan opened her eyes, immediately tucking the blade into her waistband, bringing her arms up just as Maya lunged. Maya stabbed at her chaotically with an anger that seemed personal—*they hate you for your strength, for your success*.

Sloan used the girl's inexperience to her advantage. She threw her right hand up underneath Maya's extended bicep, grabbed the girl's wrist and locked her arm back. Maya's trapped hand opened reflexively, dropping the blade. Sloan kicked the weapon away, releasing the girl. She took a step back, out of Maya's reach.

"Stop lunging, refocus," she advised the girl. But her words fell on deaf ears—Maya didn't want her advice.

Maya leaped at her wildly, one knife still in hand, and Sloan easily sidestepped.

"Listen to her, Woods, she's trying to teach you!" West's voice called out.

Maya seemed to be completely enraged, ignoring anything said to her. She moved quickly—she was fast, but Sloan was faster. More importantly, she simply had more skill and experience. Once more, Sloan got ahold of Maya's wrist, twisting it outward until freeing the second knife. She pulled Maya into a hold, grabbed her own knife and brought the holographic blade to Maya's throat.

The spar was over.

"Forty-five seconds, Woods . . . Lieutenant Radcliffe has beaten you in forty-five seconds," West admonished, stepping into the circle.

Sloan released her hold on the girl. "Maya, you have good speed but you need to—"

Before Sloan could finish speaking, Maya made a sudden move, swinging around and clipping Sloan in the jaw. Sloan backed up, cursing the pain. Maya spun wildly, driving her knee into Sloan's abdomen. Sloan managed to deflect in time, preventing getting winded. Maya, in her rookie abilities, showed panic. She lunged for a knife by Sloan's feet.

I was trying to teach you . . . Sloan shook her head. She was sick of being treated like this. She rubbed her jaw as Maya scurried on the grass for a weapon, although what she was going to do with a fake knife was beyond Sloan. It didn't matter; she was on Maya in a second, swiftly striking the side of the girl's face, anticlimactically ending the fight. Maya rolled onto her back, holding her face, her lip bleeding. Sloan shot an angry look to Elijah—he was visibly worried.

This *is what happens when you challenge us.*

Elijah wanted to take Jared's title; he wanted this girl to take Sloan's. Well, now he knew how that would go. Sloan stepped back, frustrated. She relished the opportunity to show exactly why she was the best—but she hadn't lost her temper, she hadn't truly gone after Woods; in fact, she had tried to give her advice. And a foul shot was the thanks she got for her leniency and kindness.

"Cheap shot, Woods. The spar was over." West sighed, helping Maya to her feet. He ordered the girl to the Infirmary and turned his back to the group to face Sloan.

"You alright?"

Sloan shrugged. "Of course I am, sir."

"Don't take it personally, Radcliffe. You know how the other students see you and Jared," he advised.

Sloan wanted to say, *Yeah, they love him and hate me,* but she remained silent. *Didn't they know that living with such responsibility was awful? That being the best made her a target, it made her a key player in a war that she could die in.*

West turned from her, clapping to regain the attention of the group. "Okay, all of you pair up. Sloan, seeing as you broke Daniel's partner, you pair with him."

"Major West, I would rather—" Sloan protested but West shot her a silencing look.

"You play by my rules here, Radcliffe. Now pair up with Daniels," he ordered. Sloan glanced to the other end of the field; she could just make out Jared near the archery center.

He's not going to like this.

"That was unnecessary." Elijah's voice spun her around. He was standing just inches away from her, causing her to step back.

"And her cheap shot wasn't? I was trying to train her. You having her think she's good enough to take me is your problem. She's nowhere near capable of taking my championship."

Elijah rolled his eyes at her arrogance. "You and Dawson are so obsessed with being the best."

Sloan scoffed. "Coming from the guy who is trying to organize taking our championships from us. That's rich, Daniels."

He shook his head, but remained silent. *Can't argue with that truth, can you?*

"Is she your betrothed? Is that what this is about—you two want to take over from Jared and me?" Sloan pressed.

"Get over yourself. Not everything is about you and Jared."

Sloan glared at him. "How else would we see this? You challenging Jared, training your betrothed to challenge me."

"She's *not* my betrothed—I don't have a betrothed," he admitted angrily. He obviously regretted the words, looking away from her quickly.

"That's not possible." She shook her head. "You're of age." And yet, Sloan realized, she had never seen him at a Betrothal Calling. The Calling happened shortly after their sixteenth birthdays, before the entire Academy, but she couldn't remember ever seeing Elijah take part.

Why do I even care?

He shrugged his shoulders. "I just don't." Another

part of the enigma that was Elijah Daniels. *Whatever.* Betrothed or not, Sloan was certain he had feelings for Maya. Why else would he watch their spar with such concern?

Which gives me the leverage I need. . .

"If you back out of Fight Night, I won't annihilate Maya Woods in front of the entire Academy when she comes after my championship."

Elijah eyed her up bemusedly. "Afraid I'm going to hurt your blue-eyed boy?"

"Not in the slightest. Jared is a champion, and so am I. Not you and *definitely* not Maya Woods. You two should back out before someone gets hurt. Before *Maya* gets hurt. You know the girl is no match for me."

"Well, that will be her problem."

Is he calling my bluff—or does he really not care?

Elijah took a step near her. "If you aren't worried about Jared then why are you so afraid?"

Elijah infuriated her. He seemed to be completely oblivious to the threat Jared posed him. Every opponent Jared had ever faced in Fight Night had lost, had been hurt, had wound up suffering in the Infirmary. Every. Single. One. It was all she could do to just forget her whole protest and let Jared destroy this guy. And yet she couldn't help but try to stop it from happening. *Why? Why can't I just let him fight?*

Because Jared might kill him. . .

The thought ran across her mind again, and it agitated her. Why did she care what Jared did to him? Elijah Daniels was obviously a jerk. But Sloan had witnessed Jared destroy contenders whom he had no personal feelings towards. She didn't know what he was capable of doing to someone he had an agenda against.

She crossed her arms over her chest, huffing loudly. "Because I *know* you two have some outside issue that you're trying to bring into the ring—that's dangerous."

Sloan avoided looking directly at Elijah's eyes. She studied his neck . . . and then feared what Jared might do when he got his hands on it.

Elijah laughed.

Now he's laughing at me. . . .

"You still don't know why Dawson hates me? Of course you don't; you didn't even realize why I'm not—" But his voice trailed off in a chuckle as he turned from her. She grabbed his bare arm, spinning him back.

"All I know is that you're causing a problem in my relationship—now just back out of the *damn* Fight Night."

Elijah pulled free of her grip. "Oh, yeah? How do you know it's me causing the problem? How do you know it's not your *one true love* doing all of this? Maybe you two aren't even meant—" he began, but stopped himself. She glared at him, daring him to finish that sentence.

West appeared at their side, interrupting their argument. "Radcliffe, Daniels, do we have a problem?"

"No, sir," they answered in curt unison.

West studied the two of them, nodding slowly. "Then get training."

"We just need some real blades, Major," Sloan announced. Elijah wanted to fight a champion so badly? *I'll show him what that entails.*

West nodded approvingly and pulled two steel blades from his bag, taking Sloan's holographic training weapon. She slipped the knife into her waistband, eyeing Elijah for any sign of hesitation. He showed none.

"Keep your guard up," West advised unnecessarily before leaving them. Sloan walked away from the other students, finding freer space on the green. Elijah followed, taking a formal stance. They locked eyes.

"On your ready." He smiled, his voice cool and calm.

She rolled her eyes at him. "On *your* ready, Daniels."

He eyed her up and then suddenly took a step towards her. Sloan immediately stepped into him, spinning around to bring her left leg up towards his head. He blocked just in time—he was fast. He grabbed her leg, throwing it down, and pulled her towards him with a rough tug. He wrenched her back up against his hot chest.

He tucked his head into her, his mouth over her neck, his arm crossing her chest. "We fit pretty well, Radcliffe."

She grabbed at his forearm with one hand, reaching back for his head with the other, and with all her force she threw her body up into the air and slammed down to the ground, landing on her knees. Elijah flew over her, rolling into the grass. She jumped to her feet, barely up before him. They squared off.

They stood, in stance, with loosely clenched fists. He struck at her with lightning speed, but her anticipation of his movement gave her the opportunity to block. She landed a solid hit to his face, and then a kick to his inner thigh. His knee gave in and she struck him as he struggled for balance. He pivoted on his knee, turning out from her as he got to his feet.

She went for another hit but he got ahold of her forearm and spun her around, planning on putting her in an arm lock. She grabbed onto his hand with her own, spiraling around him to turn his intended lock on himself. In an instant he was free of her grip.

He spun, aiming a kick at her head. She ducked, crouching low as she returned the favor—landing a swift kick in his abdomen. He backed up and they both retook their stances.

"Nice move," he approved.

"Jared taught me that," she answered wickedly.

He was good. He was *very* good. Sweat dripped down her body, and her abs rippled with tension. She would need to connect a *very* strong hit in order to win.

She feigned going for a roundhouse kick, swapped legs and then aimed to land a forward kick to his diaphragm. He moved too quickly. He grabbed her extended calf and pulled her forward until her thigh was up against his ribs, her calf locked around his lower back. He spun her and landed on the ground, lying directly on top of her, in between her legs, his face hovering just above her own.

Realizing the intimacy of their position, she grabbed

his throat and squeezed with all the force she could muster from her confined position. He grabbed her hand and slammed it back over her head. Finding the other hand, he did the same, heaving up to hold her arms away from her. His arching back pushed his abs against her own; his wide hips pinned her legs down. She was stuck.

He stared down at her with intense green eyes, looking at her as though he had never seen her before. He was taking her all in. *Consuming her.* His full lips fell slightly apart and his breath was heavy against her face. The beads of sweat trickling down his chest mixed in with her own, and his grip on her hands loosened enough to let her break free, but she didn't . . . and she couldn't help but really look at him.

His face was undeniably near perfect, but it was the way they had fought that had stunned her. They had been so in sync. He further loosened his grip on her hands, but still she didn't move. *Hurt him,* she urged herself, but his stare was paralyzing. She needed to look away; she willed herself to look away. Finally a movement in her periphery drew her glance. Jared was there.

Jared!

She wriggled underneath Elijah. "Get off of me."

"Pretend like that's really what you want," he whispered, just loud enough for her to hear.

She wrenched her right arm free and swiftly brought it between them, hitting him in the face with her elbow. He rolled off her. She couldn't imagine how this looked to everyone else. Or rather, she could imagine it only too well. Elijah was on his feet in an instant.

Had he pinned her on purpose? Had he seen Jared coming? She didn't care. She leaped to her feet and turned on him. With unbridled rage she swung. She clipped him on the jaw, and it surprised him.

Their fight wasn't over.

He spun, aiming a kick at her. She blocked and landed a strike to his neck. He buckled and she kneed his chin. She struck at his face and he stumbled from her. He regained his stance, anger replacing surprise. He leaped at her, striking viciously. She blocked, parried; he grabbed her arm and with surprising might threw her to the ground. She rolled back in a somersault, getting to her knees, ready to lunge—but Jared was now fighting in her stead.

He had stepped in and he and Elijah were going full force. Elijah lunged and Jared deflected, striking at him mercilessly. Elijah countered, hitting Jared in the jaw, and Jared turned out, clipping Elijah with a backhand.

Sloan got to her feet slowly, watching in horror as the two viciously brawled—Elijah was too tired for this fight. Jared was entering the spar fresh and angry. He kicked Elijah's knee in and came behind him, locking his forearm around Elijah's neck.

"Come near her again and I will *end you*," he growled to Elijah.

"ENOUGH!" West's voice boomed over them.

Jared let Elijah go, immediately walking away.

West stepped towards Jared but Jared didn't stop for

him, instead he shot a glare at Sloan, his blue eyes on fire.

"Dawson," West called but still Jared didn't stop. He left them all standing there.

West looked from Elijah to Sloan, shaking his head. "What the hell happened, Radcliffe?"

I wish I knew.

CHAPTER 3

Sloan leaped out of the pod and looked around her living quarters. Where was he? She crossed the room and turned into their bedroom. Jared was sitting on the edge of the bed, his head in his hands.

"What the hell was that?" she asked, stopping in the doorway.

He had just left her there to deal with West. He had intervened in *her* fight.

"Do you have feelings for him?" He asked the question so quietly she almost hadn't heard.

"*What?* Feelings for who?"

He raised his head, staring at her. *Had he been crying?* "Don't be like that, Sloan. For Elijah."

"How could you ask me that?"

"What do you expect me to think when you're rolling around with him in the grass . . ."

"When we were *fighting*? You think nothing of it. You know I love you. It's always only been you," she answered, softening her voice as she neared the bed. She knew how it had looked; she knew how it would hurt him.

A memory from summer crossed her mind. They were camping, wrapped up in blankets, their bodies intertwined. *"Swear you'll always be mine . . . that this will always just be ours."* The order had fallen from her lips onto his still-hot skin.

He had cupped her face, nodding. *"I would rather die than have this with anyone else, Sloan."*

Jared stood, running his hands through his short dark hair. "I can't deal with this, Sloan. You need to stay away from him."

"I'm *trying* to. If you just backed out of Fight Night or told me what the *hell* was going on it might make it a little easier," she explained, following him into the living room as he walked past her.

"That's not an option." He shook his head.

"Well, I told him to back out."

He spiraled around to face her. "Why would you do that?"

"Because I know you! If you two fight you will try to kill him. He's good, Jared, *really* good. One of you will get hurt."

Jared paced the room. "If you knew my reasons you would understand."

Sloan collapsed to the sofa, running her hands over her neck. She was sick of this. "Then *tell* me!"

"I can't!"

"I don't get it. I don't understand how you can be keeping secrets from me. You're supposed to trust me."

"I'm doing this for *us*, to protect us," he argued.

"From what? Whatever it is—"

"No. Not *whatever it is*—you need to know that I am doing what I am for the sake of you and me and I expect you to support me."

Sloan rose, crossing the room and walking to him. "I *do* support you. You have had my support our entire lives, Jare. But you're acting different . . . everything since Carson has been different. You never kept secrets from me . . ." she began but her voice trailed off under the weight of his stare.

His cobalt eyes narrowed, his jaw clenched. "*Why* would you bring up Carson?"

She grabbed his hands, willing him to hear her. "Because you've been different since that day. What are you even asking the Order to give you in Winnings? What will fighting Elijah achieve?"

"Review."

He answered so curtly Sloan wasn't sure she had heard him right.

"*What?*"

"I will have Elijah sent to Review—it's my Winnings request."

Sloan dropped his hands, stepping away from him. Sloan imagined the Order assessing Elijah. He would either be warned to fall in line or sentenced to Dismissal—execution by lethal injection.

"You—" Sloan couldn't quite understand how he was saying this. "You can't be serious."

He stared at her with a challenging gaze. "Deadly serious."

Panic seized her heart, a sharp contraction of muscles. This was absurd, it wasn't tolerable, and it wasn't *Jared*. She felt like she was staring at a stranger.

"Please don't do this."

"Why would you care if the Academy lost Elijah Daniels?" he asked, accusation hanging in his every word.

"I don't! I care about losing you, *you idiot*! What sort of person would risk someone's life over some petty dislike?"

"It's not a petty dislike! I *have* to do this. I don't have a choice," he yelled, frustration welling.

"You *always* have a choice!"

"Not this time."

"Jared, you *can't* do this."

He slammed his hand on the table, staring at her with frustration. "This isn't up for debate—I *need* to do this."

"And I don't have a say? You would just risk someone's life—"

"I *don't care* about *his* life, Sloan!"

How could he be saying these things? What could possibly have caused this vehement hatred for Elijah? She watched him turn from her, resting his palms on their dining table, head bowed low as he tried to regain his composure.

"Do you think Carson would want you to do this?"

Jared spun around, his eyes alight with fire. Sloan instinctively stepped away and in an instant he had her backed up against the wall. He lashed out, hitting the wall beside her. She stood perfectly still.

He studied her for a long moment, eyes wild. *"Stop bringing up Carson West."*

Sloan narrowed her gaze on him, pushing herself away from the wall, forcing *him* to back up. "Get the *hell* away from me." She growled the order.

He backed away immediately, realizing his inappropriate behavior. "I'm sorry."

Sloan shook her head at him. "You've been saying that a lot recently."

He nodded, barely raising his blue eyes to meet her stare. "Please, *please*, just trust me. I have to do this. I need to keep him away from you. That's why today when—" he began, but it was Sloan's turn to cut him off.

"Today when you intervened in *my* fight?"

"Yeah, I'm sorry, I just—"

"No. Don't apologize—just knock it the *hell* off. What you did today made us both look weak."

The recognition of his own words coming from her mouth stunned him. He caught her angry stare and nodded. They had their unspoken rules and Sloan had learned to follow them—she wouldn't live by any double standards.

She took a deep breath. She didn't want them to be *this* way. "Jared, you and I—we *know* who we are. We are soldiers and all we have is each other and all we can rely on is our training to ensure we get the rest of our lives together. But that requires trust; staying the way we are requires trust. I need you to tell me the truth here."

He ran his hands over his face, messing up his dark hair, his blue eyes falling on her sadly. "I am asking you to trust that I know what I am doing."

Sloan shook her head at him. *That's not how it works.*

Sloan couldn't get to sleep. She lay next to Jared, watching him peacefully slumber, the slow rise and fall of his chest. She wished they hadn't argued, she wished she hadn't brought up the fight, she wished he would tell her the truth, and that she hadn't brought up Carson . . . She wished for a lot of things.

She thought back to that day when Jared's world had shattered. She remembered General Stone prying Jared's shaking hands off of Carson. She remembered the look on Jared's face as he suddenly regained composure, wiping away his tears, his face turning cold and hard. She could hear Denise Carmichael's overwhelming sobs and she could remember thinking, *That's the sound your heart makes when it's broken.* She had seen Jared's blue eyes turn from an ocean, to a storm, to ice. *"He's gone,"* Stone had said and Sloan had never really known if he was talking about Carson or Jared.

The Friday before the Betrothal Calling the quarterly War Front Collective was held, led by the Order for the senior students to receive necessary updates on the war effort. Sloan followed Jared into the senior conference hall, a large room designed like every other space in the Academy—bleached and clinical. Academy security lined the white walls, former students posted on base instead of on the mainland. The sentries dressed in all white, toting ivory weapons, indistinguishable from one another. It was odd, the way they blended in with their surroundings so well and yet were impossible to ignore.

Sloan shuffled into the first aisle and took a seat at the desk nearest where the Order would preside. The Order hadn't arrived yet; Sloan consciously checked her uniform and hair, knowing the importance of appearances. Jared nudged her in the arm. "Stop fidgeting. You look perfect."

They hadn't said more than two words to each other since their fight. Every time she looked at him she found herself searching for his past self, for *her* Jared. The Jared who had taught her how to shoot crossbows, the boy who liked to brush her hair at night, the man who made her realize that love was as real as the war effort—something worth fighting for.

The seats around them began to fill with the loud shuffling and chatting of students. Becket Brock, lieutenant from 67, sat next to her, briefly greeting her before leaning over to speak to Jared. Sloan ignored the customary chitchat; she was too distracted by Jared and Fight Night to partake in idle conversation. Suddenly, an odd sensation overcame her.

Sloan was certain someone was watching her.

She felt heat rise through her neck and she craned around, scanning the crowd of her identically dressed peers. She glanced over them, grouped in conversation, some seated, some perched on desks. She could see Major West near the entrance, Erica and Mika two rows back, but all of them were absorbed in conversation, taking no notice of her. She scanned until her eyes landed on Elijah. He was seated five desks back, arms crossed over his chest.

Staring at her.

Their eyes locked, and she waited for him to look away first. He continued to stare, unyielding, unaffected by the bustling students and noise that separated them. Unaffected by Jared sitting right beside her. She could make out the dark shadows of bruising around his eyes but was unsure if that was her handiwork or Jared's. She couldn't hold his gaze any longer, his bright green eyes singling her out. She repositioned, forcing herself to look away. Yet, she could still feel his gaze on her. She quickly looked back, and with a half smile across his face, he winked at her.

Sloan spun around, immediately looking to Jared. He was still engrossed in conversation with Becket. The last thing she needed was Jared seeing Elijah watch her. Sloan kept her eyes trained on the panel desk ahead, determined to not look back. It took almost every ounce of willpower she had.

What have you done to Jared? Why won't you leave me alone?

Abruptly, the guards took a step forward, cueing them all to stand, announcing the arrival of the Order. The room immediately silenced as they stood to attention. The Order was comprised of General Walt Stone, Lieutenant General Amelia Brass, Major General Joseph Carr, Brigadier Hans White, Colonel Christopher Don Luke, Lieutenant Colonel Kate Barden, and of course, their highest ranking member, Grand Marshal Ludo Romani.

The Order filed through, taking their stance behind the panel desk. Romani kept them standing, a moment of long silence and stillness. He was a small man, short and wiry in build, with jet-black hair framing a narrow head and large eyebrows mounting dark, deep-set eyes. He had a small, well-groomed moustache that didn't extend past the corners of his mouth, and wherever Romani went, he wore pristine white gloves.

Their grand marshal might have been a small man, but he had an unnerving presence, a charismatic demeanor and a cutthroat nature—he was hardened by the war effort, they said. He had grown suspicious and erratic, they said. He rarely walked the halls of the Academy, like he once had, and he only ever spoke with his favored students and most trusted advisors on the Order. Sloan would be lying if she said she felt comfortable around him, but her status kept her in his good graces.

Sloan knew the Order through their day-to-day roles at the Academy—the major general, Joseph Carr, would at times lead training sessions, and Lieutenant

General Amelia Brass oversaw the Infirmary, but largely, the Order, unlike the trainers and professors, had little interest in developing bonds with most of the students. Their role was deciding the fate of the Academy from a distance, and unless you were a champion, like Sloan and Jared, then you really had little interaction with them at all.

Romani finally saluted them, cueing them to take their seats. Sloan watched him sit, resting his chin on the back of his hand—how he always sat. The attentive position made Sloan uncomfortable, and she had long ago realized that garnering such an effect was probably exactly why he did it. Sloan glanced to Jared and saw as he watched the Order with a keen attentiveness, his mouth half turned in a smile. This was comfortable for him—for the both of them, really, aside from Romani—because they were finally amongst those who valued them most. While the Order tended to disregard the students, they made a point of knowing their champions.

"Hello, my senior students," Romani greeted them. He let his gaze fall over the students, and if any had been fidgeting they were now immobile under his stare. "We shall start this conference as usual, with a brief on the war effort. Then we shall review this quarter's Dismissed, and then a final word on this weekend's Betrothal Calling."

Sloan sucked in sharply—she didn't want to hear about the Dismissed. She took a deep breath; she couldn't be emotional here, not in front of the Order.

They would have already known she was handling Tandy's death poorly, first with Paul's shoulder and now the recent tension with Jared that likely hadn't been missed by anyone. As if on cue, Jared abruptly took her hand in his, placing their clasped fingers on the table, for all to see. She wanted to pull her hand free, but knew how important it was for the Order to believe they were doing better than they truly were . . . and she couldn't deny that under his touch, however much she wanted to resist, he did calm her. Their relationship was like that; it was unique and unexplainable. Theirs was the union that most reflected the accuracy of the Order's Betrothal Calling.

Romani turned the floor over to Major General Carr. He was a stern man with a fierce temper, always critical of Stone's approach to training as well as his sincere interest in his pupils. The major general leaned forward, clearing his throat.

"The Others made an attempt to overthrow Fort Destiny, on the eastern coast of the mainland. Over the course of three nights, our forces fought them back, and on the fourth evening a tactical air assault was executed . . ." Carr continued but Sloan let her mind drift away.

She thought of the *Others*. The enemy. The Others were the reason this Academy existed. The mainland had once been a peaceful place, a place that had recovered from the nuclear war that had decimated global populations, destroyed entire cities and broken down borders. Time had passed and the survivors came together, forming a new colony: a home called *Dei Terra*. The mainland colony, first to regain fertility, was a last salvation for the survivors of the war. Treaties had been signed, a democracy formed, and people swore to never again allow such atrocity. People, though, are creatures of habit, and habit would ensure that after enough time had passed, war was once again something conceivable. Something tangible.

And then the Others formed, as a group of those who stood against *Dei Terra* democracy. They organized a coup, after years of manufacturing and stockpiling weapons and resources, years of infiltrating government operations and social-political offices. Their agents and followers sprung up on both coasts, working towards the capital. They were strongly resisted, but never defeated. *Dei Terra* was still young, low in population. So while those fit enough would stay to hold the enemy off, there was only one long-term solution: the Academy. Families nominated their children to be trained by the remaining military experts, taken to a safe and isolated island. The children would return as an army, prepared to protect *Dei Terra*.

"—and needless to say, all efforts are being directed towards the stabilizing of Fort Destiny." Carr's words drew Sloan back. Romani thanked him, once again turning to the students with critical eyes.

"You should all know that as far as our latest reports can find, your families remain alive and well, proud and hopeful that your class will be the final reinforcement our troops need."

Sloan exhaled heavily. Somewhere on the mainland her family was safe. Jared squeezed her fingers, sharing in her relief. It reminded her that he wasn't the cold person she had been living with for the past few days— the one who seemed intent on killing Elijah.

Didn't he care that Elijah had a family too?

Romani gestured to Amelia Brass. The lieutenant general readjusted her wire-rimmed glasses. She was a petite, older woman, but despite an unassuming size she was tough as leather. She ran the Infirmary and, as such, the morgue. She oversaw the administration of the lethal medications during Dismissals. Sloan glared at Brass, conflicted by the older woman. Brass had healed Sloan's own wounds, had taken her pain away countless times, but she had also been the sole individual to technically end Tandy's life, and that was a pain that greatly outweighed any broken bones.

Brass flicked over her papers. She sighed heavily before beginning. "Jennifer Devel, 17, failure to advance; Emily Slough, 16, failure to advance; Jeremy Dieter, 16, failure to advance; and Tandy Norman, 16, failure to advance."

Sloan's entire body tensed. She wanted to get up, get out, to fight her way out of here, and in the same way he had always been able to read her mind, Jared's grip on her hand tightened. She glared at him but he kept his eyes forward, holding her so tightly she couldn't feel her fingertips.

Romani leaned forward, narrowing his eyes. "Failure to advance . . . We all have families who are relying on us to return to them for their protection, for the restoration of peace and order on the mainland . . . for the sake of *Dei Terra*.

"When you came to us as children, your parents relinquished all responsibility for you. This is not to say they didn't love you, and our Dismissals are not a way of saying *we* do not love you. But we are not here to love you. We are *not* here to keep you safe. You are *chosen soldiers* and *we* are responsible for shaping you into that which will stop the Others," he explained, jabbing the table with each impassioned word.

"Those who fail to excel—they would have been responsible for your lives. For your families' lives. And they would *not* have been up to the challenge. I know it's difficult—some of them were your friends. But they would have failed to protect you. Their *existence*, despite any friendships formed during their time here, would have been, inevitably, a detriment to you all." He sighed heavily.

Were there others in the room feeling the same conflict as Sloan? *I can't be the only one*, she thought. Had someone been best friend to Jennifer, Jeremy or Emily? Were there others wondering about the truth in Romani's words, that the Dismissed would have inevitably been their downfall?

What if he was right and Tandy had been assigned to serve with Jared—what if her inabilities had led to his death?

But Tandy would have never let something happen to Jared. You know that.

"We rose up from the fire to fight." Romani spoke their motto—his voice loud and commanding as he raised his forearm, bringing his fist upward in a tight gesture. This was their motto—their communal salute.

"We rose up from the fire to fight," the students answered in unison, raising their hands into fists. Sloan was forced to lift her left hand as Jared still held on to her right with his vice grip.

Romani nodded at them slowly. "It is important to remember, in these times, that the mainland is a utilitarian colony. By culling the few, we are saving the many."

Sloan was really beginning to hate that expression. *Culling* was a hunter's term, a tactical approach, a solution to a problem. Tandy hadn't been a problem. Tandy, with her doe eyes and trusting nature, hadn't been a hunter's prey. So many people had loved her.

Kenny. He would have heard all of this, he would be here, listening to the Dismissed, listening to the Betrothal Calling plans. How had Sloan been too preoccupied to visit him, too selfish to think of him sooner?

Because that's how they want us to be—how they make us. Tandy died because she wasn't that kind of person.

And Jared and I are—we are the Academy's ideal, Sloan thought and found herself—not for the first time—feeling a sense of discomfort. The other students didn't understand; they envied Sloan and Jared because they didn't know the pressure they lived under. The way they strived for perfection in every aspect of their lives, the way their trust was slowly crumbling, the way their relationship was suffering, the way they would be expected to live and die for the Academy because they were natural leaders, gifted soldiers. They wouldn't be made sentries or receive active duty posts in some secure office; they would be out *there*, in the midst of the danger, both hoping that if neither survived then they wouldn't be the second one to go, that they wouldn't be the one who had to live a minute, a day, a year without the other.

"Let us discuss a lighter topic!" Romani's cheerful tone caught her attention. "Tomorrow night we have a Betrothal Calling! Sixty eligible students will have their partnerships announced. As usual we expect our senior students to be present, dressed appropriately and ready for the Principle dance, which, as usual, will be led by your senior champions."

His eyes fell on Sloan and Jared, who lifted their clasped hands to acknowledge Romani's words and the dull clapping of their fellow students. They had led the Principle dance at every Betrothal Calling for several years, since before they themselves had even been betrothed. It was their duty as champions.

The boys would be in mess dress—military whites—and the girls would wear their issued ivory dresses, custom-made as they entered their own Calling. Sloan had been gifted one much earlier, so she could lead the Principle dance with Jared in appropriate attire. Sloan had always loved the Calling but this one would be different . . . this one would have seen

Tandy paired to Kenny. Now Kenny, a boy of age who had completed all the necessary Calling assessments, would be paired with his next best match. Sloan could clearly recall her own ceremony, of Tandy asking what she would do if she wasn't, by some disaster, paired with Jared. *"I would want to die."*

She thought about her words now—had they been too reckless? Was death really the only alternative or was it just an inevitable result of having your heart broken beyond repair? She imagined never having had Jared in her life. She had known it then, as she knew it now; Jared was the largest part of who she was, imbedded into her existence. There was no Sloan Radcliffe without Jared Dawson. She wondered, though, how much of yourself could you lose before existing became impossible? She hoped to never find out—not like Kenny would have to.

General Stone stood, walking around the panel table. Sloan watched him lean back, arms crossed over his broad chest. If she had to guess, she would say these Collectives bored Stone. He always *looked* bored, at least.

"As you all know, we have under a month before this quarter's Fight Night. We do have exciting news— both senior champions will be entering to defend their titles." He gestured to her and Jared as a bustle of excitement broke out in the room.

"Fighting your champions are Captain Elijah Daniels and Second Lieutenant Maya Woods." He gestured to the back of the room, where Elijah and Maya would be seated. The room was alive with quick whispers, bets being offered, a laugh, even a clap of hands high-fiving. They were so excited for that which she dreaded—*because they don't understand what it means to be us.*

Romani stood, silencing the room. "We conclude the War Front Collective. Until next time—you're dismissed." At his words the seniors got to their feet, rushing towards the exit. Jared freed her from his tight grasp and she turned in her seat, searching through the humming crowd for Kenny.

"He isn't here," Jared spoke, staring down at her, knowing her thoughts.

She stood slowly. "Where is he, then?"

He pulled her close to him, lacing an arm around her. The intimacy of their closeness felt conflicting to Sloan. *I want this; I just want it with the old version of you . . .*

Jared was an intrinsic part of who Sloan was, and it scared her, more recently in different ways than usual. It had always scared her to know she couldn't—*wouldn't*—live without him. But the unbreakable bond they shared, the way they lived each day for one another, that wasn't the only thing that frightened her now. Jared had a rage, a darkness that he had molded into a dangerous quality. He had blinders on—living and breathing to be the best and to be with Sloan—and anything that threatened his ideals would be swiftly eradicated. She had grown up with him; they had grown together, sharing their thoughts, feelings and plans—he was half of who she was as she was half of him. Somewhere along the way, during their closeness, had she inherited his darkness? She *was* dangerous, she knew that, but to what extent would she exert that power onto the outside world?

She imagined a charcoal ball of anger and malice, a merciless rage, hiding somewhere inside her. Breaking Paul's shoulder, laying into Maya, every Fight Night championship, every threat that had fallen from her lip and every hit she had executed—she did it all for her status; she did it all to be with Jared. Were they more similar than she knew?

I wouldn't risk someone's life, though . . . But would she? If it meant keeping her and Jared together, if it meant maintaining their status . . . *What wouldn't I do for him?* If she ever let that darkness come through, to the same extent to which Jared showed his own, would it surprise him . . . would it scare him?

Would he even care? *He would love you more,* Sloan thought, and she pushed the thought away. The truth was a dangerous thing to think about. *Maybe that's why Jared keeps it at arm's distance. . .*

Jared tugged at her hand, drawing back her attention. "I have been visiting Kenny since the Dismissal . . . He obviously hasn't handled *it* well, but we have had a few sparring session. I think those are helping. I knew he wasn't ready to be here today, to *hear* all that, so I got him out of it," he explained, his voice hushed.

Sloan was confused—Jared hadn't even *liked* Kenny. She could easily recall him criticizing Kenny and Tandy for being too sensitive for Academy life. She stared up at him, perplexed by his kindness.

"I know what she meant to you. I know you would want him to be okay, so I'm on top of it." His words washed over her like a warm reminder of the boy she had always loved. She took his hands in hers, knowing, with frustration, that she would always love his goodness more than she feared his darkness.

"Thank you," she whispered.

Marshal Romani appeared at their side, cueing Sloan to abruptly drop Jared's hands, standing to attention. "At ease." He nodded. Romani turned to Jared. "Captain Dawson, we need to have a quick word."

Sloan flicked her gaze between them, desperately wanting to know what Romani needed Jared for, but she couldn't ask. Jared nodded to the marshal and Sloan stepped away, ready to leave, but Jared grabbed her hand, once again wrenching her back to him. "I love you."

She glanced from Jared to the marshal. He was making a spectacle of their commitment. For the time being, she didn't need to know why to understand that it was best to go along with him. Did he know something she didn't—*more secrets?*

"I love you too, Jared." He waited a moment before releasing her hand. Slowly, she turned from them, making her way out of the room. She turned down the corridor to be met with a mess of senior students still waiting to get a pod out. Leaning against the wall, she watched the crowd.

"Don't you want to know what they're talking about?" Elijah's voice startled her as he appeared at her side.

"No," she lied, crossing her arms, closing herself off to him. *How does he always find me?*

"*Liar,*" he laughed in her ear. She leaned further away and he curved into her, letting his eyes travel over her slowly. She felt the heat emanating from his warm skin and she couldn't help but recall lying underneath him during their spar. The weight of his body on top of hers and that look of interest in his eyes. She wanted to push him away; she *wanted* him to leave her alone.

"*Pretend like that's really what you want.*" His former words filled her mind and her skin tingled, fine hairs rising sharply on her neck. She shook her head at him. "Just go awa—"

Suddenly, before she could finish her sentence, Elijah was stumbling away from her. He staggered back as Jared draped a heavy arm over Sloan's shoulders. "Getting a bit too close for comfort, Daniels."

Elijah stood up straighter, an easy smile playing over his face. "Too close for your comfort or Sloan's?"

Jared tensed around her, a shield. "Watch yourself," he warned.

Elijah stepped forward. "I would rather watch *her.*" He nodded in Sloan's direction.

Jared jerked forward but Sloan threw her hand against his chest, pulling him back. "He's not worth it, Jared."

He relaxed under her touch, kissing her temple possessively. Sloan glared at Elijah. "Stay the *hell away* from me, Daniels."

He stared at her, his fiery green eyes boring into her. "Pretend like that's really what you want," he smirked.

Jared tensed up but this was Sloan's turn. She took a step towards Elijah. "What do you think I want? *You?* All I have *ever* wanted, all I will *ever* want, is standing behind me with blue eyes, mad as hell, wishing you were long gone."

Her words hurt him and for a second—a *millisecond maybe*—she felt bad. She did want him to leave her alone; she did want her and Jared to go back to normal . . . and she also didn't want Jared to get Elijah killed. And if he kept this up then he would definitely ensure that happened.

Elijah shrugged, looking from her to Jared, back to her. "Well, we don't always get what we wish for."

Keeping his eyes on her, he backed up, before slowly turning and making his way into a pod. Sloan shook her head, infuriated by him. She turned back to Jared, lacing her arms around him. She thought about the situation she had found herself caught up in . . . If she just let Jared get Elijah Dismissed, she wouldn't have to ever deal with him again, but if Jared did something like that, his darkness would become more than she knew how to bear.

She would lose them both.

Jared kissed her forehead and remained resting against her. "I hate him," he sighed.

"That doesn't mean you should get him killed."

He pulled away from her. "Sloan, can we not do this again . . ."

"Just tell me—" she began, but was quickly cut off by the reappearance of Marshal Romani.

Once again, she put distance between herself and Jared, standing to attention. "At ease, soldier. I just wanted to say I look forward to seeing you both tomorrow night."

He smiled, his tight mouth twisting upward, before turning and disappearing down the corridor.

Sloan turned to Jared. "What's he talking about?"

"Tomorrow night, before the Calling, he wants me and you to meet the Order."

"Why?"

"Don't know." He shrugged. "Some important guests are arriving or something."

Sloan nodded, no longer wanting to fight with him. Were other seniors invited or just she and Jared? What guests would be at the Academy that demanded their presence before a Calling?

"Just us two?"

"Probably. Like I said, I don't know— he just told me to get ready for the Calling and go to the Order beforehand."

Sloan nodded as they made their way to an open pod. She didn't like having plans sprung on her and she never liked being around Romani. She wanted to know what he had planned for her and Jared, but she supposed they would find out soon enough.

That night, Sloan went to the Infirmary. Jared had fractured two of Kenny's ribs, knowing injury was the only excuse to miss a War Conference Collective. She idled down the hall, glacial footsteps staggered by her own fear. There was nothing anyone could say to her to make Tandy's death less painful; how could there possibly be any words to help Kenny? Slowly, Sloan made her way to the bed number and hesitated at the curtain.

Finally, she managed to speak. "Kenny . . . it's Sloan." She hoped he was already asleep.

"Sloan?" His familiar voice cracked through her . . . what was she going to say to him? She couldn't turn back now. She closed her fingers around the curtain, pulling it back slowly. Kenny was lying in the white bed, sheets pulled up to his chest, his hands resting on his stomach. His short hair was messy and he had large blue circles under his eyes. His usually bright face was sallow and gaunt. He looked sick, like he hadn't slept in weeks . . .

Which he probably hasn't.

"Hi, how are—" Sloan began, but she couldn't ask how he was feeling. So instead, "How are your ribs?" stumbled from her with uncertainty. She approached his bed slowly.

"They're fine. The nurses offered to do a rapid fix, but I opted for the old-fashioned wait-it-out approach . . ." His tone was all she needed to hear to know how he was feeling. His voice no longer had that natural uplifting quality. Conversation with Kenny had always been easy, and despite not being on her table, he had always been with Tandy, which meant she had plenty of time to form some semblance of a friendship with him. She had viewed him as a friend, at least *before*. What plagued her now was wondering how *he* viewed her, after she had forgotten him in his time of need.

Was it too late to repair their friendship—was there even a friendship without Tandy? She had been thoughtless for forgetting about him, but she was stupid for coming here now with hopes of normalcy too. Things would never be normal again, not for the two of them. Not without Tandy.

Kenny looked past her. "Is Jared with you?" Sloan sighed at his question. She should have brought Jared—he had remembered to care about Kenny's pain. She would just say what she could and leave him be.

"Look, Kenny, her Dismissal . . . it hurt me too much, so much so that I no longer thought about who else was hurting. I was selfish and I wish I had handled it all differently." It was the truth and it was all Sloan could offer him.

He nodded at her thoughtfully. "It's okay, Sloan. Jared explained everything to me." She had barely spoken to Jared about it, so what could he have possibly explained? Suddenly, Kenny perked up, looking over her shoulder. "You did bring him! How are you, man?"

Sloan felt a warm hand against her back and suddenly Jared was standing beside her. "I'm doing alright, Ken, how about you?"

Sloan watched Kenny transform in Jared's presence. He sat up in his bed, a half smile crossing his face, eyes wide as he watched Jared. Jared nudged Sloan to sit on the foot of the bed, which she did. He stood over her, an arm locked around her. Sloan couldn't have been more thankful. Jared, once again, had somehow known she needed him.

Kenny held his hands up, animatedly talking about his rib injury. Sloan nodded and smiled, laughed where appropriate, and as the time passed she didn't think about Tandy, or her frustration with Jared, or worry about Kenny in the Betrothal Calling. She had blissfully fallen into the familiarity of their conversation, admiring Jared for his unfailing ability to captivate people. She was reminded of why she loved him so easily: Jared was the one person who could make your life seem like it was a thousand times better than it truly was.

Jared patted Kenny on the shoulder as he said goodnight to him. "Get those ribs sorted out so we can get back to sparring. I need the extra training going into Fight Night," he offered kindly. Sloan felt a weight come over her at his words. She didn't want to think about Fight Night, not after such a pleasant evening. She wanted that feeling of normalcy to last just a bit longer . . . but it was clearly gone.

"Goodnight, Kenny." She smiled at him.

"Sloan, can I have a minute?" Kenny asked, staring at her intently. *No. . .*

But she said, "Sure," and nodded, squeezing Jared's hand desperately as he left the two of them to speak.

She awkwardly sat back down and Kenny abruptly took her hand in his. Had he ever held her hand? She couldn't think of a time. He didn't seem to think it strange, though, as he held on to her. "I wanted to thank you."

Sloan stared down at his tightly clasped fingers, curling around her own. "You have nothing to thank me for."

He shook his head at her, his eyes sad. "I wanted to thank you for loving her as much as I did, for suffering a broken heart as much as I am, for not knowing what to say to me this whole time because I haven't known what to say to you either."

Sloan's hand was shaking in his. "Kenny, if I could change what happened . . ." she offered, trying to steady her voice, forcing herself to look into his heart-broken eyes.

He shook his head, his jaw clenched, holding back tears. "There is no changing it. She will never come back to us."

Sloan leaned over and pulled him into a hug, holding on to him to ease the pain they both felt. After the longest moment, she released him and stood. There was nothing left for them. A heart never fully heals. After enough time, you just learned to live with the pain, and the pain existed for a reason. A reminder that part of you had disappeared along with the love you lost.

It was the saddest realization of Sloan's life.

She shook the thoughts away, patting his knee. "Get some sleep. I will see you tomorrow."

"I will see her soon," Kenny whispered.

Sloan felt her blood turn to ice, her hand freezing above the bed, her ears pricked up, keenly aware of every noise on the Infirmary floor. A cold shudder ran down her spine.

"*What* did you just say?"

He smiled at her question, his kind eyes watching her. "I said, I will see you soon."

Maybe she was going crazy, it *had* been a long day and she could have misheard him. *I didn't mishear him, I know I didn't . . .* "Are you sure?"

He nodded. "What did you think I said?"

She stared at him and her heart pounded under his intense stare. She nodded slowly. "Nothing. Never mind." She seemed unable to shake off the uneasy feeling, even as she disappeared behind the curtain.

She turned down the hall and found Jared waiting by the exit. She broke into a run, rushing to him, into his arms. She breathed in his warmth, believing that as long as he held her, she was incapable of falling to pieces. Her heartbeat was so heavy she could hear its strained pounding against his chest. What if someone had your whole heart and they let it break? If they hurt you beyond salvation?

She squeezed him tighter and loved him for his immediate response of holding on to her with all his strength. Sloan didn't know why the thought came to her, but she couldn't help but realize that she truly felt safest in the arms of the most dangerous person she knew.

Sloan couldn't help but think about everything that went into a Betrothal Calling as she dressed for the night ahead. The assessments took the students just under six months to complete. The process tested students' personality, mental acuity, emotional response, physical ability and intelligence. The machine responsible for processing the data and creating viable matches was called Nuptia. A viable match was made when two students shared 98 percent compatibility, and while it was probable for a handful to share lower percentile compatibility, it was near impossible to find multiple matches at a 98 percent tier. During your last exam you could write down a preference for your match. Sloan figured that was for the students' benefit, to believe you had some role in deciding your future. She had written *Jared Dawson* down in thick capital letters. She had checked it and rechecked it, until she was certain no one could make the mistake of thinking she wanted anyone else.

She sighed, the memory still lingering in her mind, as she pulled her hair over her shoulders, regarding her appearance in the bathroom mirror. She couldn't help but think of Tandy while getting ready. Someone would have had to remove her friend's data from Nuptia.

Whose job was that?

"What are you thinking about, beautiful?" Jared asked, appearing in the bathroom. Sloan eyed him up and down; he was glowing in his military whites. How had she been so lucky to be matched to the boy she had fallen in love with years before?

"I'm thinking about you," she sighed, turning away from him to check her appearance again. Her long blond locks fell loose around her face, but there was nothing she could do about the slight bruising on her pink cheeks, a result of recent spars, nor could she change the exhaustion she saw in her golden eyes.

"Thinking good things, I hope." He stood behind her, locking his strong arms around her. This was her favorite place—tucked in against his powerful frame. His strength was something she both loved and feared. She had given her love to a champion fighter, certain if anyone could keep it safe, it would be him. She had never thought about the potential danger in letting someone who could kill with his bare hands hold on to her heart.

He would rather die than hurt me, she thought . . . but he was hurting her. He was keeping secrets from her. And when he held her she knew she could love him through anything. But that didn't mean she should.

She turned in his arms to face him. "I need you to change your mind about Fight Night, Jare."

At her words he began to pull away. Sloan couldn't help but feel that whenever he let her go, he was letting go of *them*. It was a fleeting feeling, but it shook her to her core.

"We talked about this already."

She grabbed his hand. "No, *you* talked. Can't you just see that you don't have to do this?"

Sloan searched his blue eyes, looking past the unrecognizable for the familiar. He looked down at her, regarding her patiently. "This is a special night for us," he said. "Let's talk about it later."

She nodded her head, acquiescing, if only because they didn't have the time to argue; they couldn't be late for Romani. He pulled her into his embrace. "There *will* be a later," she promised. She nuzzled against his strong body, resting her head against his chest.

She wanted to be able to hear his heart still beating.

Jared held on to her hand tightly as they navigated the white corridors. They were headed for a senior floor conference room, one Sloan was certain she had never been to before. They still had no indication as to why Romani had asked to see them before the Calling, but Sloan had an uneasy feeling in her stomach.

"I don't like this, Jare," she complained, tugging at his arm as they neared the large white doors.

He glanced down at her. "It's fine. We'll be in and out in no time."

She sighed, continuing down the corridor to the

doors. Jared knocked and after a minute of silent waiting, both doors opened. Two Academy guards flanked the doors, gesturing for them to enter.

Apprehensively, Sloan stepped into the room, letting go of Jared's hand. Some sort of party was going on. The large white room had a wall made up entirely of windows from which you could look down on the training field and the rest of the Academy. There were white sofas, where people Sloan didn't recognize sat, engaging in conversation, sipping on drinks. A quiet classical piano tune filled the room, as servers dressed in ivory uniform carried silver platters around, navigating through the small group.

In the corner of the room Stone stood, leaning against the window. He was speaking to Colonel Luke, but as his eyes found hers he stood up straighter, as if he was surprised to see her.

She turned to walk towards him but the sound of her name froze her.

"Captain Dawson and Lieutenant Radcliffe!" Romani called, crossing the room with a quick stride.

They both stood to attention, saluting their marshal. He smiled at their formality. "At ease, at ease, this is a party."

Since when did he have a cheery side? Sloan wondered, eyeing him up warily. Jared had spent more time with the Order; was this a side of Romani he had seen before?

He quieted down and eyed her and Jared up. "Ready for the Calling, I see, very good."

"Yes, sir." Jared nodded. Sloan ran her hands over her white dress.

"Well, I won't keep you long. I simply have a few visitors who would like to meet you both, if you wouldn't mind accompanying me?" he explained, extending his arm out to the side.

Sloan glanced up to Jared but he looked as baffled as she felt. *What is going on here?*

Romani waited, his arm still outstretched. Jared took a quick breath and then walked towards the back of the room. Sloan followed closely. Romani overtook her and guided them to where a single Academy guard stood blocking a doorway. The guard saluted and then opened the door. Jared walked in first, followed by Romani, and then slowly, she followed.

They had entered a small room with fluorescent ceiling lights and nothing but plush white leather seats. *What is this room even for?*

Romani walked to the center of the small room, directly under the lights and in front of the chairs. "I will need you two to stand here. This won't take long."

"Sir, if you could possibly tell us what you need—" Jared began, but Romani shot an enraged glance towards him, silencing him.

"Captain Dawson, have you not asked *me* to assist *you* in a favor later this evening?"

Sloan looked from the marshal to Jared—what favor? What was he talking about?

"Yes, sir. Apologies, sir," Jared answered formally, standing up straighter.

"Very good. As I said, if you two could please stand here, this won't take a moment."

His voice was tense, on the verge of cracking. Sloan rested her hand against Jared's arm and guided him to the center of the room, appeasing Romani. She glanced around but everything out of the reach of the fluorescent light was too dark to make out. The door was still open and she could see a handful of people making their way over from the party.

Romani stepped into the doorway, turning his back to them. Sloan laced her fingers into Jared's, glancing up to him. "What's going on?" she whispered. He looked down at her and shrugged, sincerely uncertain.

Sloan took a deep breath, standing close to Jared under the bright light. People began to shuffle into the room—Stone, followed by Colonel Luke, Lieutenant Barden . . . the entire Order had come, and several people she didn't recognize. Sloan felt her stomach tense, beginning to sense her and Jared's purpose here. There was a woman wearing a neatly pressed pantsuit, her dark hair pulled into a severe bun; a young man, with short blond curls and dark eyes that traveled over Sloan as he made his way to a chair; and an older man, who wore thin-rimmed spectacles and had a bushy grey moustache. Sloan watched the three take their seats, directly in front of where she and Jared stood. The majority of the Order followed suit, except for Stone, who stood, arms crossed over his chest, an angered look across his stern face.

Romani stepped towards her and Jared, stroking

his chin with his white-gloved hand, a tight smile still pressed into his face. The Academy guard closed the door and they waited in silence.

"Mr. Franc, Ms. Beaumont and Mr. Degrassi, these are the two I have spoken about to you." Romani addressed the three strangers.

Sloan eyed them up—she had definitely never seen them before and she couldn't recall ever hearing those names. The three of them looked over her and Jared and then quickly leaned into one another, exchanging hushed whispers.

Sloan didn't know what to do. *Who were these people? What had Romani told them about her and Jared?* She focused her eyes on Stone but couldn't quite catch his gaze.

"May we?" The stern woman—Ms. Beaumont—spoke. Romani nodded animatedly, seeming to understand her request.

"Yes, yes, of course," he answered, waving them over. The three of them stood and crossed the small distance, stepping into the fluorescent light. Ms. Beaumont and the older man approached Jared; standing but inches away from him, they began to look him over—*inspecting* him. The younger man came straight up to Sloan, his intent gaze traveling over her slowly.

She leaned back, wanting to put space between herself and this stranger. She glanced to Romani, wanting to know what was going on, but he just watched as she and Jared were made spectacles of.

The older man circled Jared, walking behind the

two until he came up on Sloan's side. He leaned in, studying her face. "This little girl," he began, shaking his hand at her, "is your *champion*?"

Romani stepped in. "Yes, both of them are. The best of the best."

"But she's so—" the older man continued, but he was cut off by the younger.

"Beautiful. She's so beautiful." He smiled, tilting his blond head to view her from a different angle.

What the hell is this? Sloan wanted to demand, but she could sense Romani's unsettling demeanor. If she embarrassed him, if she did anything short of allowing these strangers to regard her like property, who knew how he would react . . .

She could feel Jared tense at her side, his hand twitching.

"The boy—how old is he?" Ms. Beaumont piped up, leaning past them to see the marshal.

"Seventeen. In prime condition." Romani smiled.

"So young." She shook her head.

"I assure you, you won't find anyone more impressive than Captain Dawson, Ms. Beaumont. He is the finest our Academy has," Romani stressed.

"I have to disagree," the young blond man chided, standing directly in front of Sloan, his dark eyes flicking over her.

"Careful, Mr. Degrassi, you wouldn't want to anger Mr. Dawson." Romani laughed—his version of a joke.

"So she is spoken for?" Mr. Degrassi asked, not

seeming all that bothered by the threat of Jared, or Sloan's relationship.

"She is spoken for." Jared's voice startled Sloan. Mr. Degrassi turned his gaze, staring at Jared with a bemused expression.

Mr. Franc scoffed, leaning away from Sloan. "She is with the boy? Then surely she rides on his success."

Romani shook his head, coming closer, closer to Sloan than she could ever recall him being. "I assure you, Mr. Franc, she is quite lethal."

Sloan's chest heaved with each deep breath she took. *What is going on here?* She wanted to know who these people were and why she and Jared were on display for them. How could they speak about them like this—like they were merchandise?

"Yes, you can see it in her eyes, she's *fiery*." Mr. Degrassi smiled, turning his gaze back to her. Slowly, he raised his hand, reaching for Sloan's arm. Her entire body tensed as she leaned out of his reach.

She no longer cared what this sick display was or who these people were; she didn't care about angering Romani or the Order. She caught Mr. Degrassi's dark eyes, glaring at him as she spoke softly, "Touch me and I will break you."

His young face contorted under her threat, gauging her seriousness. Then, stepping away from her, his amused smile returned. "Feisty indeed."

A movement from the back of the room caught her eye. Stone was approaching, quietly getting closer to her.

Ms. Beaumont walked past Sloan, approaching Romani. "A presentation then. If she is his equal then have them perform a demonstration."

Sloan's fists tensed at her side. *Do you think we are circus animals?*

Stone stepped into the bright fluorescent light. "I'm afraid I have to decline. These are *my* champions and not only do they have an event to attend shortly, they are both in training for an impending fight, and I cannot risk their injury."

Romani scoffed loudly, shooting a dismissive glance at Stone. "Our good guests demand a presentation. They have traveled quite a distance to see our finest students, General."

Mr. Degrassi folded his arms, stepping back. "I concur. If you cannot provide us with some evidence as to their abilities, then I can assure you, investing will no longer be a viable option for my party."

Investing? Who are these people? Sloan wanted to demand. She turned her gaze to Jared. His fists were clenched at his sides, his jaw tense. He kept his stare trained forward—he was trying to remain calm. Sloan loosened her own fist and ran her hand against his, discreetly holding his tightly knotted fingers. Why were the Order doing this to them?

"Of course, of course," Romani acquiesced politely. Stone shook his head at the marshal.

"Romani, I must insist—"

"General, that is quite enough." The marshal's voice cut through the room. He took a slow breath, composing himself. "Please, all of you, be seated. I assure you my students are as lethal as they are obedient. You will have a demonstration."

Mr. Degrassi and his colleagues finally backed away from her and Jared, returning to their seats. Sloan watched Stone back up, but he didn't sit; he remained on the periphery of the lights.

What is Romani going to make us do? Sloan let go of Jared's hand, taking steady breaths, waiting apprehensively.

Romani approached Jared, his hands folded behind his back. "Captain Dawson, pick a number between one and ten."

Sloan watched Jared's cold blue gaze fall on to the marshal. Sloan couldn't imagine how Jared was feeling. Objectified? Humiliated? Sloan knew that whatever favor Romani was doing for Jared wasn't worth undergoing this treatment, but what choice did they have? They couldn't walk out; they couldn't disobey their highest-ranking leader.

Jared exhaled slowly. "Seven."

Romani smiled broadly. "Marvelous." He turned from them, walking towards the closed door where the Academy guard stood. He spoke to the guard quickly, quietly, and then returned, taking a seat beside Ms. Beaumont.

Sloan glanced to Stone; he was staring at her with a look of concern and apology. *Why are they doing this to us?*

Before she could think on it further, the door

opened. One by one, seven Academy guards entered the room, wearing their ivory shield uniforms—leg plates, white chest plates, bleached chrome helmets. *Was this some sort of game for Romani, tricking Jared into choosing a number of guards to fight?*

Sloan took a step back, and Jared moved with her until they stood side by side. They both knew what was about to happen. He began to unbutton his white coat as she pulled her hair back, tying it into a knot. She looked up to him, slowing down her breath, watching from her periphery as the guards neared. "I'll take lead, you finish them?"

"Works for me." He nodded, his voice low and angry as he took several steps back, leaving Sloan in the foreground.

Sloan took a slow breath, closing her eyes, feeling the adrenaline course through her veins and excite her muscles. As she entered her element she became deaf to any noises in the room. She opened her eyes, letting her tunnel vision take effect—when she fought, she had a singular goal, an entirely relentless concentration that nothing could distract her from.

There was a single second, when Sloan drew one final breath, when the room was entirely still, when she brought her hands up to guard and strike, and moved her feet to gain greater balance—and then the guards descended.

The first two charged her wildly—these were not unskilled junior students. These were Academy graduates. As one made an initial strike the other grabbed her arm, violently jerking her towards him. Sloan ducked her head, missing the guard's fist, and viciously kicked at the guard holding her arm, her flowing dress whirling around her. He released her and she grabbed him in turn, bending his arm back and striking the back of his neck—sending him falling to Jared's feet. The first guard spun, twirling around and connecting a backhand against Sloan's face.

She recovered quickly, blocking his next assault. He was fast and had a formidable size. She needed to connect a hit quickly and pass him on to Jared—in the corner of her eye she saw the next guards preparing to make their move. *One.* She ducked, blocked and struck—connecting a hit against the guard's exposed throat. He grabbed at his throat instinctively, suffering a loss of air and allowing Jared to make his move. *Two.* Sloan turned from him just in time—the third guard was about to hit her with a roundhouse.

She blocked, stepped into him, scissor kicking him and rolling to the ground with him. *Three.* She leaped to her feet, stomping violently against his abdomen before leaping on the next guard. Like a spider, she scaled his body, locking her legs around his neck and pulling him to the floor. As they fell, she pulled his helmet off and struck him against the head—knocking him out. *Four.*

Suddenly, she was being hauled to her feet, strong arms grabbing at her. She broke an arm free from his grasp, reached over her shoulder and grabbed the helmeted head. With a ferocious jerk, she slammed her body forward, flipping the guard over her. He rolled to the ground and she leaped on him, executing strike after strike on his body. *Five.*

"Sloan!" Jared's voice drew her gaze upward—in time to be grabbed by the throat. The guard heaved her to her feet, strangling her.

She punched at the inside of his arm until his grip loosened, and then, grabbing his elbow and wrist, she wrenched him forward. He buckled at the waist. "Jared!" she called, shoving the guard at him. *Six.*

The next guard connected a solid kick to Sloan's chest. She flew back, rolling in a backwards somersault as she fell. She got to her feet, her chest on fire, struggling for a breath. The guard wasn't waiting for anything. She turned, grabbing Jared's arm for leverage as she flung the guard away with a strong back kick. Jared pulled her upright, spinning around her. The guard he had been fighting was almost out—Sloan whipped an arm out, wrenching the helmet off the man violently. With a feral gasp of air and expense of energy, she struck the man with his helmet—sending him unconscious to the floor.

"You had to say seven!" she called over her shoulder, pivoting around. She stopped as her eyes fell to Jared. The guard couldn't land a strike on him—Jared was too quick; he was too good at anticipating someone's next move. He moved around the guard like a wildcat, executing strike after strike. Jared made a final hit and the guard fell to his knees. Sloan leaped.

She swung a leg around the guard's neck, locking him in between her legs, and rolled to the floor, hitting the man's head against the ground roughly. *Seven*.

Sloan took a slow breath—assessing her body for injury. Jared helped her to her feet. He had a cut lip but otherwise seemed fine. She took a deeper breath, testing her ribs. She flailed her arms and shook out her legs—she was okay.

The loud clapping drew her back to their *audience*. She turned, facing the Order and their guests. Mr. Franc was clapping animatedly, standing for emphasis. Romani stood, a wide smile painted across his face.

"I told you—*lethal*."

"Indeed," Mr. Degrassi agreed, standing, his eyes still lingering on Sloan. She looked around, the guards beginning to come to and get to their feet.

Ms. Beaumont stood. "The way these two move around one another, as though they share one mind," she spoke, nearing Jared. She stopped inches away from him and stared for the longest moment before turning her cold gaze to Sloan.

"He truly loves you."

Sloan didn't know how to respond—if she was even *allowed* to respond. She said nothing, and slowly, the woman retreated.

"I want to leave," she whispered to Jared. He nodded, closing his hand around hers.

"When can we discuss our options—" Ms. Beaumont began, but Romani raised a hand, interrupting her.

"Later, of course. My champions have a dance to go prepare for now, but we can discuss details after tonight's ceremonial event."

Sloan listened keenly, looking from Romani to his guests, wanting to ascertain the point of all of this . . . to no avail.

Romani turned to Jared. "Captain, thank you for your assistance here tonight. I will be more than happy to help you with your plans later this evening at the ceremony."

What plans? Sloan felt so lost—so confused. She needed to get out of here.

"Sir, are we excused?"

His gaze fell to her and he regarded her with such unsettling contentment. "Yes, Lieutenant. Thank you for your marvelous display of talent."

Sloan felt nauseous under his heavy gaze. How could he have treated them this way?

She pulled at Jared's hand. "Come on . . ."

He nodded, following her out of the room.

Jared stormed down the hall, half dragging Sloan into the pod. He released her hand once inside and she immediately sat down. He remained standing, pacing the small space.

"Jare, what the hell was that?"

He ran his hands through his dark hair, pivoting back and forth. "He said he would leave you out of all of this . . . he *said* . . . Are you okay? Are you hurt?"

he rambled as he turned his gaze to her, touching her chin to inspect her face.

She lowered his hand from her. "I'm fine—what are you talking about? Why would the Order do that to us and who were those people?"

"I don't know . . . I wasn't told. I didn't think he would do that, but they said guests were coming . . . I should have known better." He began to pace again, wildly talking to himself.

"Just sit down—talk to me," she ordered, grabbing at his hand. He slowly sat down, watching her with wild eyes.

"I'm so sorry," he whispered.

"Sorry for what? Did you know we were going to be made to do that?"

He shook his head. "No, of course not . . ."

"Who were those strangers?"

"I don't know. I don't know anything, Sloan. All I know is—" But he silenced himself.

Sloan turned her body, getting closer to him. "All you know is what? What do you know that I don't?"

He looked away from her. "I can't tell you . . ."

She gritted her teeth in frustration. *Of course you can't . . .*

"Jared, come on! Tell me what is going on here. We were just put on display for three total strangers and had to fight a handful of our own guards—what do you know that I don't?"

He stood and knelt before her, grabbing her hands. "I swear I don't know anything about that. I had no clue what we were walking into or who those people were."

Sloan regarded his panicked face—the desperation in his blue eyes, the worry resonating through his voice. "Then what favor is Romani doing for you?"

"What favor isn't he doing for me right now is more like it," he sighed, sitting back up on the seat beside her.

"What is that supposed to mean?"

He shook his head. "I have a gift for you . . . A present, he helped me plan something."

Sloan studied him warily. *What sort of gift?*

"You're saying we just got objectified and attacked over a gift?"

"No . . . that was over something else. He knew we couldn't say no to him. He knows *I* can't say no to him."

Sloan shook her head. "You aren't making any sense."

"Can we talk about this later? We need to get to the Calling . . . the Order will be following us there any minute now."

Sloan leaned back in her seat. She had never seen him in such a state. She didn't know what he was talking about, what he was being honest about, what he did or didn't know. She wanted to be angry, she wanted to demand the truth—demand more facts . . . but she couldn't see him like this for a minute longer. It was her duty to protect him, her role in life to support him. But, looking down at her mangled hands and blood-speckled dress, she had to wonder how much more she would be expected to tolerate.

"Jared, I have always believed that everything we have done, we have done for one another. That we would do anything to sustain us. And lately, that isn't how I feel you have been."

Her words cut through him. His mouth fell slightly open, his blue eyes widened. He grabbed her hands. "Everything I am doing, I am doing for you—I am doing *for us*. I swear it."

"Promise me. Promise me if I go to the Calling with you now and we get through this night, you will tell me everything?"

He nodded slowly before speaking. "Swear to me that whatever I tell you, however I choose to proceed once you know everything, that you won't ever leave me?"

They held one another's bruised and battered hands and sat in silence—neither of them capable of answering the other.

Sloan let the cold tap water run over her knuckles, washing away traces of blood and soothing the tender ache of bruising. She didn't have time to go to the Infirmary; she barely had enough time to duck into the bathroom to clean up before going into the Calling.

She had a million thoughts racing through her mind—who were those three people she was made to fight for? What did Romani have over Jared and did it somehow relate to his recent behavior changes? She wanted to sit in silence, to think out what had transpired this night—but the night was just beginning.

As group after group of giggling, white-dressed girls came rushing in and out of the bathroom, she couldn't concentrate on tonight's events—on Romani or the fighting or the way that Degrassi man had leered over her. Her mind was overwhelmed by a sense of déjà vu, bringing forward memories of her own Betrothal Calling.

She had been standing in the partitioned room, waiting to hear her fate. General Stone's familiar voice had echoed out. "Sloan Radcliffe to be paired with . . ." Sloan was certain she was about to faint. There was no world in which she didn't belong with Jared. "Sloan Radcliffe to be paired with Jared Jacob Dawson." She felt her heart stop. Relief stole her breath away, paralyzed her muscles, slowed her senses.

Relief felt an awful lot like dying.

The auditorium erupted in cheering. She stumbled under the amber lights and all she could see was Jared. He stood there, hands in pockets, dark hair flicked to the side, his easy smile . . . He didn't walk to the Order, like he should. He took confident, easy strides across the stage. Towards her. She willed one determined foot after the next until she was in his arms. He spun her round and she held his neck, kissing him as he lowered her. The students cheered and whistled and all she could do as he set her on her feet was look at the way he glowed golden. "I told you," he whispered. "I told you that you were mine."

"Excuse me." A junior student bumped into Sloan, knocking her hand into the faucet. Sloan hissed at the pain.

She wanted to get out of here, to find Jared and talk this out. She needed answers, but if he demanded promises from her, could she make them?

She turned the taps off and regarded her appearance. Her cheek was red and swelling; a small cut framed her lower lip. She shook her head . . . This night couldn't get any worse.

She made her way out of the bathroom, navigating the busy corridor until finally making her way into the hall that she usually trained in—it had been transformed into a grand room. Soft white and golden lights glistened over the walls. Where there had been training equipment, there were now tables of food and drink, and in the corner, the student band had set up. The usual viewing stands were draped in white cloth and to the far left of the hall, a massive platform with two partitioned rooms flanking either side had been erected. Center back on the stage was the panel desk, where the Order would preside.

The Order . . . They were the last people she wanted to see again tonight.

Sloan walked closer to the platform. She knew the seniors would be called up first, reliving their own Calling, before commencing the Principle dance—a formal performance that honored the Calling. Sloan remembered practicing with Jared, learning the dance for the first time. He had lifted her into a dramatic dip. *"Don't let me fall!"* At her order, he had safely placed her on her feet.

"Never."

Tandy had been watching their practice, commenting to Sloan afterwards, *"He holds you like he'll never let you go."* Sloan had shrugged to her best friend, eyes still on the boy she loved.

"He won't."

How had so much changed between then and now? How could Jared be keeping such secrets from her, planning such dark plans; how could the Order be treating them like this; how could Tandy be gone?

Thinking of Tandy made her think of Kenny. He would have spent today preparing for the ceremony. Which poor girl would now be forced to live with him, to live with Tandy's ghost?

Sloan followed the stage, running her hand over the cloth edges, making her way behind the partitioned rooms. When had her life begun to fall to pieces?

As though on cue, a hand fell on her lower back— Elijah Daniels appeared at her side. She jerked away from him, letting his hand fall.

"Don't *ever* touch me," she growled—a flash of Mr. Degrassi's smile crossing her mind.

He smiled at her anger, leaning in, closing the gap between them but careful not to touch her. "I know you were invited to see the Order earlier. I don't know why but I thought it worth telling you that Jared won't back out of Fight Night, and neither will I, if that's what you were talking to them about. Dawson and I— it's been a long time coming."

"I am not in the mood for this, Daniels." She was already infuriated—everyone baited her with their insistence that they wouldn't back out of this fight, but no one would tell her why. She wasn't an idiot—she *knew* she was somehow involved. She knew Romani knew something, that Stone knew something, and yet, everyone sidestepped the truth.

Jared had become murderous overnight and Romani had them acting like dancing puppets. Elijah taunting her was the last thing she needed.

He rested an arm against the stage platform, encircling her with his broad body. *Why does he have to look at me like that?* She tore her gaze from his brilliant green eyes.

"You need to stay away from me," she ordered.

"I'm not afraid of Jared," he whispered.

She looked at the small gap between their bodies—how could so much complication fit into such a small space? How could she feel such anger towards him but want so badly to keep him alive?

She glanced up to his face, his mouth so near her cheek.

"You should be."

He brought his hand up to her face, gently moving a lock of her hair. He liked her . . . He liked *this*, being able to be near her. Was it a crush? Was that the stupid cause of Jared's irrationality?

She didn't immediately pull away from him, hoping to use his interest to her advantage. "What did you do to upset Jared?"

He leaned down, his breath running over her cheek, hot down her neck.

"I'm doing it right now."

His words broke her from trying to play his game. She scowled, pushing him away.

"I told you *not* to touch me. You get that I love him, right? That I will always love him. I am *rightfully his*."

Then why wouldn't you agree to his promise in the pod tonight? Sloan pushed her conscience away, honing in on Elijah's hurt face.

"Are you sure that you're *rightfully* his?" He stared at her, challenging, but she stepped further away.

What the hell is that supposed to mean?

But it didn't really matter right now. She didn't want to be *here*, she didn't want to be with Elijah, she didn't want to spend one more minute of this night parading around for the Order—but she had no choice.

"I don't know why I care what he does to you, but if you have any sense, you will leave Jared alone." Her words were filled with her natural fierceness, and no matter who he thought he was, he was smart enough to know that she was being serious. She turned from him, ready to leave.

"But you *do* care?"

The question stopped Sloan in her tracks. She turned back slowly. He stood there, shoulders curves awkwardly, green eyes hopeful.

"You do care about what happens to me, don't you?"

She didn't know what to say to him. She didn't know why she felt the way she did—she feared losing Jared, and that's exactly what would happen if he killed Elijah.

She settled on a partial truth.

"I care that he doesn't kill you, sure." Then she walked away.

Sloan found Jared near the entrance, watching the room around him. She leaned against the wall next to him and he fastened an arm around her small waist.

Her world felt fragile—everything about this night brought reminders of her life when it was seemingly perfect, and yet, it all felt so deeply wrong. What the Order had done to them; Tandy being gone; the fact that Kenny would be paired to a stranger; everything with Elijah . . .

"I hate this," she sighed, knowing he would know what she was referring to.

"So do I . . . I promise, Sloan, if you can just see this through, it will all work out."

She looked up into his familiar blue eyes and while she wanted to say a thousand and one things, she remained silent, kissing him instead. Was he right? If she had blind faith in their love would things work out?

With a loud step from the adjacent Academy sentries, the double doors to the hall flew open, and the Order, *led by Romani*, filed in. Sloan's entire body tensed up, rage filling her. Jared held her closer, keeping a narrowed eye on their leaders as they shuffled past.

"Let's join the others," he whispered, pushing away from the wall and leading her to where the other senior students had gathered near the platform. The Order had made their way up to the stage and had sat at their large table. Romani waited a moment—as usual—and finally saluted them.

He leaned forward, resting his chin on the back of his white-gloved hand. "I speak for the entire Order when I say we are most excited to greet the Academy's newest unions."

Sloan glanced around, wondering where Mr. Degrassi and his associates were. *Still at that sick party probably.*

Romani pressed on. "Junior students, I have invited you here tonight to witness that which you too will soon be endeavoring. The Betrothal Calling is a practice near as old as this very establishment. We pair up the finest unions and we create more than just marriages.

"You are the chosen soldiers, those shaped by us to perform great duties in this world. We provide you with your one ideal partner, the sole individual who knows your mind better than you do, who will help push you to achieve the greatest of feats, who will watch your back when you descend upon the enemy, who will help nurse your wounds and who will have blind faith in you, no matter what."

Jared tensed beside her, curling his arms across his chest. Sloan didn't know if he was simply still mad about earlier tonight or if it was something Romani had said, but she knew that his words had struck a chord in her. " . . . *have blind faith in you, no matter what* . . ."

Was she failing to be what Nuptia had assured Jared

she would be—was she capable of offering him her blind faith? She felt an odd sensation of inadequacy and frustration. Maybe she wasn't exhibiting blind faith in him, but he wasn't putting any faith in her either—he didn't trust her enough to be honest with her, and she didn't trust him enough to believe he had valid reasons to be acting the way he had been.

Romani's voice pulled her back. "My senior students, I ask that you make yourselves available to those newly paired, to lend them your experience during this transition."

Sloan bit her lip, resisting the urge to roll her eyes at the hypocrisy of his request. How could he, just the other day, tell them to coldly disregard their Dismissed peers only to then ask them to care about their fellow students?

"We shall commence the evening with the Principle dance." Romani leaned back in his chair, speaking softly with the Order. They would each call out a name, ordered by the surname of the partner with the highest ranking. Sloan loosened Jared's arms, pulling his hand into hers.

She loved him—she *truly* loved him. Why couldn't they trust each other, though? She would do anything for this boy—she would give up her own life for him—but she couldn't do it blindly; she couldn't do it on pure faith alone. She needed to see that he trusted her too, that he trusted her before anything else.

She closed her eyes; she didn't want to think about this anymore. She wanted the clock to turn back on their lives; she wanted to be back at her own Calling. She leaned against Jared, letting those memories return to her.

"*Tell me you will be mine forever,*" *he whispered. Sloan had thought he had fallen asleep. She ran her fingers over his back as they lay on the mess of their bed in their new room. Their room. The thought was enough to make her smile. He turned on to his side to face her, watching her in the darkness.*

"*I'm yours . . . forever.*"

In an instant he was on top of her, perched on his elbow, his face inches above her own.

"*Promise, Sloan.*" *His words were an order, a desperate request. Sloan freed an arm from underneath him and touched his perfect face. She ran her thumb over his lip.*

"*I promise.*"

He hesitated before finally relaxing, resting next to her, kissing her bare shoulder.

"*Sloan, you know I would die for you.*"

She leaned over, kissing the top of his head. "I know."

They lay still, breathing rhythmically, and Sloan couldn't help but think that her life was as close to perfect as she could ever hope for. He was hers, truly, only hers. The Calling was over and now no one could take him away.

"*Sloan?*"

His voice was a soft murmur in the dark.

"*Yeah?*" *She stroked his arm, opening her eyes slowly. His head rested on her chest, rising and falling with each breath she took.*

"*I'm never going to let you go.*"

She smiled and affectionately squeezed his arm "I'm not going anywhere without you."

He nodded.

"You should get some sleep," she added, gently readjusting him in her arms.

"I will . . . I just like lying here with you. I love you so much. I always have."

Could her life get any better? She had the love of her best friend, of the Academy's favored student, of Jared Dawson. "I love you too."

"Sloan?" he asked again, turning in her arms to once again face her. She laughed at his persistence to keep talking. It was late and they had to wake up early. She couldn't blame him . . . they had just had the perfect night.

"Yes, Jare?"

He raised his hand and cupped her face.

"I would kill for you."

" . . . Captain Brett Crews-Tyler and Lieutenant Lara Elizabeth Rhodes," Amelia Brass called out. Brett clapped Jared on the shoulder as he and Lara made their way onto the stage. They saluted the Order, clasped hands and exited off the stage to take their position on the floor.

"Captain Graham Anthony Danners and Second Lieutenant Jordan Chey," Romani called out. Graham and Jordan made their way onto the stage, saluting the Order before boldly kissing. Sloan barely noticed, though. She couldn't help but wonder where Elijah had gone. He didn't have a betrothed, no one to perform the Principle dance with. Had she ever even seen him take part in a Betrothal Calling?

Before these past few days, had she ever even noticed him at all?

"Captain Jared Jacob Dawson and Lieutenant Sloan Radcliffe." General Stone called their names.

Jared led her forward and helped her up the steps and together they crossed the stage to the Order. Sloan kept her eyes on Stone, refusing to look at Romani as they saluted.

She began to step away when Jared grabbed her arm. Romani abruptly stood.

"Pardon the brief interruption," the marshal spoke, pulling a small box from his pocket. Sloan could feel her jaw tensing—*what now?*

He made his way around the table, a tight smile on his face still. He was pleased with them, with their little performance earlier.

"When Captain Dawson arrived at the Academy, he had a chain around his neck. Hanging from that chain was a token from his mother. After much deliberation we have agreed to let Captain Dawson present that very token to Lieutenant Radcliffe this evening."

Sloan stared up at Jared, shocked. *What is going on?* She could hear the sighs and murmurs of the Academy, just as she could feel a hundred sets of eyes on her. Jared had never told her about any token—he had never even *spoken* about his mother. Yet, here they were. Was this the big favor Romani had done for him? Was giving her this gift so important that they had been forced into that disgusting presentation earlier?

She watched as Romani handed Jared the box, and then Jared guided her out further onto the stage, in full view of their fellow students.

He smiled broadly—no longer seeming distracted by his anger or their recent fighting. "As an acknowledgment of my love and commitment to Sloan Radcliffe, I present her with this, my mother's ring." Jared shot his hand up in the air, revealing a small gold band. The students erupted in cheers and Sloan realized her mouth was open, her eyes widening—she was shocked. Not only could she have never guessed this was his big surprise, but she knew students didn't regain the possessions they arrived with until Departing Ceremonies.

How had he managed to convince the Order to let him do this—was it in exchange for showing up to perform for them tonight? Had he truly not known what he had agreed to when he planned this surprise for her?

Jared leaned into her. "Tell me you're mine." His words were soft—she was the only one who could hear him now.

"I am yours."

It was the only response she knew.

He slipped the ring onto her finger. The band was small, but Sloan was surprised at its astounding weight. He pulled her into a kiss, a tight embrace. She didn't understand why he was doing this—was the ring an apology, a promise, a tie to him? His mouth was soft against her neck as he held her.

"Promise you'll never leave me?"

He phrased it like a question. She knew better than to believe it was.

Sloan mirrored Jared, turning in circles as they danced. With an easy grace they spun counterclockwise, raising palms to meet one another again. "Do you like the ring?" She spun out, returning back to him.

"Of course . . . I'm just surprised."

What did you have to do to give this to me?

He leaned into her. "Good, I'm glad I can still surprise you after all this time."

She shot him a knowing look. "You certainly can."

She whirled under his arm, his hand landing lightly on her side. He spun her out and brought her back for their final dip. He held her thigh with one hand, his other firmly clutching her back, as he lowered her to the ground in one slow controlled motion. She couldn't help but think of the promises he had demanded from her—and the promises she had wanted from him.

"Swear you'll change your mind. Promise you won't get another student sent for Review." She forced the words out of her mouth as he held her precariously above the ground. He raised her slowly, taking a final pose. The Academy cheered, clapping for them. She barely heard him as he spoke.

"Everything I am doing, I am doing for you," he answered through his smile.

But Sloan wasn't smiling. She couldn't help but

notice that he asked every promise of her, but couldn't make one himself.

Sloan sat between Jared and the others of 27, crowded on the stands. The newest couple appeared on stage, saluting the Order, and took one another's hands for the first time. "Captain Mary Jo Nielsen to be paired with Lieutenant Michael Grate."

The Order continued to call out names; unions continued to form. Sloan felt claustrophobic. The weight of the ring on her hand, Jared's secrecy, Elijah's taunting and that disgusting performance the Order had forced her to undergo earlier—it was all too much to think about. She needed air—she needed to think clearly. Could she just step away without drawing attention to herself?

Before she could move, General Stone cleared his throat loudly, leaning forward to announce his next pairing.

"Lieutenant Kenneth Merose to be paired with—" Sloan sat up straighter, her heart racing.

"—Lieutenant Cassie Flatt."

Cassie Flatt. Sloan didn't know the girl. She rolled the name over in her mouth. It tasted wrong.

After a moment of silence, Kenny appeared. Slowly, he stepped away from the partitioned room, his eyes downcast. Opposite him, Cassie appeared. She didn't have Tandy's dark skin, she didn't have a mess of wild brown locks, she didn't have doe eyes, or hands that fluttered like butterflies at her side. She was just a girl, with heaving shoulders, crying.

Kenny and Cassie approached the Order, saluting dismally. The Academy was silent as they turned to face one another. Kenny took the girl's hand, his eyes still trained on the floor. Cassie covered her quivering lip with her free hand, choking back tears.

Sloan turned to Jared. "This is devastating." He offered her a helpless shrug.

Seeing two students suffer through the pairing was heartbreaking. There weren't many who formed relationships before the Calling; it was too much of a risk. She and Jared had, though, lucking out in the end. Kenneth and Tandy had as well . . .

Was this the alternative to having all your dreams come true?

As soon as the Order began to draw the ceremony to a close, Sloan rushed out of the hall. She couldn't stay there; she could barely remember why she had ever assumed the Calling was as wonderful for everyone as it had been for her. She climbed into a pod and jetted off to the outdoor training field. As the doors opened she sprung from the pod, running as fast as she could to reach the field. She fell to the hard ground, grasping at the blades of grass with her trembling fingers. Fingers that still ached from tonight's fight, fingers that still trembled under the weight of Jared's gift. She closed her eyes and saw Tandy's face. She had held Kenny's hand and talked about their loss, but she hadn't felt

Tandy's absence so keenly until seeing him hold hands with the wrong girl.

Her heart ached for her friend's pain, and it ached for her own relationship . . . She loved Jared for who he was, his confidence and easy grace, his competitive drive and charismatic nature. She loved him for who he had been for her, for the way he was ingrained in every memory she had of her own life. She toyed with the ring, imagining his mother, a blue-eyed woman who gave her most precious possession to her boy. A token of such value that he had now given to her to take care of . . . And once more a thought filled her head.

How can someone filled with such love be so heartless?

Sloan thought of Carson and how the older boy's death had changed Jared so greatly. Carson had suffered from a heart defect, one he had never spoken of. Jared and Carson had been sparring, laughing as the captain continued to pin Jared in front of Sloan.

Carson helped Jared get to his feet again. *"Dawson, if you keep watching her you're going to get hurt."*

Jared had smiled, shrugging helplessly. *"I can't take my eyes off of her."*

Carson had studied Jared skeptically. *"What are you going to do if you don't get paired in the Calling then?"*

Jared had walked over to her, kissing her forehead as he pulled her into his arms. *"Then I will burn this whole place to the ground,"* he promised, his words hot on her skin.

"What about you, Radcliffe? Are you in love with this

messy kid?" Carson had smiled at her; she tightened her grasp on Jared.

"Of course I am."

He had nodded at her approvingly, leaning over for his water bottle. *"Good. Then promise you won't break his heart,"* he had ordered, swigging his water.

"I prom—"

It was at that moment, Carson collapsed. Jared wrenched free from her, falling to his mentor's side. He pulled the older boy over, calling out his name, demanding he wake up. Carson's weak chest heaved, his hand resting on his heart, and before anyone could try something to help, he stopped breathing.

Stone had explained Carson's defect to her and Jared afterwards. The Infirmary had been monitoring him with medications, preparing for a surgery he never got to have. She had often thought about what his last words had been to her, how he had been speaking of love when his own heart had lost the ability to work. It hadn't taken long for Sloan to realize that the moment Carson's heart stopped, Jared's *had* broken.

Sloan looked up to the sky, wondering if she could still keep the promise she had tried to make to the older boy, the one she had always thought would be impossible to break.

I had made a promise, in my heart, to never hurt him— but why can he find it so easy to hurt me with these secrets, with these plans?

And there it was. Sloan could finally admit to herself that Jared was hurting her. The most defining aspect of love was trust—and somewhere along the way, she and Jared had stopped trusting one another. How could she ever trust him with her life when she could now see how easily he would end another's?

It wasn't just about their promises to each other; it was the promises they had made to their Academy. To their *families*. Sure, they spent their lives learning to kill, but that was under the threat of their own possible execution; it was a necessity for their family's safety. They, more than most, were meant to understand the *sanctity* of life. Needing to kill and choosing to kill were distinctly different.

More and more it seemed as if Jared had begun to lean more towards *choosing*.

Sloan wasn't just afraid of who Jared was becoming, she wasn't just afraid for Elijah . . . she was afraid of who *she* was becoming. Because she knew the truth. That however much Jared scared her, she wished she could be more like him.

She wished she could simply stop caring too.

As Sloan got to her feet, prepared to go back home, a single shot rang out in the night, a cracking whip in the darkness.

"**S**loan!" Paul's voice startled her, jerking her attention back. She dropped her fork, crossing her arms. She looked to Jared, who pushed food around aimlessly on his plate. It had been six days since Kenny's suicide—six days since she and Jared had formed any real conversation.

"We were asking if you were worried about Fight Night," Paul said.

"Worried about *my* fight? No, not at all." She shrugged. She had nothing to be worried about for her fight; Maya wasn't any real threat to her. But that was the last thing on her mind.

She had heard the gunshot. No one knew how Kenny had managed to get a pistol from the guarded lock safe, just as no one had seen him pocket a single bullet earlier in training. But he had. She had been the first to find him, followed by a swarm of sentries. She had screamed at them to get Amelia Brass, to get anyone from the Infirmary, to fix this. His pool of blood had stained her white dress. It was ruined, just as the Calling would always be for her from now on.

"Fight Night is going to go like it always does," Jared said, snapping her back to the present. "Sloan and I will remain reigning champs," he added, his usual confident voice sounding distinctly disinterested.

Six days. It had been six days since they had been forced into that disgusting display for the Order and he still had told her nothing—he refused to trust her with whatever reasons he had for wanting to send Elijah to Review, for whatever reasons the Order had for parading them out for those strangers.

"What if we don't win?" The question blurted out of her, an angry, demanding challenge.

"Look, I'm upset about Kenny too—" he began, taking in her temper.

She shook her head at him, cutting him off. "Since when did *you* give a *damn* about other students' lives?"

He stared at her with wide-eyed ferocity, silent and fuming. She didn't care anymore. How could he see the pain Tandy's death had caused everyone and live through Kenny's suicide and *still* plan on risking Elijah's life so carelessly?

"Go ahead, *champ*. Tell them what you're asking for at Fight Night." Her voice was low and provocative. If she was hurting him, she didn't care—he no longer cared about how he was hurting her.

Jared had pulled her out of the blood; he had dragged her away from Kenny's body. She hadn't realized she had been crying, hadn't realized she had been speaking aloud when she demanded to know why Kenny had done this. Hadn't realized until Jared had actually answered her.

"He was weak."

Jared's words had stunned her. If she had been the one to die instead of Tandy, would Jared have been *stronger* than Kenny, would he have survived her death despite every word he had ever spoken to the contrary? She had shoved him away from her, disgusted by his answer. Just as she was disgusted with him now for pretending he cared about Kenny's death in front of their table.

"What are you going to ask for?" Will pried. They all leaned around one another to look at Jared.

Jared shrugged nonchalantly, but his glare stayed trained on Sloan. "When I win, I am having Elijah Daniels go up for Review." His voice may have sounded confident, but Sloan could hear his nerves.

A piece of orange fell from Paul's hand. "Are you joking, man?"

"No, I'm not. The Academy relies on unions like Sloan's and mine. If Daniels can't respect that he deserves to go to Review, to be warned to toe the line or face Dismissal."

Will shook his head at Jared nervously. "Daniels is just messing with you guys. You can't risk his life for *that*."

"Shut up, Will," Mika snapped. "You would feel the same way if it was us."

"Well, I think it makes perfect sense, Jared." Erica smiled sweetly.

"Same here. Who cares about Daniels?" Devon laughed.

Jared pushed his food tray away. "Just shut up, all of you. None of you know why I need to do this."

"He's not a threat to our *union*, Jare. I'm betrothed to you; he just has a stupid crush," Sloan argued.

He narrowed his gaze on her. "You don't know what you're talking about. You don't know *everything*, Sloan."

She leaned across the table. "Then tell me."

"I *can't*."

Sloan recoiled. *Wrong answer.* She had waited long

enough, she had been patient, she had tried to reason with him, and he gave her nothing in return.

"Is he risking your life, Jared? Is he risking *mine*?" she demanded, hitting the table angrily.

Jared stood, staring at her with anger and desperation. "He is risking *everything* I have."

She stood, squaring off with him. "*How?* Tell me what he's doing."

He leaned away from her, crossing his arms, silent. She shook her head at his defiant reticence.

She took a step away. She was done with this. He had always sworn to do anything for her, do *anything* for their relationship, and when all she asked for was honesty, he couldn't give it.

"I love you, Jared, but I hope Daniels takes your championship. You don't deserve it."

"You don't know—" he began but she was already walking off. Crossing the hall.

Looking for Table 82.

The students on Elijah's table stared up at her expectantly. A blond boy nudged Elijah, cuing him to notice her. He smiled, flicking his dark hair out of his eyes. She was keenly aware of just how many eyes were watching her, wondering what Jared Dawson's betrothed was doing at Elijah Daniel's table.

"I need to speak to you."

He shrugged nonchalantly. "About what?"

"Not here."

He followed her gaze, taking in the watchful students around them. He stood, nodding a goodbye to his table. She needed answers.

She gave 27 a wide berth as she made a beeline for the pods, Elijah in tow. She dialed in the training hall and stepped into the pod. As the doors closed, the last thing Sloan saw was Jared's shocked face.

"So, are you going to tell me what's going on?" Elijah asked, sitting on the floor of the training hall. Sloan paced.

"No, you're going to tell *me* what's going on."

"What's that supposed to mean?"

She spun, glaring at him. "*Do not* play games with me, Daniels. I want the truth. What are you doing to Jared? What are you going to ask for in Fight Night that's so important you won't back out of it?"

He shook his head at her. "I don't want to talk about that."

"Why?" she snapped.

"Because I don't want you to hate me."

She had to admit that was the last thing she had expected him to say. More than ever, she knew this Fight Night was a bad idea.

"What is that supposed to mean? It doesn't even matter. You *need* to back out."

"I told you, I'm not afraid of Jared. I can beat him."

How could he be so naïve?

"He is *the* champion. He has seriously hurt people and he didn't even hate them."

"I already told you—I'm not afraid of him."

Sloan shook her head at him. "Just consider what *he's* going to ask for when he wins."

"I could wager a few guesses," he laughed stupidly.

"This *isn't* a game, you idiot! He is going to send you to Review."

She had been afraid that she wasn't going to be able to say it. That her love and loyalty to Jared—still tugging at her incessantly—would keep her silent. But the words fell from her with relief, a secret she no longer had to hold. She studied his face for some look of shock, but he stared up at her calmly. She moved to stand before him.

"Don't you understand? You're risking—" she began, but he raised a hand, silencing her.

"I already know . . . the same way he knows what I am asking for." He reached out to touch her hand but she snapped it away.

"You *know*?" She felt like the idiot now, dragging him here to help him avoid Jared's wrath. He *knew* the risks and didn't seem to care. It dawned on Sloan that perhaps Elijah Daniels wasn't so different from Jared Dawson.

Sloan shook her head at him, confused and angry. "There is nothing worth risking your life over." Even as she said it, though, she could hear Jared's long-ago promises.

"I would die for you. I would kill for you." It had never dawned on her that she wouldn't want him to.

As if echoing her thoughts, Elijah asked, "Really? You wouldn't risk your life for the Order? For Jared?"

"That's different . . . risking *my* life for duty or the one I love is not the same." She wouldn't risk her life for a championship title; she wouldn't risk someone else's life because they had an infatuation with Jared. Elijah could have all the feelings in the world for Sloan and it wouldn't be a threat to her love for Jared. How couldn't Jared see that?

"Well, what if I told you I was doing just that?"

"Doing *what*? Fighting for the sake of the Order?"

"No," he answered, shaking his head slowly. "Risking my life for love."

Sloan turned around. She didn't need to hear any more of this. Nothing she said seemed to have any impact.

"I'm not going to lose." His words followed her as she started to move to the exit. In an instant, he was in front of her.

"I can explain everything, Sloan—" he began, but was interrupted by the loud slam of the entrance doors swinging open, revealing Jared. He took measured steps across the hall, hands curled in fists, eyes alight.

"Sloan, I told you to stay away from *him*," he growled.

"Go to *hell*," she snapped, shaking her head at him boldly. She had spent her entire life being ordered around—she wouldn't take it from him too.

He stormed towards her. "You are *not* a captain, you do *not* need to know why Daniels and I are fighting, and you need to *stop challenging me* in front of the entire *damn* Academy!" His voice echoed through the auditorium, shaking her. She wouldn't be cowed. Not by this *person*—this *stranger*—standing before her.

Elijah stepped forward to meet Jared. "You need to calm down, Dawson."

"Screw you, Daniels. You're loving this, aren't you?" Jared snapped, shoving Elijah away.

Elijah stepped back angrily. "She deserves to know!"

"Know what?" Sloan yelled, getting in between the two.

"Do *not* say a word," Jared warned Elijah.

Sloan turned to face Jared. "I don't want to hear it from him anyway. You tell me. What are *you* keeping from me?"

Jared shook his head at her, staying silent. Elijah took that as an invitation to speak.

"Something went wrong in your Betrothal Calling, Sloan."

Sloan stumbled back as Jared leaped past her, punching Elijah. Elijah fell away, touching the corner of his mouth where a stream of blood appeared. He wiped it away, rounding on Jared.

"You know this fight won't change a thing. Even if you win, even if I get Reviewed or whatever happens to me. She *will* find out!"

"Find *what* out?" Sloan screamed. This time Elijah rounded on her angrily.

"Figure it out—you're a smart girl!"

Nothing came to her, though. Nothing had happened

at her Betrothal Calling other than being paired with the one she loved. She backed away from their expectant gazes, glaring at them with disbelief. *How did I end up here, with these two? Elijah, who has done nothing but try to ruin my relationship, and Jared, who has become unrecognizable?*

She studied his face—his blue eyes filled with frustration.

Doesn't he understand that he's a part of who I am? That when he changes, I change?

Sloan wanted everything to go back to how it used to be . . . to the days where she knew with certainty who she was because Jared knew who *he* was. To a time where she wasn't surrounded by secrets strong enough to kill.

Elijah was the first to move, taking a step towards her hesitantly. "You can fight it all you want, but there is *something* between you and me, something that you didn't know existed until I was a part of your life . . . But I knew it existed, Sloan, I knew there would be *something* between us—I knew it since the Calling when you got paired to Jared."

Sloan looked to Jared, but he turned away from her. How could he stand to hear Elijah say these things?

"There is *nothing* between us," she said, sidestepping him. She grabbed Jared's arm, pulling him round to face her. "Look at me!" she demanded, forcing his face towards her. "What is he talking about?"

She wanted him to tell her Elijah Daniels was a liar, to tell her that nothing had gone wrong in their pairing. He placed his large hands on hers as she cupped his face. She could see it in his eyes. She could see the truth before he said it.

"Something did go wrong . . ."

His words washed over her and she was certain she would fall. He quickly locked an arm around her waist, holding her steady. Sloan thought back to that night. *"I told you . . . I told you that you were mine."* He had been so certain . . . but he knew something had gone wrong. Her chest tightened as she tried to hold herself together, and a creeping realization made its way into her mind.

"Are you saying . . ." She shook her head, trying to brave the truth that she had, just minutes ago, been dying to know. "No. You and I—*we*—are not a mistake," she whispered.

This wasn't happening. This wasn't possible. Tears burnt her eyes, blurring the image she had of Jared, but she could see, through her pain, the look on his face and that was all the answer she needed.

"So what? Were you matched to someone else?" she asked him, so quietly she wasn't sure he had heard.

She remembered Jared's words to Carson. He would burn this school to the ground if he weren't paired to Sloan. Had he pulled strings, made a deal with Romani to get a different life than the one Nuptia had organized? How many people knew the truth that she had been too dumb to see—that she wasn't *truly* his?

The word *mistake* didn't seem big enough to hold the weight of its own implication. If she wasn't meant to be Jared's, it was more than a mistake. It was something that stole her breath away; something that filled her mouth with the metallic taste of loss and helplessness.

It was heartbreak.

He loosened his hold on her. "No," he answered.

"Then what?" she demanded.

"*I* wasn't matched to someone else."

She was confused—if he was meant to be hers then what could have been wrong? "But, then . . ."

Elijah spoke, shuffling in her periphery. "Sloan . . . *you* were matched to both of us. To Jared *and* to me."

She glared at him as he stood there, shoulders tensed up, uncomfortable with his own admission. Where were his cocky taunts now? Where was his attitude and bothersome persistence?

It was one thing to imagine a world where Jared was promised to someone else, someone who was his *true* soul mate. It hurt, but it was conceivable. But there was *no* world where she was meant for anyone but him.

She needed more space than this massive room had to offer. This room—where she had been promised to Jared. This room—where her reality was now being shattered. She stumbled away from them, dizzy. Jared reached for her, a look of fear painted across his beautiful face.

"There is no way you should have compatibility with both of us . . . it never happens . . . but you were a 98 percent match to us both and you got me because we wrote preferences."

Sloan was actually shocked that writing a preference had served a purpose. How long had he known and kept this from her?

She almost choked on her words. "Why didn't anyone tell me I had a choice? Why didn't *you* tell me?"

Jared took a deep breath. "They asked me if I wanted you to know you had a choice to make."

He had lied. He had omitted. He had betrayed her. He took a step towards her. "I did it because I love you . . . I couldn't risk losing you," he explained desperately.

She understood *that* but it didn't change the fact that *he* had ultimately made the decision for her. What had he done to ensure this secret remained kept from her? Who knew the truth and had been using it against him ever since? Stone? West? *Romani?* Who else allowed this to happen?

"How was *not* telling me your decision?"

"The marshal did it as a favor . . ." Jared's voice trailed off.

Sloan thought of the other night. Of the fight they had been forced into by the Order for those strangers. Those people who had viewed her as property, as some object.

"At what cost, Jared?" she yelled.

Her words cut into him, his pain reflected in his eyes. "I'm sor—" he began but she cut him off.

"How could you have been so blind? Don't you understand that you're the only person I ever loved? How could you think that by telling me I would have ever chosen *him*?" she asked, jerking her head in the direction of Elijah.

"*Dammit*, Sloan, I was afraid! Losing you would have killed me. I am only what I am because I have you. *We* are only who *we* are because we're together." He was on the brink of tears and it took all her strength to not wrap him in her arms and forgive him. But she couldn't. She looked to Elijah, a bystander to her and Jared's suffering. She hated him for existing, for being paired to her.

She glared at him with all the anger she felt. "What do you even *want*? Now that I know your big secret, what do you want from me?"

He stared at her with a perplexed expression. "I just want you," he answered boldly. As if it were the most obvious thing in the world.

Jared stepped in front of her, squaring off with Elijah. "Well, she doesn't want *you*, Daniels."

Elijah shook his head, sidestepping him and approaching Sloan. "You weren't so certain of *that* this whole time, were you, Dawson?"

Jared shoved him back from her. "Get away from her," he growled.

Sloan backed away from them both, her slow retreat drawing their attention. In disturbing unison, they reached out to her: Elijah stepping forward, Jared extending a hand, willing her to stay.

She shook her head, unsure which boy she was addressing when she spoke.

"Just let me go."

CHAPTER 4

When Sloan woke up, Jared was sitting at the end of their bed. She had a headache; her hair was damp with sweat. She felt disoriented and her eyes burnt with dried tears.

"I'm sorry," he whispered, leaning over to her.

Her throat was hot and swollen. "I don't know what to say to you."

"Say it's me. Say you would choose me." She wanted to reach out to him, but she was too upset to comfort him. Refusing her instincts felt wrong—she had only ever known how to love him, how to help him. She had never learned how to hurt him. And she didn't want to. She wanted to love him so much she could forget he had ever figured out how to hurt her.

"I *did* choose you, Jared. And I would have if presented with the choice too. Do you know how much it hurts that you didn't know that? That it has always been only you."

It's still only you. Sloan studied the dark outline of this man who had hurt her and saw instead a memory of the boy she had first loved. She had been four years old—crying in the dining hall—missing a family she now couldn't really remember having ever known. He had walked over to her, sat down beside her and held her hand. *"I'm all alone,"* she'd said. He squeezed her small fingers tightly, inching next to her.

"Not anymore."

He moved closer to her on the bed, relief on his face. "So, you see why Elijah has to go now, right?"

What? It was not at all what she had expected him to say. Sloan pulled away from him, sitting up slowly. "Wait—you're *still* going through with Fight Night?"

He nodded slowly. "I have to."

"But I choose you."

He shook his head at her, his eyes narrowing. "You still don't understand."

"Jared, pull out of Fight Night and I will stay with you, I will marry *you*, I won't ever tell anyone he was paired with me."

"He won't ever let that happen, Sloan. He will go into Fight Night and demand the Order give you to him as his Winnings. I can't back out; it's the only way to ensure you stay rightfully mine."

What?

Elijah's former words crossed her mind. *"Are you sure you're rightfully his?"*

She wasn't *rightfully* either of theirs. She had been

wrong to ever use that word; she hadn't meant it the way Jared and Elijah had.

She stood from the bed, steadying herself with the wall. "I am not rightfully yours—I choose you. I made a choice. I'm not going to just be *given* to him."

He stood. "Can't you see? You don't have a choice."

"Then let him ask! Let Elijah ask for me, beat him in the fight and we will carry on with our lives. But, Jared, *please* do *not* ask for him to be sent to Review."

He cursed under his breath, and with a sudden jolt, he hit the wall. "*Dammit*, Sloan. I don't have a choice either. He won't stop until I lose you—he will challenge me in championship fights again and again until the Order gives you to him."

Sloan stared at him. This wasn't possible—there was no way they could just *give* her to Elijah. And then she recalled how easily they had objectified her before, and the thought became much more terrifying.

"But they *can't* do that. I want you, I won't leave you."

"Yes, they can."

Sloan walked out of the bedroom aimlessly, shock overwhelming her. They couldn't do this—this couldn't be a possibility. He followed her into their living quarters.

"I'm *not* property, Jared."

"The Academy's favored daughter is given to their favored son. Daniels and I are neck and neck here . . . If he takes my championship, he will ask them to change their decision about our pairing."

Sloan felt sick. She needed to get out of here, to scream, to run, to fight her way out of this mess. She urgently searched for her shoes.

I am not something the Order can gift to the Academy's best captain. I am not a prize. She thought of the strings Jared had pulled, of Fight Night, of the threat of death happening in her name. She would *not* be the spoils going to their prize stud, like she apparently—unknowingly—always had been.

Sloan took deep measured breaths of the cool night air. It was late and the field was bare, completely dark barring a few floodlights on the perimeter. She ran to clear her head but couldn't get Jared off her mind. She sped up her pace.

She thought of their love and all they shared. Their laughs, their tears, their bodies . . . Had it all been a reward for having been the best? Had she made herself this trophy by pushing herself so hard? She had only ever worked to achieve such status *for* Jared, not for anyone else. Even, she could admit, not for herself. Yes, a part of her *wanted* to be the best, but it didn't define her. The responsibility that it had brought on was enough to buckle her most days, but it had been worth it to be with him. Had she let love blind her so greatly to what was going on around her?

She pushed past the pain in her heart, extending her legs further, curving away from the reach of the floodlights and turning into the darkness. With a sharp smack Sloan went flying into the air. She fell, tuck-and-rolled and lay sprawled in the grass.

"OW!" another voice barked.

She had tripped over someone. She quickly rolled to her knees, looking back. She strained her eyes in the dark. Adjusting to the low light, she saw Elijah sitting up, brushing off his knee.

"Of course it's you . . ." she hissed, rolling back to lie down, catching her breath. She could feel a graze on her elbow. "Just go away, Daniels."

He crawled over to her anyway. *Because apparently what I say or want means nothing.*

"Couldn't be nicer to someone you just trampled?"

"You don't deserve it," she said, feeling no remorse. She didn't care about him. He nodded, remaining silent.

"I told you to leave," she reminded.

"Well, unlike you, I have the right to make my own choices."

Sloan bolted upright, furious. "Don't you *ever* speak to me like that."

"Relax," he added quickly. "It was just a joke."

"I don't care if it was a joke. I don't want to hear *your* jokes. I don't want to hear *anything* from you at all."

He remained silent—effectively scolded.

Sloan took a deep breath, brushing grass off herself. "What are you *even* doing out here?" she demanded.

He shrugged his large shoulders. "Getting perspective."

She shook her head. *That's rich.* "On what? The fact that you're ruining someone's relationship?"

"*No*," he answered through grinding teeth. "I just like to look at the sky sometimes . . . It's the same sky that our families are seeing . . ."

Sloan might have hated this boy with a fiery passion but she wouldn't poke fun at him for trying to reminisce over his family.

Slowly, she turned her gaze upward. The midnight blue span was bedazzled with a million marvelous crystals. It *was* incredible but it didn't help her put a face to the parents who might also be looking up at it. She watched the sky transform above her, stars dancing and shooting. She didn't want to be out here with *him* and she didn't want to be inside with Jared.

"It all reminds me that this is just a place, just a time in our lives, that there's *more* out there." He spoke softly.

She turned to him. "It might be *just a place* but it's the place that made *us*—and it might just be *a time* in our lives, but the way you're going it could be where your life ends, and it could be where you ruin *my* life."

"I'm not trying to ruin your life," he whispered softly.

That seems to be exactly what you're trying to do.

He took a deep breath before adding, "The *Academy* ruins lives."

His words shocked her. Whether there was truth in them or not—*no one* spoke about the Academy like that.

"If you think the Academy ruins lives then why are you so hell-bent on having the Order honor Nuptia's pairing between us?"

He looked away from her. "Jared told you that's what I'm going to ask for?"

She didn't need to answer. Of course she knew now.

He sighed heavily. "Look, Nuptia might ruin lives, but it's not wrong about who makes good partners. I *need* someone I can trust, a partner."

Sloan thought of Kenny, of Cassie Flatt, of the very situation she found herself in with Jared and Elijah. It *did* ruin lives.

"I get that, Elijah, I really do . . . but it won't be *me*. Jared will ultimately try to get you Dismissed and you need to know, regardless of the fight, regardless of anything, I won't choose you."

If Jared went ahead with his murderous plans, though, she didn't know if she could choose him either.

He nodded at her slowly. "I won't need you to choose."

His words mirrored Jared.

She leaped to her feet—she had heard enough. "*Screw you*, Daniels."

As she stormed off she gasped for air, her emotions finally overwhelming her. She *wasn't* property. She deserved to have a choice in all of this—she couldn't just be given away by the Order. As she made futile attempts to hold back her tears, the skies above thundered, breaking the night open, releasing a shower of rain on her. She picked up her pace, but her mounting sobs began to ripple through her body, taking her over.

Her wet hair stuck to her face and she tried to push it out of her eyes with trembling hands. Her clothes clung to her small frame and slowed her. She heaved for a breath. Suddenly, Elijah was in front of her, his arms locking around her. She struck at him wildly, hitting him in the chest, trying to push him away from her.

"I *hate* you, don't you understand that? I will *never* choose you," she cried. He pushed past her sad assaults, past her hard words, and pulled her against his chest, letting her cry, letting her lash out against him.

"He doesn't love me enough to change his mind," she sobbed. He held her tightly, letting her break in his arms.

Through her mounting wails and the thunderous sky, she couldn't be sure, but she thought she heard him whisper, "He doesn't love you the way I do."

Fight Night was a week away. Sloan and Jared had barely spoken to one another. He was hell-bent on following through with his plans, despite her best efforts to change his mind. How couldn't he see that if he became someone *murderous* she couldn't love him the same way she always had? All he knew was that if he won his fight, he would keep her, with or without her consent. It was the only thought Jared and Elijah cared about. They didn't seem to care that if they won her over *that* way, she would never forgive them. She would never love them the way they hoped their win would ensure.

For a while, she had felt perpetually sick, knowing how much of her life wasn't her own. Until she remembered something that finally offered her a small degree of relief—*she* would have Winnings in Fight Night too.

General Stone circled a group of senior girls practicing Krav Maga. "Sir, can I speak to you?"

"Lieutenant, I will be with you in a minute for training," he answered dismissively.

They too had barely spoken recently. She hadn't known what to say to him about the fight the Order forced her into, and he seemed to have nothing to say to her about it.

"Sir, this isn't about training."

He shot her a questioning glance, but lifted his whistle and signaled the girls to stop.

It's nice to know there are still some privileges for being their champion.

"My office," he ordered, leading her to the back of the hall. She followed quickly, slamming the door shut behind them.

He sat down heavily in his chair, running his hands over his grey hair. She sat opposite him. She had never really noticed him ageing, but seeing him now, weary and tired, she could see it. His haggard hands and the deep lines around his eyes were all more prominent under the dull fluorescent lights.

"What's going on, Radcliffe?" He leaned back in his seat, crossing his arms over his broad chest. She explained what she was going to ask for from the Order when she won and she watched the incredulous look grow on Stone's face. He stifled a laugh and rubbed the back of his neck.

"All I can tell you is no one has *ever* asked for that."

"But I am allowed to ask for it?"

"You can ask for anything aside from a direct Dismissal of another student," he answered.

To Jared's great annoyance. . .

He cleared his throat. "But it is unorthodox and—"

"But, sir—"

He raised a hand to ward off her protest. "I'm not saying don't do it, Radcliffe, I am just saying"—he lowered his voice, speaking softer but somehow more seriously—"you're walking a fine line when you try to defy the Order . . ."

Sloan took a deep breath, taking in his ominous words. She knew that he was right. She thought of the fight they had forced her and Jared into; she thought of how they could give her away to Elijah if they so chose; she thought of Romani and his objectification of her; she thought of Tandy and Kenny . . .

Screw the Order—they were the ones walking a fine line by testing her limits.

"I'm not afraid," she answered boldly, acknowledging the fact that she did have something to be afraid of by pursuing this train of thought.

He nodded at her slowly, understanding her motives.

"Radcliffe, about the other night, and everything that is going on with you and Dawson and Daniels—I *am* sorry . . ." he offered, lowering his gruff demeanor, regarding her with sincere apology in his eyes.

She shrugged, dejected, resigned to her role

here—to the way the Academy saw her . . . but she wouldn't go quietly, she wouldn't accept objectification without putting up a fight.

"All I am in this place is property," she admitted boldly. What did she have to lose in being candid? She trusted this man with her life. She expected him to understand, but even if he didn't, what would it change? The Order didn't care if she knew how they saw her; they believed there was nothing she could do about it anyway.

"No, Radcliffe, not to me you aren't. You're the greatest student this place has ever seen. Believe me, I've trained them all." He leaned across the desk, speaking so softly she almost didn't hear him. "And that makes you *dangerous*."

Fight Night Prep was the preview sparring session between all the contenders—while it was meant to be an opportunity to display exercise and control in the ring, it was really just a highlight reel of what was to come. Sloan paced, stretching out her arms. She looked to Jared, warming up with Will; to Maya Woods, speaking to a group of her friends; to Elijah, who watched her warily as he loosened up . . . and she felt *nothing*. She felt *numb*.

Jared didn't love her enough to change his mind, Elijah wanted her so badly he would hurt anyone in the process of getting her, and the Order—the people whom she had put all her faith in—viewed her as their property, as a prize. There was only one person in this entire Academy who could see her for what she was—Stone. She *was* dangerous. She had been pushed too far.

Stone cleared his throat loudly. "Daniels and Radcliffe, Dawson and Woods, front and center. Everyone else, take a seat—this is Fight Night Prep!" His voice boomed through the hall. Students began to file into the stands as the four of them congregated on the training mats, circling Stone.

"Dawson—spar with Woods; Daniels, you take Radcliffe. When I blow my whistle, you swap whom you're sparring with."

Sloan squared off with Elijah. She hadn't spoken to him since that night in the rain. She didn't *want* to speak to him.

"Are you okay?" he asked, eyeing her up cautiously. She said nothing, her hands tightening into fists, squaring off with him.

She found her balance, rolling her head around, loosening up her neck. At the sound of the whistle, she gave in to her basic nature. She felt the adrenaline speed through her, she found the silence in the room despite all the noise, her vision narrowed in on her target, and she jumped—aiming a spinning kick at Elijah.

He blocked, narrowly escaping her assault. She spun and connected a roundhouse against him. He had a startled look in his eyes—surprised by her unbridled attack.

Still want me now? she thought, leaping forward and locking him with her legs in a scissor kick. He rolled to the ground with her—and she came out on top. She struck at him violently with quick, precise jabs. She got his cheek, his neck and his temple. With a swift shove, he sent her flying off him. She was on her feet first and made the first strike—she was too fast for him now.

He swung at her but she ducked, coming up behind him and pulling him into a chokehold. He flung his body forward, sending her flying over the top of him. She rolled to the ground, ready to make her next move, as the whistle blew.

Maya had leaped at the opportunity and Sloan barely caught the girl's foot as it came flying towards her face. She wrenched Maya's ankle, rolling to the side, and kicked at her knee. She jumped to her feet as Maya fell to her knees in pain.

You really think you're any match for me? She leaped, spiraling in the air, landing a back kick on the other girl. Maya fell back, rolling to the side, pushing herself up to her feet.

Sloan took a confident step towards her, lowering her guard. "Is this *all* you've got?" she berated her. Maya swung but Sloan caught her wrist, twisting it inward until Maya buckled at the waist. Sloan kneed her in the chest, and if that weren't enough, she kicked in the back of Maya's leg, forcing her to the ground— for good measure.

Sloan held her down forcefully. Incapacitating her gave her a chance to see Jared and Elijah—fighting full force for the first time.

Every strike, every hit and kick . . . they were too

similar. They moved with dangerous speed. Jared performed double roundhouse kicks, which Elijah blocked and answered with spinning hook kicks. They moved one another into locks as quickly as they broke free from them. They were incredible to watch.

It filled Sloan with terror—and with loathing. They fought so hard for her, to control her, to *win* her. She watched them move and saw the brilliance in their abilities and knew, with absolute certainty, that there was only one other student here who could fight like that—*her*.

She kept her eyes trained on them and found a deep desire to hit them—to *hurt them*, the way they had hurt her.

The whistle blew and Elijah immediately stopped his intended assault and turned away from Jared. Taking his exit as an easy opportunity, Jared nailed Elijah's ribs with a heavy side kick. They all heard the deafening snap. The look on Elijah's face confirmed the break.

Stone blew his whistle sharply. "Dawson!"

Jared paid no attention to Stone. He grabbed Elijah, ready to hit him again. *The rules don't apply to us—not anymore*, Sloan thought. She flung Maya's small body away from her, and leaped towards the guys.

She blocked Jared's next hit and the look in his eyes was pure anger—but it paled in comparison to her rage. He had devastated her—she *wanted* him to know her pain.

She hit him with a double upper cut, and stepping

into him, she cuffed him with an elbow strike. Before he could pull away, she kneed him in the abdomen, and as he lurched back, she landed a forward kick. He moved to grab her, to cage her with his arms, but she was too fast. She ducked, grabbing his arm and pulling it back in a lock, using all her might. She kicked at his legs, landing him flat on his stomach. She kneeled, holding his strong arm back, and kneed him in the ribs, feeling him break against her.

It hurts, doesn't it—being betrayed by the one you love?

Sloan was startled as a strong arm began to pull her away from Jared—it was Elijah. She spiraled in his grip, hitting him forcefully. He let her go and she struck a forward kick against his diaphragm. Jared was in front of her in an instant, in obvious pain, fear in his eyes as he watched her lose control.

"Sloan," he began, but she didn't want to hear it. She backhanded him, turning in time to kick Elijah back away from her. In her periphery, she saw Maya leap.

Stay out of this, amateur.

Sloan caught the girl, striking her in the temple as she flung Maya to the side. Elijah and Jared stood beside one another, both bruised and broken, both keenly aware of her rage.

Jared reached for her hand—*big mistake.* She grabbed his wrist, viciously turning it back as she twirled in, landing a back kick against his chest. Elijah moved to grab her, and she struck at his throat. She fell to the floor and spiraled on her foot, using her extended leg to kick his feet out from underneath him.

And then there was perfect silence—a moment of pure stillness. She rested, perched on her haunches, ready to strike out. The boys rolled to their feet, slowly rising. Maya was still on the floor, nursing her wounds, barely moving.

"Radcliffe." Stone's voice filled the room. She ignored him. Jared and Elijah, probably unbeknownst to them, raised their hands slowly, offering peace as they regarded her with fear.

Jared took a slow step towards her, extending his hand. She leaped to her feet, backing up. *"Don't touch me!"*

Her angry order echoed through the room. Stone slowly stepped onto the training mat. Sloan was aware that *everyone* was watching—she didn't care.

"Sloan," Elijah began but Stone grabbed the boy's shoulder and held him back. "Don't touch her. No one touch her."

Sloan's breath began to return, slowly filling her lungs. She could see the look of fear in all of their eyes, she could sense the tension in the room, and the way they all circled her—like she was a wild animal.

She regained her composure, pulling her shoulders back tightly, looking at the damage she had done. She looked at the shock, the concern and the pain in Elijah's and Jared's faces. She shook her head. She didn't need to be here—she didn't need to stay here. She looked from the boy who broke her heart, to the one who had wanted to win it, to the man who had trained her to be *this* lethal—and she had no idea which one she was addressing when she spoke. *"See what you've made me?"*

CHAPTER 5

Jared had opted to sleep in the Infirmary for the rest of the week, managing to skillfully avoid her. She had taken to eating in her living quarters, a concession granted by John, the kitchen head, based on her promise to train his son privately. Even now, as she sat in class, trying to ignore Mika and Erica's snide words about her, she played out the conversation she was going to have with Jared.

Since her display at Fight Night Prep virtually everyone had given her a wide berth—too afraid of her volatile nature. She glanced at the empty seats on either side of her—she had become a pariah. She didn't really care—no one understood what she was going through. The path all this insanity had put her on was one she was certain she would have to walk alone . . . but she missed *him*.

She wanted to tell him that hurting him had only

hurt her more. That he was part of what had pushed her to such limits—that his darkness had finally brought out hers. She wanted him to understand—to change his mind about Fight Night while he still had time to do so. She wanted him to know that if he changed back into the version of himself she knew and loved then she would change back too.

With a dull beep, the large metal door of the classroom slid to the side, revealing Elijah. Sloan eyed him suspiciously—he wasn't enrolled in this class. She watched as he walked over to Professor Masse, handing over a note. Masse looked it over, nodding. "Very well, take a seat."

He crossed the room, obviously still nursing broken ribs, and tossed his bag on the desk next to Sloan. "Is this seat taken?"

Sloan felt the stares of her classmates, but she ignored their speculative eyes as she looked up at Elijah with confusion. "What are you doing here?"

He winced in pain as he rummaged through his bag, taking a seat next to her. "I changed my classes around."

"*Why?*" she asked him in disbelief. He should have been as afraid of her as everyone else was now—*more so* than everyone else. He had helped unleash her rage and he was a prime target of it.

"Has anyone spoken to you since Fight Night Prep?" he whispered, arching his brow at her. She looked away—he knew no one was speaking to her.

She didn't have time for his games. "What do you *want*, Elijah?"

He readjusted in his seat, keeping a hand on his broken ribs. "I told you," he whispered, "I only want you."

She narrowed her gaze. "I *attacked* you," she reminded him.

He shrugged indifferently. "I still want you."

At that moment, Sloan experienced a feeling she had never expected—flattery. His persistence was strong enough to survive her violent attack against him, and that—being the *exact opposite* of the response she had expected—surprised her.

A hand tapped Elijah on the shoulder, and Sloan glanced back to see who it was. Tim Smith—a captain on 38—leaned over from the desk behind. "Careful, Dawson, *her* friends drop like flies." Elijah looked back at Smith's hand, resting on his shoulder, and then stared right into Tim's amused face.

"Talk about her again and I will break your hand, Smith." Elijah's whispered threat caused the boy to recoil, falling back in his seat. Even with broken ribs, there weren't many people in the Academy willing to challenge him. Sloan looked to Elijah, silently thanking him for his determination to win her over. Having him, she supposed, was better than having no one.

Sloan's dislike of the Infirmary had intensified threefold recently. She walked the narrow corridor, feeling

Tandy's and Kenny's presence at her side. She held her arms around herself, quietly navigating the clinical floor. The Infirmary had incredible technology: lasers that cauterized wounds, machines that scanned bodies in seconds and chip readers that could help identify unseen injuries. She wondered what damage would show up if she could be scanned now.

As she moved through the rows of rest beds, she looked for number 314, where Nurse Patty had told her Jared was. As she approached the bed number she was surprised by the sound of voices.

"She's unhinged. She broke your rib, Jared."

"You deserve better."

Sloan pulled the white curtain back and found Jared, sitting up, flanked by Mika and Erica.

She stood up straighter, glaring. "What are you two doing here?"

Erica stood, crossing her arms over her chest. *"Us?* What are *you* doing here?" Sloan took a confident step towards the girl. She had no reservations about putting Erica down, not after everything. She was supposed to be Sloan's friend—but all of 27 had completely ostracized her since Fight Night Prep.

"Get out of here," she ordered the girls. They didn't move.

Sloan took a measured breath. "I said *get out*," she repeated, her low voice an authoritative command. They would listen to her because she could pull rank on them or they would listen to her because she would physically enforce her order—but either way, they *would* listen. Slowly, under her threatening glare, the girls grabbed their bags and filed past her.

She waited until she heard their footsteps disappear down the hall. She glanced to the glass touch screen behind Jared's bed; it flashed images of his ribs, as well as his vitals and monitors on his nutrition and medication. She touched the end of his bed gingerly.

"I wanted to apologize," she began, looking down at him.

Jared scoffed. "For *breaking my ribs?*"

She maintained eye contact. "Yes."

He shrugged his shoulders dismissively. "Whatever, you wanted to hurt me, so well done."

She sat on the end of the bed. "*You* pushed me to that, Jared . . . You and the Order and Elijah."

"Well, none of it will matter for much longer."

"Jare, even if you win and send Elijah to Review, you know he's too good to be Dismissed. Not even your *bond* with the Order could get them to get rid of someone like him."

Jared let his heavy gaze fall on her. "You have to know by now that I'm not sending him to Review."

Sloan's breath caught in her lungs. *Has he finally changed his mind?* She reached over, grabbing his hands. "Thank you, I can't tell you how—"

He snatched his hand away, cutting her off. "Sloan, I'm not sending him to Review because I'm going to ask for him to be Dismissed."

She shook her head at him. "We all know that's not allowed."

He cocked his head to the side, seemingly enjoying telling her this. "Stone lied to us. It's been granted in Winnings before."

Is that true? What kind of monster would have asked for someone to die in the ring? *The kind like Jared.* The dark answer quickly crossed her mind.

"You can't do this," she pleaded.

He smoothed the bedding over his legs, his hands still and controlled. "You will learn to live without him."

"Will *you* learn to live without me?" she snapped back.

"We've been over this . . . I won't have to. When I win, you will remain mine."

She shook her head at him, swallowing heavily. "Stop talking like that."

He said nothing. The pain she felt was immeasurable. She had learned that heartbreak was something you could physically feel. She had never endured a pain that she hadn't overcome—would this time be different?

She stood and walked up to the side of the bed, leaning over his face. An odd calm came over her, a stillness before a storm—this was their goodbye.

"I love you, Jared Dawson, and I always will," she whispered into his hair. She kissed him, bringing her hands up to his face, running them through his hair, pulling him in and savoring him. She wanted to breathe him in and remember this feeling. She ran her lips over his, tugging at them softly, experiencing him the way she had countless times before. Pulling away finally, she rested her forehead against his. They breathed in one another's air, eyes closed, and she could hear his heart beating, slow and certain, undeniable proof that he still had one.

"Whatever Elijah asks for, remember *you* have a choice. You always have a choice," she whispered, stepping away from him.

"Haven't you realized it yet, Sloan?"

She stared at him quizzically, his beautiful eyes watching her pensively. She said nothing. This time it was he who sighed, a half smile on his beautiful face.

"Choices are the one thing we don't have."

The pod doors opened and Sloan stepped into Elijah's living room. He was lying on his sofa, a book in his hands and an ice pack on his ribs. At her intrusion he dropped the book and struggled to sit upright.

"What are you doing here?"

She crossed her arms, watching him get up. "Jared is going to ask for you to be Dismissed."

Elijah stared at her doubtfully. "No, he's not allowed to. The worst he can do is send me to Review . . . or kill me in the ring."

Sloan shook her head. "Apparently Stone lied—Jared said it's been done before. So, are you going to back out of Fight Night now?"

"I . . . can't," he answered, his voice sullen.

How could you be so stupid? Fight Night is tomorrow and it could end in your execution.

Sloan suddenly felt exhausted by all this insanity. Jared wouldn't listen, Elijah wouldn't listen—there was nothing more she could do.

"You should know, I'm going to ask that no more students get Dismissed this year," she added, finally revealing her Winnings request to someone other than Stone.

Elijah looked up at her hopefully. "Would that save me from Jared's Winnings then?"

She shook her head. "No, Winnings are granted to all Winners—I imagine if they grant my request, you would be the last one Dismissed, a way of appeasing both Jared and me—*if* we win," she added politely.

His face dropped. "Okay . . . but, Sloan, you really shouldn't risk upsetting the Order with that kind of request."

She wasn't worried—she knew what she was doing. The Order would view her request as an undermining of their authority; they would have to yield power to grant it. Romani would be beyond angry and it would destroy whatever image the Order had of her. It would cement her newfound standing as an outsider. But as far as she was concerned, they had it coming. How could they not see the risk in creating students as dangerous as herself, as Jared, as Elijah, and then provoking them into anger?

"I want you to know something else," she added, leaning against the wall. He stood and walked over to her, crossing the room in quick strides.

"If—by some miracle—*you* win Fight Night, I will

never love you, I will never *be* with you the way you would want me to be, I will not be anything more than someone you share a roof with."

"Sloan—" he began but she cut him off.

"You think I could ever love someone who views me as a trophy?"

"You love Jared," he shot back.

She slapped him clean across the face and turned to leave.

"Wait!" He grabbed her wrist and pulled her back. "I didn't mean to say that . . . but I can't back out of Fight Night. It's all gone too far now—Jared will ask for my Dismissal in this fight, or the next, or the one after that. And he doesn't *need* to fight me in order to ask for it as Winnings, and even then, you know it as well as I do, he would probably try to kill me outside of the ring.

"There's not another student here who stands a chance of beating him. At least this way, I have a chance of saving my own life."

Sloan pulled her arm from him—she *finally* understood. They had created a cyclic feud, spurred by the Calling. Jared was convinced that if he backed out, Elijah would fight whomever and ask for her to be given to him, and at least this way, Jared stood a fighting chance of keeping her and killing Elijah to prevent him from coming for her again. In turn, Elijah, even if he swore he didn't want her, had already convinced Jared of the contrary, and fighting was his only chance of not winding up dead. If Jared backed out, Elijah would still take her in Winnings; if Elijah backed out, Jared would still get him Dismissed.

What if he could convince Jared, though? If he could convince him he would leave her alone.

"He's only trying to get you killed because you want me—prove to him that's not the case anymore, *stop* wanting me," she reasoned.

He shook his head at her sadly. "I would rather die."

Sloan stepped away from him. "Elijah, *I don't love you*," she told him firmly.

He shrugged. "According to the Calling—you were born to love me."

She shook her head, backing up to the pod doors. "You can go to hell, Elijah. You and Jared both . . ."

Sloan stepped into the pod, ignoring Elijah's muffled objections as the doors closed around her. She turned, catching her reflection in the mirror. She studied her face thoughtfully. Her golden hair fell around her milky face. Her full lips were a deep red; her yellow eyes a slow burning fire. She shook her head, clenching her fists. Was this a face worth dying for—worth killing for? She lashed out, punching the mirror. Her reflection shattered, and she found peace in seeing herself appear as broken as she felt.

CHAPTER 6

Once again the hall had been transformed, except tonight, it was not the romantic, gold-lit room befitting a Betrothal Calling. Tonight, it was showing its true purpose: an epic stadium apt for Fight Night. A grand boxing ring was set up in the middle, with large dimensions to host two simultaneous fights, separated by ropes. Blue and white lights shone out across the room, flickering and dancing over the crowd, seated in viewing stands that now circled the giant ring. A viewing box had been craned above the stands, a panel for the Order to officiate from.

Sloan ducked into General Stone's office, avoiding the crowd of students. She couldn't remember the last time she'd felt this nervous . . . this helpless. She prayed that one of them, Jared or Elijah, would be brave enough to change their requested Winnings, and that it would influence the other to follow suit. She had wanted to speak to Jared last night, after speaking with Elijah, to tell him she understood the trouble he was in, that she understood he wouldn't back out of the fight in order to keep her. But she hadn't been allowed back in the Infirmary, since Jared had instructed the nurses to ensure he had no visitors.

More than anything she hoped he changed his mind about sending Elijah to Dismissal, but Sloan couldn't help but feel torn between what she had learned in the past few weeks and this new information. Jared was still the sort of person who would send another to their death. Did it change anything, knowing he was doing it for her? Perhaps just as important, *was* he doing it solely for her, after everything he had said to make her believe she was little more than a trophy?

Pacing, she caught her reflection in the mirrored glass of Stone's window. Her golden hair was pulled tightly back, her skin seemed pale, her narrow jaw and slender nose shadowed, her cheeks gaunt; and her yellow eyes seemed to burn too bright—filled with anxious anticipation. Her whole life was about to come crumbling down around her. If Jared won, he was a monster who killed another student; if Elijah won, he was a selfish traitor who forced her into his union.

Either way, *she* wasn't winning.

Taking a seat, she readjusted the strapping on her hands and ankles, tightened the drawstring on her shorts and ran her fingers under the elastic of her sports bra. She pulled at the makeshift necklace she had formed—a strap of leather from which Jared's ring now hung.

"Nervous about the fight?" Stone's voice startled her. She turned to see him in the doorway.

"Not mine." She shrugged. He walked around the desk, taking his seat opposite her.

"Well, it's yours you need to concentrate on, because I have heard bad things about what Maya Woods is asking for . . ."

Sloan waited expectantly for details.

Stone shook his head wearily. "She's going to ask for Daniels to go to Dismissal too."

Sloan was shocked. "*What?* Why—he trained her!"

Stone raised his brow. "Forgotten just how much sway Jared has over people when he wants to?"

How could he have convinced her of this—and *why?* Maya was no real contender for Sloan, so was it just to rattle her, or to hurt Elijah?

She shook her head, readjusting her hair band. "Well, it's a good thing Woods isn't in the same league as me then."

Stone nodded slowly. He leaned back in his seat and loosened the collar on his formal uniform.

"Sir, aren't you supposed to be up in the box, watching the juniors fight?"

He shook his head. "One fight is already in the bag; the other is being dragged out—I needed a break . . . and I needed to check in on you."

Sloan didn't understand. "On me? Why?"

He arched his brow, crossing his arms over his broad chest. "You're coming undone, kid."

She sat back in her chair, leaning away from him.

"The other day, Fight Night Prep, you completely lost it . . . and I get it. You're pissed off at the world. And you proved your point—no one can control you when you're doing your thing—but you've got me worried."

Sloan felt awkward. She didn't want him to worry but she also didn't want to be harangued about her recent behavior. She hadn't started any of this—*they* had.

She shrugged. "All I am is what this place made me—that's all you're seeing."

Stone stood, walking around the desk. "If you really believe that then you aren't giving yourself enough credit, Radcliffe."

He paused, briefly touching her shoulder. "Good luck out there tonight." She remained seated as he walked out of the room.

She couldn't think about Stone's feelings on her recent volatility—she needed to concentrate on Fight Night. She knew that Elijah needed to win. If he won, she would have to live with him for a year, but after Departing Ceremonies, she could find Jared. Sure, it was unsanctioned, but she didn't care—she loved *him*. If Jared won tonight, it would destroy her image of him, and it would end Elijah's life. She stood; she needed to go find Jared.

She knew as she stepped out of the office, crossing through an onslaught of lights and noises, that she and Daniels had the advantage walking into this Fight Night—they were fighting for his life. Winning had never been more important.

Jared, Elijah and Maya stood in silence, separated by Major West, out in the corridor. She went straight up to Jared. "Could we talk for a minute?"

He raised his brow at her, crossing his arms over his broad chest. Reluctantly, he took a few steps away from the others, yielding to her request. She stood close to him, wanting to keep her words private. She took a deep breath and reached for him, resting her hand on his shoulder.

"I understand now . . . I understand why you're afraid of backing out tonight, but if you ask for *any-thing* else, I swear I will fix this—I will find a way to stay yours."

He shook his head down at her. "He'll never stop, Sloan. I've got to do this."

Sloan knew he was right—Elijah wouldn't stop—but that didn't mean he should die. She wasn't worth his life. "We can find another way to get through this. *Please* reconsider."

"He'll be gone by daybreak and we won't ever have to worry about this again."

He seemed to not even be listening to her—he was so fixated on Elijah *taking* her that he didn't even realize he was *pushing* her away.

She perched up on her toes and kissed his forehead. "I love you," she breathed against his skin, holding on to him for the longest moment.

She thought back to the night of their Calling, of her promise to him. *I'm yours . . . forever.* Forever had been reduced to thirty seconds before a fight, their future dashed with fear and blood and a championship title. He just didn't realize it yet.

"I love you too."

She turned from Jared, reluctantly letting go of him to face Maya. The girl was chewing her lips, wringing her hands and bounding on her heels—she was nervous. Sloan crossed her arms, glaring at her.

"Is it true—what you're asking for in Winnings?"

Maya shrugged, still defiantly bold despite her nerves. "Yeah, it's true."

Sloan shook her head at the girl. "Big mistake, Woods, *big* mistake." For having ever thought it was okay to ask for something like *that*, for getting involved where she shouldn't be, Sloan was going to make this process painful.

"I'm not afraid of you," Maya said, but she instinctively stepped away from Sloan.

Sloan eyed her up and down. *No, you're not afraid . . . you're terrified.*

Before she could say anything more, the loud booming voice of Marshal Romani reverberated from the hall into the corridor. "Presenting your Senior Fight Night contenders—reigning champion, Captain Jared Dawson!"

West opened the door and Jared jogged through it, taking one last lingering look back at Sloan. *Please, please change your mind.* She willed that he could, like he had been able to so many times before, read her thoughts. She wanted to run after him, to tackle him, to force him to be better than this . . . but she wouldn't take his free will away—she wouldn't do to *him* what he was doing to her.

"For the first time, presenting Second Lieutenant Maya Woods!" Romani's voice surrounded them. Sloan's heart was racing. Maya shoved past her and ran through the door.

She and Elijah were next.

"Woods is asking for your Dismissal," she told him, taking her stand next to him. He shot a shocked look at her.

"I don't plan on letting her get you killed—now you just ensure Jared doesn't succeed either . . . He doesn't block well on his left, and *do not* get him on the floor—he will win on the floor," she told him plainly.

He stared down at her with confusion. A year of misery for her, if Elijah won, would never compare to him losing his life. She felt rushed. Even though this night had been advancing on them all term, she suddenly felt flustered.

" . . . Captain Elijah Daniels and reigning champion Lieutenant Sloan Radcliffe!"

Elijah smiled down at her nervously. "That's us."

"Get out there." West hurried them, holding the door open. Elijah jogged in and she slowly trudged after him.

"Sloan!" Elijah called, circling back to her in the dark. Violet lights streaked over them and, just as suddenly, left them standing in the pitch black behind the stands.

"What?"

"In case I don't win." He shrugged, and before she knew what was happening, he had kissed her. As quickly as it had begun it ended. He released her just in time for the lights to land on them, so that no one ever saw what she had never expected.

She ducked through the ropes, entering her side of the ring. The crowd went wild, the majority of them simply excited to see a champion Fight Night. Missing from her usual applause were the once-distinct hollers from Mika, Erica and the rest of 27. She watched Jared and Elijah strip off their shirts, discarding them to their corners, warranting further howls from the rowdy crowd. Both boys had strapped their ribs, indicating neither had yet to fully heal. She shot a final, pleading glance towards Jared. He looked back, offering her a helpless shrug.

As the crowd quieted down, lights landed on the Order, illuminating Marshal Romani. Sloan looked up to General Stone—he was watching her keenly. Romani leaned into the microphone. "Hello, senior contenders. Welcome! We thank you for your willing participation this evening. Now, let's get down to business!"

He cleared his throat, resting his chin on his white-gloved hand. "Let us hear from our senior girls first. Second Lieutenant Woods, what would you like to request as your Winnings should you manage to defeat your champion?"

Sloan watched Maya shift nervously from foot to foot. She had never been in a Fight Night. Having to address the Order was nerve-wracking enough, but doing it in front of the entire Academy—especially with such a heinously intended request—would be enough to scare anyone.

Anyone except Jared.

"I would like to ask . . . I would like my Winnings to be that . . . I mean . . ." Maya stumbled on her words.

"Any day now, Second Lieutenant," Romani advised impatiently. Sloan smiled at the girl's inability to express her disgusting request.

"I would ask that Elijah Daniels be Dismissed," she finally spat out, her voice small but determined.

Her demand quieted the hall—the Academy was in shock. The Order would have had some inclination as to what she was going to ask for; after all, Stone already knew. Whispers began to fill the large room. Sloan watched the Order speak amongst themselves as the crowds of students began to speculate. Sloan enjoyed seeing the unimpressed reaction of the Academy—she hoped it showed Maya how vile her request truly was.

"Thank you for your request, Second Lieutenant." Romani smiled.

Sloan shook her head in disgust. *You're really going to grant it, then, aren't you?*

Romani leaned back into the microphone. "Champion Lieutenant, welcome back to the ring." As he spoke, he leaned forward to stare down at her from his box.

Sloan held his stare, uncomfortable as he made her. "Thank you," she managed through gritted teeth.

"What will *you* be requesting this evening, Lieutenant?"

Sloan cleared her throat—*here goes nothing.* "I would request that for the duration of my time at the Academy, no student be Dismissed and that never again can a student be allowed to request another student's Dismissal."

Romani narrowed his eyes at her. The great hall was completely silent, everyone unsure whose request was more serious—Maya's or Sloan's. The Order was accustomed to granting trips to the woods, holiday time, extended training hours . . . they would not appreciate the magnitude of tonight's requests. They certainly wouldn't appreciate their senior students' defiance or audacity. Moreover, they would not appreciate relinquishing control or being forced to abandon the role of executioner. The Order had always had the final say. And in the first two requests, they now faced being *forced* to kill or forced to *refuse* killing again.

Finally, Romani forced his gaze away from her, turning to the boys. "Champion Captain Dawson, I imagine you have an equally *unique* request?"

"I too, sir, would have Elijah Daniels Dismissed." His voice was clear and confident and Sloan felt a striking pang in her chest. She'd still had hope that at the last minute, he would change his mind. But no—it had happened; he had really done it.

He had asked for another student to die.

Romani tapped the table in front of him, studying his fluttering hand for a long moment before shifting his concentration to Elijah.

"Captain Daniels, you have clearly not made many friends . . . Please, enlighten us as to what you may be requesting tonight?"

Elijah shot an apologetic look to Sloan before speaking. "As the Order well knows, Sloan Radcliffe has been living under the misconception that she was solely matched to Jared Dawson in her Betrothal Calling. The truth of the matter is, she was also paired to me, a 98 percent match, and I request that should I win tonight, that pairing is honored, with Lieutenant Radcliffe relocating to my quarters immediately so that we may . . . *catch up* on lost time."

Sloan's face was on fire. It was finally out there—the whole Academy knew the truth. There was a moment of silence, followed by an outburst of noise: whispers, speculation, laughing, shocked gasps. She could feel every eye in the room trained on her; she felt heat rising in her neck. She gritted her teeth, locking eyes on General Stone, the only face she could bear to see.

Romani stood, waving his hands slowly to quiet the room. "What a mess you three find yourselves in."

What a mess you put us in, you mean, Sloan thought. She had been humiliated enough by this man and his Order.

Romani took a deep breath before speaking. "Very well. *If* you survive the night, Captain Daniels, your

Winnings will be honored, as will any of yours," he said, looking over the rest of them, "should you win."

It was clear, though, that Romani didn't think Elijah stood a chance, not now that both senior fights had to be won in order for him to survive. Sloan took a deep breath and looked to Jared. His fists were shaking, a ticking flutter in his broad chest, his eyes trained downward—he was furious. Sloan couldn't believe the Order would acquiesce—how could they let students gamble the lives of their peers?

How could they just give me away like some crown? She couldn't believe any of it—hell, she couldn't believe they accepted *her* request. Sloan sighed heavily, shaking out her shoulders. She needed to concentrate on her fight.

A dark thought crossed her mind—if she lost her fight Elijah would die and she would stay with Jared . . . *That is not an option*. She shook the thought away. She would rather lose a year with Jared than be responsible for an innocent boy's death.

Romani sat down slowly, a small smile creeping across his face. "Let Fight Night begin on your ready."

Sloan turned on Maya, who was pacing like a caged animal. Sloan flung her arms back and forth, stretching out. She let her instincts overcome her. The people in the stands blurred from her vision, the noise disappearing into muffled murmurs, nothing in her line of sight except for Maya.

And then the adrenaline began to fill her. She honed in on Maya. "Scared yet?"

Maya said nothing; her eyes darted around the ring . . . and then, she abruptly lunged. Sloan easily sidestepped, finding her natural rhythm. *This* was *her* playground—Maya was out of her depth. The girl continued to spring at her, hands reaching for a grasp, but she wasn't fast enough, wasn't controlled enough. Sloan weaved around the girl, light on her toes. She glanced across the ropes to Elijah and Jared; they circled one another, mapping out their fight before engaging.

Maya aimed a kick at Sloan, but she easily deflected, grabbing the girl's ankle and kicking out her resting leg, causing Maya to land on her back. As the girl fell to the floor, Sloan landed an unforgiving kick on Maya's ribs. Maya gasped under the strike, and Sloan kicked again—the all too familiar *crack* sounding off. Ribs broken. She retreated, allowing Maya to get to her feet whenever ready. Sloan rested against the far ropes, flaunting her ease in this ring. Jared and Elijah were boxing, quick jabs, still not fully engaged in their fight.

Maya got to her feet slowly, holding her side. Sloan resisted smiling as she eyed Maya up—*I promised you pain*. Sloan leaped with deadly speed, landing a kick to the inside of Maya's knee. The girl fell once again. Sloan circled her.

"Come on, Woods—you came for my championship. Is this all you've got?" Sloan mocked. Maya shot her an angry glare, lunging from her knees to grab at Sloan. Sloan sidestepped once more, slapping Maya quickly. She slapped her again, circling her, taunting her with quick hits.

"Get up!" she ordered, walking away from Maya, willfully showing her back to the girl. "I said *get up*," Sloan growled, eyeing the crowd. Half of them were cheering, half of them looking away in horror. Sloan hadn't been hit once. She heard the scuffle of Maya finally getting to her feet. Sloan spun, falling to her knees and sliding across the floor, landing before Maya's legs. With a violent thrust, she punched the inner side of the girl's knee—the one she had already done so much damage to—with a force that dislocated the patella. Maya screamed, falling towards Sloan. In an instant, Sloan drove her palm up, connecting with Maya's nose—*another* break. Maya fell backwards.

Ribs. Nose. Knee. The girl couldn't walk—she couldn't fight. Sloan rolled away, getting to her feet.

She once more leaned against the ropes, watching Jared and Elijah. Jared landed a roundhouse kick to Elijah's ribs, a front kick to his chest, a vicious series of assaults. Elijah recovered quickly, though, rolling into Jared, back to back. Elijah reached up and clawed at Jared's jaw, flipping his body over Elijah's shoulder. As Jared landed on the floor, Elijah kicked at his broken ribs, and the snap of further breaking echoed. Jared rolled away, getting to his feet.

She wanted to rush in. She wanted to stop their fight. She wanted to wring Elijah's neck for hurting Jared—it was her basic instinct to protect him . . . But she couldn't. This had to happen.

The frustration rose within her, and she looked

back at her own opponent. Maya was trying to sit up—she had an admirable persistence. Sloan sauntered over to her, kneeling beside her. She grabbed Maya's throat, nailing her back down against the mat. "Tell me, are you afraid now?"

Maya's face was covered in blood, her eyes wide as she gargled for breath. She nodded, her bloodied face bobbing over Sloan's tight grasp on her throat.

"Do you think I might kill you?" Sloan pressed, squeezing tighter. Tears welled in Maya's eyes. She reached for Sloan's tightly clenched fist, but she didn't have the strength to free herself. Sloan gripped harder.

"Are you afraid to die?" Sloan's words unintentionally came out a scream, a furious cry. Her words silenced the bloodthirsty crowds. She looked up to the Order. Stone was on his feet, Amelia Brass was covering her face, but Romani continued to smile.

"You think it's okay to ask for Elijah's death when *you* are so afraid of dying?" She might have been speaking to Maya—but she was directing the question to the Order.

She looked down at the girl and leaned forward, putting all her weight into Maya's throat. "The only two people in this entire *damn* place who can stop me are a little bit busy right now," Sloan explained. "And the one who *would* stop me, the one who would care about saving you—you just asked for him to be killed."

Maya's eyes began to flutter back. She knew every

person in the room was listening to her. Slowly, Maya's hands fell helplessly away.

Sloan *was* killing her. *You're not Jared*, she thought. *Let her go*. With an angry hiss, Sloan recoiled, releasing Maya and backing away.

She spun on the Order. "Do I have to kill her before you name your victor?" she screamed up to them. Romani looked down at her with narrow eyes—*no one* yelled at the Order. What would they do to her—she was *their* champion and they knew as well as she did that what she'd said before was true. There were two people in this entire Academy who could take her—and they were fighting to the death in the next ring.

"Sloan Radcliffe, you remain reigning champion . . . Your Winnings will be honored." His voice was tight and words measured. Sloan looked to Stone, who offered her a slow solemn nod. He was afraid for her—*or afraid of her* . . .

She looked away, moving to the side of the ring to allow nurses from the Infirmary access to Maya. She remained on the ropes, watching Jared and Elijah's fight escalate.

Elijah landed a double kick. Jared lunged, an assault of quick-fire punches. The silence she had brought to the crowd had disappeared—the pairing of Elijah and Jared had them roaring.

My words have already been lost on them . . .

Jared flipped Elijah, striking at him on the ground. Elijah's face was maimed; a mess of blood and sweat. The animal cries from the crowd spurred Jared on—he was in *his* element too in this ring. Sloan had truly realized that Elijah *had* to win. Even if his winning ruined her life, broke her relationship with Jared and destroyed everything she had worked so hard for—he *needed* to win. Losing her happiness was not the same as losing his life.

But as Jared rallied on, she just wasn't sure it was possible.

She watched as Jared's brutal onslaught continued. His muscles tensed with every rearing hit, sweat dripping down his body, blood streaking his face. Elijah flopped like a doll under each strike, and if he didn't do something soon a Dismissal wouldn't be necessary.

"Elijah!"

It took Sloan a moment to realize that it had been her terrified scream calling out his name. Somehow, over the cheers of the wild crowd, he had heard her—his battered face rolled towards her. His dazed green eyes found her, blinking the blood away. He watched her for the longest moment and Sloan didn't know what it was that he saw in her face, but it spurred him into action. With unbelievable speed, Elijah caught Jared's fist before it connected.

The crowd was on their feet, stomping, crying out, raising their fists into the air—their emblem of prevailing. Elijah threw his legs up and dragged Jared off of him. The two rolled away from one another, getting to their feet. They circled, wiping blood off their faces. Jared lunged first, but Elijah grabbed his fist once more, turning it into an arm lock, bending it until Jared buckled. Forced down and hunched over, Elijah kneed him in the face. Jared staggered, allowing Elijah to grab him from behind and lock his arm around Jared's neck. Sloan knew that was a mistake, though—Jared was too strong to be choked down, too adept at grappling. In an instant, he had flipped Elijah over his shoulder.

But Elijah was ready for the maneuver—even as he flew over the other boy's shoulder, he dragged Jared down with him, pulling his forearm into an arm-bar lock. Jared was too good at grappling—he rolled towards his arm, *into* Elijah, breaking free.

They were on their feet in an instant.

They squared off. Jared swung. Elijah blocked. He seemed revived, once more fighting for his life. He elbowed Jared in the face, landed a forward kick, and sent him flying into the ropes. Sloan felt her throat tighten—she couldn't watch the one she loved in so much pain and she couldn't pull her eyes away.

Elijah landed a succession of punches before grabbing hold of Jared's arm, bending it back, pulling up at the elbow—*snap*. Sloan's bloodied hands flew to her face, watching in horror as the love of her life broke before her. Jared howled in agony and Sloan's heart yearned for him, to save him, to hold him, to—even though she knew what it could lead to—hurt Elijah for him. Jared fell against the ropes; Elijah spun in the air and landed a kick against Jared's wounded face.

Jared hit the ground—unconscious.

He lost . . . and so have I.

Sloan had rolled under the ropes, kneeling beside Jared, holding his face in her lap. He came to, gazing up at her with sadness. She stroked his face, wiping away his blood.

"Elijah Daniels, you are the new champion. We honor your Winnings—Sloan Radcliffe is now your betrothed." Romani's voice cut through her, and she could see them wash over Jared. She couldn't look at the Order, she couldn't hear the storming crowd of students cheer for their new champion. She leaned over, kissing Jared's forehead.

"I'm sorry," she cried, resting her face against his. She didn't care that the entire Academy was watching, and she didn't care if they thought she now *belonged* to Elijah—they were wrong; she loved Jared too much. She just wanted to take him home. She stroked his dark hair back and held him tightly. She assured him he was okay, that he wasn't too badly hurt. She squeezed his hand against her chest, and was surprised when she heard his voice.

"Sloan . . ."

Her name fell from his mouth, a gargled whisper. The Infirmary nurses were crawling into the ring, preparing to take him away.

"What is it?" she asked, leaning close to his beautiful broken face.

"Get away from me."

His words were a slap. She let her hands fall from

him. Before she could think or say another word, the medics had lifted him away from her. This wasn't her fault—she had *begged* him to find another way, to let her find another way, to be honest with her from the start, to not underestimate Elijah.

She was devastated—she was furious. She didn't know how to feel. She watched them lead Jared out, then her eyes fell to the floor, where blood pooled around her. She glanced to Elijah, who stared at her hopefully, and she stood, turning away. Ducking under the ropes, she took a deep breath. She just wanted to go home.

The problem is, I don't know where that is anymore.

CHAPTER 7

All of her belongings were already there, in Elijah's living quarters. *Efficient in war, efficient in everything*, she thought of the Academy. Her clothes in the white lacquer drawers, her shoes lined neatly by the bed . . . and her photograph—the one of her and Tandy, which had been so safely tucked away—now rested on Elijah's bedside table. She gingerly lifted the photo and then slammed it facedown. She walked through to the bathroom and although Elijah's living quarters were identical to her own, she found herself hesitant to move about.

This was *not* her home.

She flicked the light on and found her own appearance terrifying. A war-mask of blood, streaks and freckles, sweat matting her hair, bright teary eyes. She looked down at her taped hands; they were crimson.

This was not her blood. She turned from the mirror, resting on the brim of the tub. She fiddled with the taps until steaming hot water began to pour out.

Returning her attention to her hands, she hesitantly began fingering the soggy tape. She had broken knuckles. She winced with each small tear, and with frustration began to rip the bindings off mercilessly. She stepped to the sink, tossing the bloodied dressings to the side, and ran her mangled hands under water. She watched the swirling pink pool and could see the fear in Maya's eyes—drowning in the loch of blood and water. She used the heel of her hand to turn the tap off. She needed to get her clothes off . . .

Slowly, she inched her sore fingertips under her sports bra, shuddering as her broken fingers strained to pull the garment off. The unforgiving pull of the armored material set her hands alight, and she bit into her lip as she stripped down naked. A small yelp escaped her as she tore her elastic tie out of her hair, the tight band snapping against her broken fingers. All that remained was the strip of leather she wore around her neck, with the small gold ring hanging from it. She couldn't take it off—it would hurt too much.

Her breaths quickened. *"Sloan Radcliffe is your betrothed . . ."* Romani's words tore through her. She had been *gifted* to Elijah. *What better prize for the new champion than the reigning champion?*

She could see Jared's desolate eyes—a look that would forever be etched into her mind. *"Get away from me."* She stepped into the scalding water, lowering her body slowly. Maya hadn't touched her, yet Sloan couldn't remember ever feeling more hurt.

Flashes of the night, of her life, sped before her, tears drawing blood into the tub. She could see Maya's fear, Jared's anger and Elijah's hopefulness . . . *Romani's glare*. Tandy—the day she came out of Review. Kenny—with a hot gun and a cold smile. She felt as though she were drowning and launched herself out of the water.

She stumbled towards the counter, wild and unnerved. Sweeping her arms out over the smooth surface, she sent soap and toiletries flying. She pulled her broken fingers into a fist and beat at the mirror, shattering it, making herself disappear. She fell to the ground and slammed her hands against the cold linoleum. She wanted to hit something—*hit everything*—she wanted to see something as broken as herself. She wailed in pain, but she could no longer feel her hands. Tears coursed down her cheeks; shudders ran through her bare skin. She bit into her forearm as she screamed—muffling her own agony. The weight of her pain snapped something in her body and she twisted into a ball, sobbing.

She barely noticed the towel being wrapped around her, just as she barely gauged that it was Elijah, covering her up as he pulled her into his lap. He leaned against the tub, tucking her face under his chin. She cried until the pain became normal, until this agony became a baseline, until she was certain it would take a bullet in the chest to feel anything worse. She cried until she fell asleep, dreaming of a world where normal didn't hurt so much.

When Sloan finally woke, she was cold. She had a damp towel curled tightly around her, and wet hair framed her face. She sat up quickly and then remembered she was in no hurry to live this day. She was not in her living quarters. She was not with Jared. She was the girl who had made a scene at Fight Night, the girl who had been traded by the Order, the girl whose private life had been made a spectacle of. Out of everything—angering the Order, terrifying Maya, the humiliation of her life being put on display for all her peers—she could only think of Jared. She took a deep breath and was amazed that, despite all her certainties of the contrary, her body knew how to live on without him there.

She stood up slowly, readjusting her towel. She glanced into the bathroom; Elijah had cleaned up most of her wreckage. She sighed heavily, wondering if he had now been able to see what losing Jared had done to her. She walked away, stepping into the living quarters. The milky daylight streaked into the room—it was still early. Elijah was asleep on the sofa—he looked *awful*. Bruises and slashes streaked his face. His hands, resting peacefully above welts on his chest, were cut and shaded dark green and blue. His ribs had extended into purple mounds and he still had a streak of blood across his temple. Was that *his* blood—or Jared's?

As if he could sense her, he woke up, blinking slowly. He had a black eye. He sat up too quickly and then jolted to a halt, grimacing. "*That* was uncomfortable," he sighed, padding his abdomen with his hands.

She watched him carefully, lowering herself into a seat opposite him. "It looks pretty bad."

He shot her a critical look. "Yeah, your hands look as bad as my mirror feels." She shied at his words—that had been the second time Elijah Daniels had held her as she broke. He stood slowly, physically assessing his wounds, running his fingertips over his bruises and cuts. "I'm sorry you slept in a towel—I didn't want to wake you once you were out."

She shrugged. "It's okay . . . Thanks for sleeping out here." She glanced at the too-small sofa.

"I had no intentions of sleeping anywhere else."

They stared at one another in awkward silence. They had achieved what was necessary—he was alive—but Sloan hadn't anticipated that in keeping him alive she would end up feeling like she were dying.

He ran a hand through his dark locks. "Look, Sloan, I didn't want to hurt anyone—" he began, but Sloan snorted, cutting him off curtly.

"Well, you failed then."

"Sloan," he sighed.

She shook her head at him. "I get it, Elijah. The Order should have told me about our pairing from the beginning, I would have chosen Jared and you could have been rematched. I get that *they* are responsible for all of this. But *you* could have done things differently, you could have insisted on a new pairing instead of *coming after* me—Jared might have tried to kill you, but you didn't give him much choice . . . Nothing changes the fact that we all got hurt."

He nodded at her slowly. There was nothing to say. The Order had set all of this into motion by bending the rules and by pitting Elijah and Jared against one another.

Elijah shifted on his feet anxiously. "It had to be you, Sloan. You're the only one— *Never mind*." He shook his head. "I'm just going to go shower."

She didn't know where he was going with that train of thought, and she didn't care. She got it—he was obsessed with her. She had run out of ways to tell him those feelings would never be reciprocated. She watched him make his way to the bathroom. She didn't understand how her life had been diminished to such a state—*she* had played no role in this and yet she was the one forced to suffer the consequences of others' decisions. The humming of the pod doors alerted her, and she stood, spinning around.

Stepping into the room with a confident stride was Marshal Romani—the man who had ruined her life. The man who could control whether she lived or died each day. The man she had greatly angered last night.

She stood to attention, saluting him swiftly. "Marshal, sir."

He looked around the room, he let his gaze slowly trail over her, and with slow steps, he approached her. "At ease, Lieutenant."

He took a deep breath, keeping his dark eyes locked on her. "You made quite the scene last night."

Sloan stood in silence. He had diminished the quality of her life—in turn she had diminished the reach of his power. She held his gaze and realized the difference in their relationship now. Thanks to the Order she had *nothing* left to lose, but they stood to lose a great deal. And last night marked her first move against them— she wouldn't suffer the consequences of *their* actions alone.

"To be frank, Lieutenant, I *do not* appreciate your grandstanding. In the future, do not use the ring as a podium to lecture on the *morality* of Dismissals."

She nodded slowly. "Yes, *sir.*"

His mouth pulled into a tight smile. "I must say, I was *very* surprised by last night's outcome. Captain Dawson hasn't lost a fight in *so many* years, and yet, when it comes to fighting to keep *you*, he somehow loses."

It took everything Sloan had to remain calm. *How dare you?* she thought, grinding her teeth back and forth.

"I wonder if he had reason to sense that your pairing to Captain Daniels was more than just a technical error," he pressed.

He was provoking her—pushing her into anger. Sloan took a slow deep breath, forcing herself to remain calm. But before she could say anything, Elijah's voice had rung out.

"That water is great, babe!"

Romani raised an eyebrow at her, his smile pulling smugly across his face. She felt her cheeks light up.

Why the hell did he just call me babe?

Romani tapped his foot on the ground with amusement. "Well, *that* answers that."

She wanted to kill him—*right after* she killed Elijah.

"Apologies, Marshal, sir." Elijah's voice turned her around. He stood in the room, a towel hanging precariously around his hips, water trailing down his body, his muscles tensed as he stood upright to salute.

Romani nodded to him. "At ease, Captain. Congratulations on your newfound championship and on your . . . *Winnings.*" He smiled, nodding in Sloan's direction.

He refocused on Sloan. "I am sending you two on leave—several days in the forest. Your absence will give Jared and the Academy an opportunity to *calm* down—let the dust settle, so to speak."

"Thank you, sir." Elijah nodded, but Sloan remained silent. Despite Jared's losing a championship, Romani still had such interest in him.

How much does that have to do with the people they were forced to fight for?

Romani eyed them both over slowly. "Leave within the hour." With his final words, he turned and dialed a pod. They saluted as he exited, and remained staring at the closed doors long after he had left.

"This is perfect . . ."

At Elijah's voice Sloan spun on him, still reeling. "Don't you *ever* call me babe—" she began, but before she could finish, he had grabbed her arm, forcefully pulling her into the bathroom.

"What are you doing?" she demanded, jerking her arm free as he pushed her towards the shower. He didn't answer, though—he just fiddled with the taps until the loud pour of water filled the room.

She shoved him away. "I am *not* showering with you."

He looked from the shower to her, perplexed. "Oh, no, that's not what I meant—I mean, feel free to shower with me whenever, but that's not why I dragged you in here . . ." he mumbled. Clearly being flustered didn't shake his ingrained sense of confidence.

Sloan crossed her arms over her chest. "Then *what* is going on?"

He grabbed her arm, pulling her close. "Shh . . . *keep your voice down.*"

She struggled to pull free from him, his grip firmer—not hurting her, but not letting go either. "What is your problem, Daniels?"

He pushed her closer to the shower water, leaning into her. *What is he doing?* She leaned away from him, pulling out of his grip.

"Stop fidgeting, Sloan!" he ordered, seizing her with both hands.

She froze, the serious gaze in his bright eyes stilling her. He finally loosened his grip, once again leaning towards her.

Don't you dare kiss me again, she thought, turning her face from him. He brought his mouth to her cheek.

"They might be listening," he whispered.

She didn't understand what he was saying—she didn't know who *they* were—but the ominous inference sent shivers through her. She lifted her face slowly, holding his stare. His green eyes were dark, serious.

"Pack your bags and I will explain everything later," he instructed quietly.

He released her, stepping to the side, and left the bathroom.

He was clearly neurotic—*paranoid*—a lunatic. *What have I gotten myself into by saving his life?*

She turned the taps off and hesitantly stepped into the bedroom. Elijah had pulled civilian clothes on, jeans and a T-shirt. He was furiously shoving clothes into a duffel bag. She kept her distance, walking close to the wall to get to her drawers. It took her a minute to find her rucksack. She tossed clothes to wear aside and began to pack. She slipped in to jeans underneath her towel, keeping her back turned to Elijah when she had to finally let the towel fall away. She clasped her bra and pulled a shirt on, turning around quickly to continue packing. She caught Elijah's eyes, watching her longingly.

He immediately looked away. "Sorry."

She eyed him up, unnerved by his erratic behavior. His longing for her already filled her with discomfort— she would *not* tolerate that on top of this crazy-person behavior. She continued to get ready, contemplating how she would handle complete isolation in the woods with him.

Sloan apprehensively followed Elijah out onto the garage platform. The large concrete area was filled with vehicles—driverless automobiles that had their destinations preprogrammed daily by the techs. Jared had once told her that approximately 65 percent of the island had been GPS mapped. The coordinates were recorded and routed to the vehicles, which would operate on autopilot without a driver.

She glanced past the vehicles to the hover bikes— road motorcycles without wheels, operated through rapid air recycling. Further off in the distance were the hangars, where the Skyshells were kept. The latest in aero-tech, the machines were paneled in reflective glass, and unlike historical aircraft, these had no wings, but instead a sole top propeller and parallel side turbines. She envied the aviation students—they got to be out here all the time, learning how to fly.

They were rarely used as pawns for the Order's amusement . . . she thought bitterly.

Elijah walked across the garage with easy confidence, comfortable navigating the engine parts and oil slicks. She followed him as he expertly weaved through the metal chaos and made his way to a back office. He rapped on the door, calling out, "Donny!"

After a moment, a young, redheaded guy with a broad smile and big eyes appeared. He pulled Elijah into a big hug. "How are you, man? Missing us already?"

Elijah clapped him on the back. "Miss it every day, man, I really do."

Had Elijah been in the aviation program? Sloan wondered how much more she didn't know about this person she now had to share a life with.

Donny grabbed Elijah's chin. "Look at your face! You really fought tooth and nail last night!"

A look from Elijah warned Donny off the topic but it didn't stop Sloan from glaring at the young man, forcing him to step back awkwardly. Seeming to remember himself, Donny waved them into his cramped office. Screws, nails, oilcans and rubber were scattered across the room. Tires were piled on top of one another in the corner, and a mess of paperwork covered the desk. Donny offered her a rueful smile.

Sensing the awkwardness, Elijah spoke. "Sorry! Donny, this is Lieutenant Sloan Radcliffe. *My* betrothed." He smiled. Sloan pursed her lips at the introduction, uncomfortable with his words. She shook Donny's hand, nodding a hello.

"She's even more beautiful up close—I can see why you would leave *this* place!" He laughed, and despite his infectious kindness, Sloan didn't appreciate being spoken about that way.

Cool it; don't waste your energy. She urged herself to remain calm.

Elijah broke the silence. "Have you been told we're off on excursion?"

Donny jumped frantically, tearing his eyes from Sloan. "Oh, yeah—of course! They radioed up an hour ago. I will take you out to her." He shuffled out of the room, Elijah and Sloan in tow.

She stared daggers at her *betrothed* but he ignored her. The only thing keeping Sloan from getting out of here was her knowledge that she had no choice in being here . . . and, to a degree, some curiosity.

They followed Donny around a series of modified automobiles, coming up to a dark grey terrain vehicle. These were modifications of cars from long past, with overhauled engines that were redesigned to burn hybridized fuel, ensuring the burning process was silent and powerful. No vehicles, neither terrain nor aviation, moved faster than those designed by the Academy.

"This is her, similar to the one we built last summer"—Donny smiled, tapping the hood—"with a few minor adjustments." The grey metal formed a rectangular vehicle, built to fit four passengers, and yet it was extremely compact—if it didn't rest on six tires it would likely only stand three feet off the ground.

Elijah ran his hand over the doors. "Beautiful," he commented. He opened the door with a single push mechanism. Sloan walked around the vehicle, noting the two hover bikes latched to the back. She came back around to see Elijah hauling their bags into the backseat. He leaned back and looked at his friend. "Is autopilot off?"

Donny nodded. "Yeah. If you want to drive her, go for it."

"And everything *else*?" Elijah asked, lowering his voice.

"The radio is all good, man," Donny answered quietly. "Go have fun." Elijah smiled back, but looked around them cautiously. Sloan didn't understand what he was looking for or what they were talking about—she was beginning to feel genuinely concerned.

Elijah pulled Donny into another hug but she just offered him a quick goodbye before making her way to the passenger side. She pushed the metal door and it gave way, swinging open. She got inside and looked around the interior. The grey panel dashboard held multiple switches, a GPS screen and a holographic image of the internal engines, lit up against the base of the windscreen. On the driver's side, a hand-sized silver disc rested on a joystick—the steering wheel.

Elijah jumped into the vehicle and placed his hand firmly on the disc. A light scanned his biometrics and the engine whirred on, the holograph lighting up the display of igniting pistons. He turned his hand on the disc and pushed down with his palm, jolting the vehicle into a quick, controlled reverse. Sloan watched him press the disc forward, zooming away from the garage.

"How do you know how to drive?" she asked, eyeing his every movement.

He shot her an amused look. "Know how to drive? I know how to *build* one of these babies!" He laughed as he directed them towards the gate. She had never learned how to drive since it wasn't necessary for her—she was a martial expert, an on-foot militant.

Sloan realized she was more than a little jealous . . .

Gate 03 was constructed of ten-foot-tall chain-link wire—a rudimentary boundary that merely served to show where the *real* fence was: a current of electricity that ran around the Academy, so powerful that anyone who crossed it without a chip scan—or preapproval to lower the barrier—could die.

Elijah lowered the windows as the gate sentry appeared, a silver scanner bracelet in hand. "Identification," the man barked. Sloan reached through the window, offering her arm out. The guard ran the bracelet over her hand, up her forearm, removing it once it flashed green. He walked around and scanned Elijah. "We expect you back within three days."

"Of course," Elijah said.

The guard grunted, but the gate pulled to the side. Without any hesitation, Elijah zoomed off, flying onto the tarmac. As he flew down the road he began to press on the dash, fiddling until a compartment flipped open. He rummaged through it until he pulled out a small black serial drive. He pushed the drive into a port behind the steering disc. The drives stored files, and Sloan half expected music to begin playing. Instead, a deafening screech pierced her ears.

"What the *hell* was *that*?" she shrieked as the noise ended.

"That's how we know the drive is working," he explained, slowing down the vehicle, seemingly beginning to relax.

Sloan eyed him warily. "Working *how*?"

He glanced at her, an anxious glimmer in his eyes.

He chewed his lip, flicking his gaze between her and the road.

"Elijah—tell me *what's* going on," she ordered. She wouldn't live with any more secrets.

He took a quick deep breath. "It's a signal jammer . . . anyone who taps into this car's radio won't be able to hear what we say."

Sloan's jaw dropped, thinking back to the start of his peculiar behavior this morning. *"You're actually insane."*

Somehow, he kept his eyes on the road, but she could see a flush crawling up his neck. He was legitimately unstable—and she was now stuck with him. "Elijah, first this morning, now *this*—no one is listening to us."

He glanced at her and she was surprised to see a playful smile crossing his face. "No, not right now they aren't." He laughed, nodding at the serial drive port.

"This *isn't* funny anymore," she said, lunging at the port, trying to grab the serial drive.

Her grabbed her hands, holding her back. "Leave it alone," he ordered, his voice deep. She pulled away from him quickly, her broken knuckles smarting—she wished she had been able to go to the Infirmary before leaving.

"You're scaring me, Elijah."

"This is the first time we've been able to speak candidly—enjoy it." He shrugged.

"Speak candidly? Alright, try this on for size—I think *you're insane.*"

He seemed unaffected. "Think what you want, soon you'll see I'm right."

"Right about *what*?"

He shot her a frustrated stare. "*Everything*. The Academy, our lives here . . . it's all wrong."

Sloan was barely listening—she had fought to keep this *mad* person alive? She had sacrificed her relationship with Jared for this lunacy.

He had been right all along—Jared had known something wasn't right with Elijah.

"Stop the car," she ordered.

He glanced at her quickly. "No."

Sloan grabbed the steering disc, suddenly jerking the vehicle. She didn't know how to control it, but she didn't care if they crashed—she needed to get away from him. Whatever he was thinking—whatever he was doing—she wanted no part in it. It was one thing to challenge the Order; it was another to act the way he was suggesting.

Treason resulted in immediate execution.

"Stop it!" he yelled, trying to regain control of the vehicle. She fought at his hands furiously.

"I said stop the car!"

"*Dammit, Sloan!*" he yelled, quickly double tapping the disc—abruptly cutting the engine. The vehicle screeched to a halt.

Before he could say anything, she leaped out and began to walk back down the tarmac, heading for the gate. Elijah was quick to cut her off.

"Get out of my way," she growled.

He shook his head at her. "I can't let you go back."

"*Let* me? *You* don't *let* me do anything—now get the *hell* out of my way!" She sidestepped him, but before she could carry on, he grabbed her arm, spinning her back.

She twisted around, violently striking him across his bruised face. "Do *not* touch me—don't *ever* touch me." She turned away from him, continuing to walk down the road.

"You *know* I'm right!" he yelled, his voice following her. "This place is *wrong*—what happened with our Calling, what we are being trained for—*all* of it. I know you know that."

She slowed to a stop. Some part of his words resonated inside her—everything did seem wrong, but that hadn't always been the case. Her life had *gone* wrong when he had come into it. She turned around slowly.

"You need help, Elijah. Actual psychiatric *help*."

He nodded at her sadly. "I know what's going through your mind. I have stood where you stand now . . . but I need you to know the truth."

"*What* truth?" she demanded, storming back up to him angrily.

"I will explain everything—but I need to make sure that when *everything* goes down, you're somewhere safe." His voice cracked over his words—*was he nearly crying?*

She crossed her arms over her chest, certain he had lost his mind. He shook his head at her.

"I promise you can trust me, Sloan. I know you

have spent the past fourteen years watching Jared, but I have spent them wishing you could just *see* me. The day Nuptia matched us . . ." He spoke softly, impassioned, as if he were all alone.

"Well, that day, I felt like I finally had a reason for being here. It gave me purpose. *You* were my purpose. And then when I kissed you on Fight Night . . ." He offered her a half smile, standing a little taller. "I was walking towards my likely death, but it was the most alive I had ever felt."

Sloan stood there, speechless.

"And when I was losing that fight and *you* cried out *my* name . . . it was you, Sloan. You were the reason I won. I realized I would lose you forever—I had never felt that before. I had never felt I had anything left to lose."

No one had ever spoken to her like this before. Jared had been intimate, loving and passionate. But *this* was different. Elijah's feelings—which she dismissed as a crush, an obsession—seemed to be real; he was really *in love* with her . . . and she didn't know why. He had a certainty that she was meant to be with him—he had the blind faith that she and Jared had somehow lost.

He sighed heavily. "I can't lose you, Sloan. I *need* to keep you safe." When she began to interject, he held up his hand. "I know, *I know*, you don't need anyone to keep you safe—you've proven that again and again. But, once you know the truth, you'll need someone watching your back—and *I* can do that."

She had a million questions and a thousand differ-

ent responses playing up in her mind. She could turn
and walk away, go back to the Academy and tell someone that there was something wrong with Elijah. *Or*
she could stay. She could hear a little more; she could
maybe finally hear what she had been demanding for
so long—the truth.

Finding out the truth didn't help change Fight Night . . .
But at least I knew what I was walking into when I entered
the ring—I wasn't ambushed.

She took a deep breath and he reached for her wrist,
pulling her closer to him—and she let him, taking a
hesitant step towards him. She couldn't tear her eyes
from his. He had opened his heart to her. Something
about his sincerity, his deep concern for her well-being,
overwhelmed her. She didn't love Elijah Daniels—hell,
she didn't *like* or even *trust* Elijah Daniels—but she
couldn't deny that his words had a draw on her.

Before she could think any further, he was kissing
her. And she let him.

He felt electric, like a live wire. He ran his hands up
to her face, drawing her in with every movement. For
the briefest moment, Sloan knew she could get lost in
this—she could acknowledge the fact that some part
of her *wanted* him. But he wasn't Jared, and she pulled
away.

"Please, come with me?" His words were a whisper
in the wind.

The Academy had taken everything from her—
Tandy, Kenny, Jared, her autonomy. Yet, Elijah's words—
his offer of truth—scared her. She glanced down at the

road leading back to the Academy, and she felt with un-wavering certainty that there was nothing waiting for her back there. She could hear Jared's voice in her mind. *"Get away from me . . ."* She had nothing left to lose.

Slowly, looking up into his green eyes, she nodded. She thought about his words as she got back in the vehicle and watched him warily as they began to drive on.

"Elijah, what did you mean when you said *when it all goes down?"*

He glanced to her, chewing his lip. "I'll explain later." Before she could complain he motioned for her patience. "I promise I will tell you everything . . . But for now, I don't want to break your heart before it's even mine to break."

All the certainty she had just felt drained away— replaced with absolute terror. He was being serious— there really was something left to be afraid of.

CHAPTER 8

The other students had often called the small wooden cabins relics, but Sloan liked their antiquated look. She found them oddly charming, even if she wouldn't admit it aloud. Elijah grabbed their bags, his boots loudly crunching the fallen pines. She nudged an ashen stone into the grey heap—someone's abandoned fire pit. Elijah made a beeline for the nearest cabin, number 13. Sloan shook her head. "No, not that one," she protested.

They had gone the remainder of their trip in silence, speculation plaguing her. She had led him away from 13—that was her and Jared's cabin . . . or, at least, it *had* been. Elijah followed her, too polite to argue. She halted at the steps leading up to the deck, letting Elijah go first. He pressed his thumb to a discreet scanner, entering the cabin via biometrics.

She waited until he was inside before walking back

over to 13. She ran her hand over the cedar deck. She braved a step. She closed her eyes— the overflying birds called to her, the light breeze played through her hair, urging her towards the cabin door—towards her past life. She brought her hand to her neck, pulling the leather band out from under her shirt and holding the gold ring tightly against her palm.

Her eyes flew open and she retreated from the cabin. *This place holds too many memories of him.*

She spun around and took quick steps towards the new cabin. She stepped through the door and was thankful that this cabin wasn't a replica of 13. It was a large open-plan room, with a kitchen area, a sofa, a fireplace and one massive bed, covered in quilts. "I'll go get the food containers," Elijah announced, walking past her to get the food the Academy kitchen had stocked their car with.

She was alone. She looked at the bed and sighed heavily—she felt uncomfortable. She didn't belong here, not with *him*. And though it was too late to deny the hold he had on her, she felt like everything she had thought she knew about him had been wrong. He wasn't just a cocky pest, as she first knew him to be, nor was he a calm introvert, as she had seen him in his quiet moments. He was an eccentric lunatic who carried contraband signal jammers and suffered from paranoia. That he loved her was not in doubt, but whether she could trust that kind of love—or *anything* about him—was impossible to tell.

He reappeared, walking past her to drop a chrome

cooler box down in the kitchen. He watched her from across the room before finally speaking. "Let's go for a walk?"

She shrugged at the suggestion but followed him as he strode out the door anyway. He walked to the vehicle, leaning through the window, and pulled out the serial drive and a small black box she hadn't seen before. *Not with the signal jammer again . . .* She sighed heavily but continued to follow him. It dawned on her that if she was willing to follow someone whom she believed to be insane then maybe she was a little crazy herself.

For some reason, it was the first thought that had made her smile in a long time.

She pushed her boots hard into the sloping hill, treading over the soft terrain with concentration. Elijah found a grassy mound beside the lake and took a seat. She sat across from him, running her fingers through the lush green blades, the cold dew soothing her injuries. The lake was clear as glass, framed with a perimeter of green and gold trees. She had always loved this place—but watching as Elijah shoved the serial drive into the black box certainly took away from the joy she usually felt being out here.

"Do I *even* want to know?"

The box began to flash with a small green light. "This is *their* island, Sloan. They could have devices anywhere—*everywhere*—to hear every word we say. Hence, the signal jammers out here, speaking to you under the sound of the shower earlier . . ."

"Stop. Just . . . stop."

He nodded at her, unaffected. "I know it's all pretty overwhelming."

"That's not a word I would use to describe *this*," she explained, shaking her hand at the blinking box.

After a long silence he drew a deep breath. "I know things . . . things you would want to know."

She arched her brow at his vagueness. "Well?"

He sighed heavily. "Your family is alive. They run a hospital in a small town on the eastern coast, outside Fort Destiny."

She was surprised at his words—but they *didn't* really prove anything. The Order had told them all their families were fine in the last War Front Collective. The rest he could have found out somehow or was simply making up.

Wait—Fort Destiny. Where the attack had just happened?

As though he could read her mind, he spoke again. "They're alright, they weren't hurt by what happened there."

She shook her head at him. "You couldn't possibly know that."

"I made a point of finding out—I knew I would need to tell you when I finally had the opportunity to show you the truth."

"How? Found out how?" she demanded.

He shook his head, chewing on the side of his mouth anxiously. "The Others told me."

It took her a moment to react. Then she was on her

feet, backing away from him. He was a traitor. "You're a defector . . ." She turned and began to scramble back up the hill. She had been lured here by the enemy and a thousand thoughts rushed through her mind. How had they gotten to him? Were there more at the Academy? If he was right about the Order *listening in* then could she get far enough away from that blinking box and scream for help?

"Sloan, come back, calm down," he called after her.

"Stay away from me," she yelled over her shoulder, getting back up to the campsite.

"*Dammit*, just stop for a minute and let me explain!"

She could hear he had stopped following her and slowly she turned around to face him.

"Why should I trust *anything* you say?"

"Because if you have learned one thing about me it's that I wouldn't *hurt you*—that I wouldn't betray you."

He took a step towards her, the black box still in hand. She took a step back. He raised his hands, as if to show he wasn't a threat.

I'll hear him out and then turn him in, she thought.

He kicked at the ground, seemingly frustrated. "I didn't want to tell you this bit so soon—I wanted to wait till—" he began, but she cut him off.

"Till my heart was yours to break?" She echoed his former words. "It will *never* be yours to break. You have *no* hold on my heart, Elijah; just get that into your head!"

She could see her words wash over him and a resolute look overtook his face. She had hurt him.

"Fine. Then here it is—the Others aren't *others* at all. They're *us*. Our families, *our* people. The Academy, Romani—*they* are the real enemy from *Dei Terra*."

What? She shook her head at his cold admission. "That's not possible . . ."

He took a step towards her. "We weren't volunteered by our families, Sloan. We were kidnapped, taken to be brainwashed to fight *for* the enemy *against* our own people."

Sloan started to pace back, certain she couldn't hear any more of this. She took another step but tripped over a pine branch, falling hard to the ground. He made to move towards her, but halted as she pointed at him wildly. *"Don't* touch me, Elijah!"

He knelt down across from her. "I didn't believe it either. When first contact was made a few years ago, I resisted. But then I spoke to my family—I still *had* a family, and I learned the truth." His words were rushed and anxious, as if he could feel the clock ticking before she fled again. She slowly pushed herself to her feet and he stood, paralleling her.

"There are people on this island that you *cannot* trust," he said.

Like you, she thought, backing away from him. His green eyes held on to her, his mouth curving with each word, and she couldn't help but think of how she had *let* him kiss her. She felt nauseous. And for the first time in her life, her body betrayed her. Her legs buckled; she fell and crashed to the soft earth. Her mind whirled with incoherent thoughts. She lost all sense of the world around her, but she could feel herself being lifted from the ground. She blinked—Elijah's face was a blur. For the first time ever, Sloan Radcliffe fainted.

Sloan woke with a stir, disoriented. It was dark out and it took her a minute to recall where she was, and as suddenly as that recollection transpired, she remembered *whom* she was there with. She lurched to get off the bed, but found her hands had been bound. She wriggled over to her side and saw Elijah sitting in a chair, watching her attentively.

"Untie me."

He shook his head slowly. "I'm sorry, but *that* is for *my* protection," he said, gesturing to the ties. "I swore I wouldn't hurt you, but I won't let you hurt me either."

Sloan pushed herself upright. "Trust me, I *am* going to hurt you. I will kill you with my bare *bound* hands if you don't untie me."

Elijah got to his feet, raising his hands in a gesture of peace. "Fine—I will untie you. But only if you swear you'll listen to me."

"To more of your lunacy? Why would I listen to anything you had to say? You're one of *them*."

He crossed his arms, staring down at her. "Your anger doesn't exactly compel me to set you free."

How was I so easily deceived? He had fooled everyone—even Jared, who for all of his hatred of Elijah hadn't known the depths of this boy's madness.

She glared up at him. "Do you think I need my

hands to kill you?" she threatened and as the angry warning escaped her lips, she saw a glint of metal in his hand. He was holding a small knife.

She began to look around the room—mapping the space she would need to fight him, the space she would need to cross in order to escape.

"Promise you will listen?" he pressed, nearing her. She nodded, seeming to acquiesce. Quickly, he pulled his hand out, revealing the knife—she had to make her move now. She leaped off the bed, landing heavily on the floor. She kicked at his knee and fell to her side. Viciously, she kicked him in the abdomen—aiming for his broken ribs.

"Sloan, stop it!" he yelled.

She lurched herself to her feet, but before she could get away he grabbed her ankle and yanked her back. She fell on her shoulder—hard. She had been in far greater pain before and she wouldn't let one injury stop her.

She kicked at him furiously from the ground, screaming, *"Get off me!"* She tried to shimmy free, but he held her legs down, battling her as he crawled on top of her. He pinned her, the knife still in his hand. She wriggled underneath him, desperately trying to escape. She watched as he brought the knife closer, a quick slash of the blade . . .

. . . and suddenly her hands were free—he had cut her ties.

She froze, uncertain of what to do next. If he had wanted to kill her he could have. He tossed the knife across the room, but remained on top of her. "I told you I would *never* hurt you," he reminded her.

Sloan glared up at him expecting to see his maniacal face, but instead, she found the sincerity in his eyes that had first brought her here. "You want me to trust you after you tied me up and came at me with a knife."

He shook his head, seemingly exasperated. "I told you—I tied you up for *my* safety. You're one dangerous girl when you're angry. The knife was to cut you free—which I *did*. I would never hurt you."

"You're hurting me right now," she countered. She glared at him as he stifled a chuckle, but he also stood up, freeing her. He offered her his hand but she rejected it, getting to her feet on her own. They stood there, staring at one another. Then she noticed blood beginning to pool through his shirt. She must have hit his knife into him when trying to break free. "Elijah . . ." She gestured. He looked down and cursed under his breath, otherwise ignoring the wound.

Sloan thought about the situation—she was stuck in the woods with him. She had two options—buy more time or kill him. And she hadn't just ruined her life in an attempt to save his just to kill him now. "You have till tonight to convince me—otherwise, believe me when I say I will kill you."

He nodded slowly. "Fine."

She had watched him clean the small slash on his side. She had watched him build a fire. Now she watched him stare at her from across the fire pit. She was done waiting. "You said you could prove you were telling the truth—so do it."

"It's not the easiest thing to do . . . Tell me this—been forced to show off for any strangers recently?" he asked, leaning into the firelight.

She thought of Mr. Degrassi and the others, of the way she and Jared had been forced to fight for them.

"How do you know about that?"

He shrugged. "They're investors. They help keep this place going and in return, they come and handpick their next bodyguards—their personal security who keep them alive and well on the mainland."

She wanted to point out that he hadn't actually answered her but he carried on speaking.

"Your conversations being listened in to—your every move being recorded. That really happens. How else would I know Jared called you a slut and then you two had sex?"

A wave of heat rushed over her. "How *you* know those things?"

She felt violated hearing him describe a part of her private life aloud.

"Stone told me you and Jared were struggling and the Order was worried about it. He told me it was ti—"

Sloan cut him off. "*Stone* told you?"

"Yeah, he's kind of our de facto leader . . . He wanted to be the one to tell you, to bring you into the fold, but it couldn't be organized that way. So he suggested to Romani that we go on excursion and I tell you."

Sloan leaned away from him. Stone—*her* general, *her* mentor, *second* in command at the Academy. She had trusted him with her life and now she was hearing that he was one of *them*. That he and the Order—*and Elijah*—knew about parts of her life with Jared that should have been private.

She shook her head. "He's been manipulating me this whole time. Just like you."

"No, it's not like that—"

"*Really?* It sure seems that way."

"Sloan, he wanted to bring you in a long time ago."

She rolled her eyes at that. "Sure, I—as his closest pupil—was too hard for him to reach."

"You surrounded yourself with people who wouldn't hesitate to turn us all in!"

"Like Jared? Stone could have told him too but—"

He cut her off, raising his voice. "Jared is *not* like the rest of us, Sloan. His family isn't out there suffering somewhere."

Sloan stood. "What's *that* supposed to mean?"

"His family is involved—here, in this place, they had a role in making it and they have a role in maintaining it. Romani is *his uncle*."

Sloan fell back onto her seat. "*What?*"

There was no way Jared knew that. No way he would have kept all of that—all of *this*—from her.

Elijah took a deep breath. "He doesn't know, if that's what you're thinking . . . but that doesn't change anything. He might have been treated the same as the rest of us, but he would have never been Dismissed, and he's definitely had closer eyes on him this whole time. So no—we couldn't tell him and we couldn't tell you until we got you away from him."

Sloan couldn't believe this. She *had* been manipulated—she had been fooled. *"Get me away from him?"*

He ran a hand over his face, struggling with this conversation. "Needing you to get away from Jared so you could learn the truth has had nothing to do with the way I feel about you. I wanted you long before I even knew the truth."

Sloan narrowed her gaze at him. *"Sure,"* she said sarcastically. "It just worked out so well for you that you had Stone and whoever else helping you *get me away* from Jared."

"Dammit, Sloan! Can you just let me explain everything before you start with the accusations?"

She recoiled at his angry voice, but she crossed her arms over her chest and listened. And as he spoke, her anger turned to shock and she became more intrigued. He began to tell her the story of their lives, but not as she knew them to be. He explained the Academy was an enemy base, but not all its students had been kidnapped. Those—like Jared, allegedly—whose parents knew and supported them had their children willingly trained up. It simultaneously made no sense and perfect sense. Everything that had begun to bother her at the Academy—or perhaps always had bothered her—could be explained by Elijah's version of the story.

"Romani is the leader of the rebel faction," Elijah

carried on. "He goes to great lengths to ensure we hear warped versions of the war. The War Front Collective is pretty much a complete fabrication . . .

"They train us to fight our own people, the ones trying to *defend* the mainland. Haven't you ever wondered why no one returns to the Academy after deployment? Those who *always* knew the truth hunt down those who survived long enough to discover the truth. No one ever makes it back to reveal Romani's lies . . .

"But there *is* a small group of us, those who know the *real* story, here at the Academy. Stone brought us all in—Donny, me, a handful from Aviation, a few captains . . . It's all been opportunistic. He handpicked every student he believed could handle the truth—you included. So many of us are from Aviation because of his time in the wings, where he could lead our excursions growing up. You're the first one who would have been difficult to enlist—and *damn*, you have been difficult—but he insisted . . ."

Sloan couldn't quite put her finger on how she felt—*mad, betrayed, humiliated, doubtful?* She barely knew Elijah and yet it seemed he had a greater bond with her mentor than she did, that he knew intimate details of her relationship with Jared, that he knew things about Jared that Jared didn't even know.

She shook her head. "So, in essence, you found out you could be with me, knew Stone wanted me in his little fold of defectors, so helped manipulate the end of my relationship with the love of my life, to then tell me all of *this*?" she summarized.

"Sloan, it's—"

"It's *not like that*? Sure . . . you have developed some sick infatuation with me and now—" But he cut her off this time.

"You know that's not true. You know how I feel about you."

She stood, looking down at him. "You don't even know me!"

He rose from his seat, squaring off with her from across the fire. "Don't I?"

"What?"

"Don't I know you? I have held you each time you needed me most. I have carried you to bed. I have watched over you. I held you in my arms to try to keep you from breaking."

She stared at him in disbelief. "Elijah, you're part of the reason I was breaking in the first place."

He shook his head at her. "I'm so sorry I ripped you away from your perfect bubble of illusion—" he began, his voice once again rising, but she interjected.

"*Don't!* Don't you dare pretend to know anything about *who* I am. You have been champion for a day—I have been it for years. You don't know *anything* about being viewed as the best. You don't know anything about the constant pressure, the pushing, the objectification and humiliation and isolation of being this way . . .

"The responsibility that comes from being the Order's prized possession—*you* do *not* know what my life has been and you helped rip me away from the only other person who understood."

He glared down at her. "I saved you from a life of being some glorified bodyguard."

"At least I would have been with Jared!"

He lashed his hands out at his side, enraged. "You talk of responsibility, Sloan, well here it is—*this* is real responsibility. You have a family who needs you, people who need you, and you're saying you would have rather carried on blissfully ignorant as long as you had *wonder boy* at your side?"

She stepped away from him . . . He was right. If he was telling the truth—he was right. She did have a family, out there, somewhere, who needed her. She had people she had sworn to go out and protect. Elijah was offering her the opportunity to do what she had always believed she was going to, and she was too mad to acknowledge it. Losing Jared had hurt too much.

She turned from Elijah, stumbling into the dark, as forceful memories pushed into her mind. Tandy, the day of her Review, flashed before her. Her best friend, shaking, eyes wide, lip quivering. *"Don't let them take me, Sloan."* She had been forced to the Order by sentries, resisting tearfully.

"Don't fight, Tandy. It's just a conversation; nothing will happen to you." She had let them take her best friend. She had failed her. She had failed Kenny. She had lost Jared. She had now angered the Order. She had—

Sloan choked, hacking icy water out of her mouth. The cold lake flooded her eyes, ears and throat. She struggled to her feet, gasping for air. She blinked water from her eyes and found Elijah standing there, knee deep in the lake. *What just happened?*

"You were screaming," he explained, raising his hands defensively.

She coughed up more water. "What?"

"You were screaming . . . you kind of lost it. Like *really* lost it."

She slumped into the lake, running her hands over her face. "Well, what did you expect?"

He stood there in silence.

After a while, she looked up at him. "You're telling the truth, aren't you?" The night sky behind him, the milky moonlight playing over his strong face. He nodded solemnly.

"Yeah, I am . . . I'm sorry."

She struggled to her feet; he helped her up and out of the lake. She wrung her hair out, shivering in the night air.

Sloan paced the cabin, watching Elijah sleep on the sofa. They had exchanged an awkward moment before deciding to go to sleep, whereby she promised she wouldn't kill him. But she couldn't sleep. She could only think. And pace. She wanted to speak to Jared— she wanted to tell him everything. But if everything she had been told *was* in fact true, she couldn't risk it, could she? If he really was under the constant watch that Elijah seemed to believe he was, if he really was

Romani's nephew and his family had some role in the Academy—how could she tell him?

Would he even believe her if she did—did *she* even really believe it all? She finally stopped pacing and looked down at his dark silhouette. She studied him thoughtfully. She had fought to keep him alive and it had meant the end of her relationship with Jared. She didn't want to resent him, but everything he had said made it difficult to not do just that.

She couldn't understand how he had ever had any draw on her. Maybe it was natural to develop feelings for someone you fought so hard to keep alive—maybe it was because Nuptia really had paired them, so he had some unexplainable pull on her, or maybe it was because some part of her knew he was telling her the truth, and that made him different from everyone else in her life.

"Why are you watching me sleep?" His voice just about gave her a heart attack—*how long had he been awake?*

Well, you threatened to kill him—it would be amazing if he slept at all.

She glanced to the countertop to see the blinking signal jammer box—it was still on; she could supposedly still speak candidly. She didn't answer him, she just asked a question. "If you're so against the system then why do you believe they were right in pairing us?"

He rolled over, blinking as his eyes adjusted to the darkness. "The machine, Nuptia, doesn't make mistakes. *People* make mistakes."

Sloan nodded in the darkness before slowly retreating to her bed. She fell asleep wondering how many mistakes had led her to this stage in her life.

"Stone helped transfer me out of Aviation when the Calling happened, knowing I wanted to be closer to you," Elijah explained. He had told her about his life at the Academy, how he had streamlined into Aviation early on, learning how to fly before any other student there. Sloan had never really thought about it—the aviators generally trained with the rest of them—but they were sort of a separate group of their own.

They had been having a relatively pleasant morning—more conversations with fewer death threats. That had to be progress . . .

She dipped her toes into the cool lake. "Then why didn't you ever just talk to me?"

He shot her a challenging look. "Would you have ever looked past Jared to me or anyone else?"

"Maybe if I thought you weren't just lusting after me—I do have friends, you know." Even as she said the words she thought about the level of truth in them— *did* she have any friends anymore?

"I don't think I ever saw you speak to one person without Jared by your side," he pointed out.

She wanted to protest but she couldn't . . . Loving someone like Jared had a blinding effect on you. She wondered, if all of this was true, what sort of person Jared would have been if he had never been sent to the Academy. She wondered what sort of person she would be, if she had been left with her parents. Would she still be the sort of girl he would have loved?

"Maybe if he knew, he would see things differently . . ." she spoke, voicing her thoughts from the previous night.

"Knew what?" Elijah asked, looking up from where he sat on the bank.

"About all of *this*," she said, waving her hands about.

He shot her a worried look. "You *cannot* tell him—that's Stone's call. I'm serious—if we told everyone we wanted to, some—*many*—would resist. Romani has the power here—imagine what he would do if there was an uprising?"

Sloan tried to imagine exactly that—a handful of students standing up and announcing all she knew now. She knew how she would have reacted—how she *had* reacted just yesterday to all of this. She would have defended the Academy. She would have put any traitor down.

As if reading her thoughts, he spoke. "They will all find out at some point . . . and it might not be too late for Jared. You could—*I don't know*—work things out . . ." He let his voice trail off. She watched him deal with his own sad hypothetical scenario.

"I can't pretend that's not what I want, but I can tell you that, whether you're telling the truth or not, we are all marching towards a war. What's the point in worrying about anything other than staying alive?"

Sure, it was true, but she said it more for his benefit than anything else. If she could be back with Jared right now she would do it in a heartbeat.

He fidgeted in his seat, looking up to her. "Because there's always *more*. Always something else—something better." He took a deep breath. "But if *this* is all I ever get, just this time with you, well—that's enough for me."

Sloan stared at the ceiling that night, this time knowing Elijah was asleep, as he snored loudly from the sofa. They had spent the entire day talking. They spoke about his version of the war and the Others and the Order. They spoke about training and Stone. They talked about how they had never known one another before the Calling. She was talked out. And yet, she couldn't sleep.

She had been raised on the belief that her parents had volunteered her for this, and that her superior skills and success would have made them proud. Who she was, the things she had done—the things she *could* do—it would probably horrify them. She imagined a woman whom she resembled, with blond locks and golden eyes, running a hospital with her husband. A hospital where many of the patients had probably been victims of someone just like Sloan . . . She wiped away the errant tear on her cheek. How could two people who saved lives ever be proud of a girl trained to end them?

Sloan stared at Elijah with apprehension, arms crossed over her chest. He had an easy smile painted across his face.

"You won't hurt yourself, just trust me," he laughed, resting his hand on the central yoke of the bike.

"It would be easier to trust you if you weren't laughing."

He laughed louder at that. Finally, he regained his composure. "Okay, do you know what a horse is?"

"Of course I know what a horse is." Well, she knew the animal, despite having never seen one.

This time, he stifled a laugh, clearly seeing through her. "Okay, these bikes are like horses. Hands on either side of the yoke. When you lean forward, you go forward; when you squeeze your thighs—lean right, go right; lean left, go left—so on and so forth."

She kicked at the ground, not liking feeling incapable. "How do you turn it on?"

He smiled, pointed to a scan pad on the side and brought his forearm to it. The pad registered his arm chip and the bike whirred to life—a low hum—and then it elevated several feet off the ground, hovering powerfully. She couldn't help but smile—she definitely wanted to try.

Elijah turned the bike off; it lowered slowly to the ground. "Mount up," he ordered and she leaped on. She ran her fingers, still sore, tentatively over the yoke. She touched the scanner pad; she squeezed the cool metal with her legs.

"Good—now turn it on."

She lowered her chipped arm to the scanner and gasped as the bike came to life, raising her off the ground with ease. He let go of the yoke, mounted his own bike and turned it on. "Ready?"

She nodded keenly. He ran her through the instructions again, having her follow him in slow circles. She leaned, the bike leaned; she rested back and it slowed. She found the machine easy to control and in a fit of inspiration, she jerked her body suddenly, causing the bike to turn in a full circle. She couldn't contain a laugh.

"You're a natural." Elijah smiled, drawing her attention back. He nodded in the direction of the woods. "Let's go." He leaned his strong body forward and took off. She watched him for a minute before flying after him.

They zipped over bushes, weaved through trees, flew over the glades. Sloan didn't know how fast this bike could go—but she wanted to find out. She leaned sharply and took off—the wind beat through her hair, the sun streaked after her. She quickly overtook Elijah, soaring through the woods, navigating around the foliage, taking sharp turns around errant tree trunks.

She bolted upright—they had reached the lake. She eyed the water suspiciously.

Can I . . . ?

"What are you waiting for?" Elijah's voice laughed out as he flew past her, confidently navigating the machine over water, creating rippled waves. Sloan didn't hesitate, leaning in and taking off after him. She performed sharp turns, donut circles, and raced forward. She laughed uncontrollably, loving the sensation, loving the speed.

Loving the *freedom*.

She flew across the water, back into the far end of the woods, leaving Elijah far behind. Leaving *everything* far behind: the cabins, camp, the Academy, Jared—it all fell behind her in a storm of whipped-up leaves and dust.

Pulling into a clearing, she brought the bike to an abrupt halt. The glade was beautiful—a small brook veined through tall matted grass. The sun glinted against the verdant shades—gold and green, like Elijah's eyes.

"Elijah." The name fell easily from her lips.

"I'm here." His voice startled her. He was hovering behind her in the tree line, happily watching her. She watched him over her shoulder.

"I thought I'd lost you."

He smiled, regarding her with reassurance. "Not for a second."

Sloan let Elijah grab her wrist, helping her up the escarpment. For their last day they had decided to go for a hike, trying to avoid conversation about the Academy and all he had said. They had swum in the lake and her damp clothes clung tightly to her. She followed him up the massive boulder and stripped her outerwear off to dry. Looking around, she realized she had been here before—this was the rock she had jumped from with Jared. *That seems like a lifetime ago now. . .*

She glanced over the edge, the lake far below them. She retreated, pushing the memory from her mind. Elijah lay on the stone, baking in the afternoon sun, and Sloan lay beside him. She glanced at his face, his bare chest—his bruises were slowly coming down, his cuts slowly closing. This time *was* healing.

"I will need to speak to Stone when we get back," she announced, breaking their promise to avoid serious conversation.

Elijah nodded, eyes closed. "He's expecting it."

Sloan rolled onto her side and watched him. "What's going to happen when we get back?" She thought of Romani, of the Order, of Stone and Jared . . .

"I won't let anything happen to you," he answered confidently, turning to face her. Sloan could take care of herself—that wasn't her concern—but it was nice to hear someone say those words anyway.

Suddenly, she leaped to her feet. She could face anything that came at her; she wasn't afraid. If this past week had taught her anything, it was that she could take the pain.

"Want to jump?" She broached the ledge confidently. Elijah was on his feet in a second, reaching out for her.

"Don't! Students have died jumping from here," he warned her, his voice panicked. Sloan couldn't help but smile at his candor—he had told her what Jared had long ago kept a secret. *Again.*

"I know," she said, inching towards the edge. He was by her side in an instant.

"I don't want you to get hurt."

She shrugged her shoulders. "I know . . . but it's a little too late for that."

He grimaced at her words.

"You don't have to jump, but I'm doing it," she declared, determined, turning towards the edge.

He grabbed her hand tightly, and for a moment she thought he was going to haul her back.

Instead, he simply said, "Where you go, I go."

And then, without any hesitation, they leaped together.

They hadn't spoken since the fall, but their silence was comfortable. She pushed against a tree trunk, winding over a bush. A light breeze chilled her bare arms. "I forgot my sweater," she gasped, picturing the garment resting on the boulder.

Elijah halted. "I'll get it."

She shook her head. "It's fine. I'll meet you back at camp." Before he could object she turned on her heel, quickly taking off back towards the rocks.

She took a deep breath, making it back up quickly. She took tentative steps on the boulder, pushing herself up higher. She threw her body up and was on her feet, spotting the sweater exactly where she had left it. She scooped it up, shaking it out before pulling it on. She glanced to the ledge, thinking of their jump. He had held her hand all the way down. He had held her hand as he wrenched her up from the water, gasping for breath too.

An unnatural crack of squawking broke through the silence of early dusk. She turned on her heel, seeing a black swarm of birds fly out from the trees near the cabin—they had been scared by something.

"Elijah . . ."

Sloan flung herself over the rocks, ignoring any pain. She jumped from the last boulder and took off with an urgent speed. She weaved through trees, leaped over logs and ducked branches. She cleared the distance faster than she could have ever thought possible. As she pushed through the bushes she saw the cabins ahead—and she came to an abrupt halt. She fell to her knees, ducking behind a bush. Slowly, she pushed the leafy twigs aside.

Elijah was kneeling by the fire pit, his hands behind his head. Standing in front of him was a white-clad Academy sentry. In one hand the sentry had a gun, in the other, a signal jammer, its flashing green lights playing through his fingers. She crept forward, inching closer, coming up behind the nearest cabin. Eventually, she got near enough to hear what the guard was yelling, all the while waving his gun at Elijah.

" . . . contraband! As soon as I tell Romani, you and your girlfriend are as good as dead!"

Sloan was chilled at his words, and yet she couldn't imagine what a lone guard was doing out this far. Did Romani suspect something? Had he been sent here with purpose or was this a routine patrol?

"She doesn't even know I have it," Elijah yelled up to the guard. "She had no clue." But the guard was having none of it, and struck Elijah with his weapon. Elijah swayed, spitting blood. The guard trained the gun on Elijah's head, fidgeting at his hip for his radio.

If he turns it on, we're done for.

Obviously thinking the same thing, Elijah made a move, leaping at the guard—but he was too slow. The guard jumped back, alarmed. He abandoned his search for his radio, lowering his aim at Elijah's heart.

"Attacking a sentry is an offence that warrants immediate Dismissal."

With a flick of his finger, the guard took the safety off of his weapon.

Without thinking, Sloan raced from the cabin wall. Maybe the guard saw her in his periphery—maybe not—but either way, it was too late. She grabbed the cold metal of his gun barrel and, twisting his hand inward, she wrenched it free, tossing it to the ground. The guard struck at her wildly, but she ducked, kicking the outside of his knee. He fell and Sloan swung herself around him, wrapping a forearm under his neck. Grabbing his jaw with her shaking hands and locking her spare arm behind his head, she wrenched his neck to the side.

"SLOAN!"

Elijah's yell echoed through the woods, covering the sound of breaking bone. It muffled the *thud* of the guard's lifeless body hitting the ground.

She reached for Elijah—he was bleeding. He recoiled from her outstretched hand, a look of horror on his face. She didn't understand. He lunged forward to her feet—his hands rolling the guard over. Sloan stepped back. Elijah stared at the man's motionless chest. He touched the sentry's face and he cursed under his breath when the guard's head rolled to the side.

"Stop it, Elijah," she ordered. He ignored her.

He rested his hands on the man's chest. *"Dammit, Sloan . . ."*

He pushed on the man's chest—*was he trying to revive him?* Elijah began to pound harder against the guard, as though he were willing him to wake up.

Sloan was barely listening. Barely present. She knew what she had done—*what she had been trained to*. She felt her hands twitching uncontrollably at her side.

"I said *stop it*, Elijah." At her low growl he looked up at her, horror in his green eyes.

He shook his head and leaned over the guard, resting his ear above the man's heart. He checked for a pulse. He grabbed his wrist, a second location for proof of life. "Come on, *come on*," he grumbled.

She needed him to stop. She needed him to stop *checking* what she had done. She took a step forward and pushed Elijah away. He fought her but she used all her might. "He's gone—now *stop it!*"

He fell away from her. "What is *wrong* with you?"

She barely heard him. She stepped away from the

scene . . . she had done *this* for *him*. She had saved him . . . she had killed a man. She turned back, looking down at the sentry's motionless chest. His nametag read YOUNG. She felt nauseous. That man had been alive, awake, moving, speaking, *hurting Elijah* . . . Now, he was motionless—inanimate. She had touched him and ended his thoughts, his voice, his ability to exist.

"Forgive me," she whispered, turning away from the body. She had taken a human and made a corpse. Without hesitation, she bolted, taking off into the woods to escape her mess—to escape the look Elijah was giving her.

She fell onto the ground and stared at her own hands. She could feel a tear falling from her. She could hear her heart beating, her breaths racing. She wanted to be sick. She could see Elijah's horrified face; she could hear the *cracking* of Young's neck. It turned out, the one thing she had fought so hard to avoid doing, the one thing that filled her with this sick feeling, was the one thing she had been trained all her life to do.

CHAPTER 9

Elijah had dropped the body from a small cliff, certain the fall could lead to a broken neck. They had packed in silence—neither of them had slept. Now, as Sloan hoisted herself into the vehicle, eyeing the ground where Young's body had lifelessly fallen, she knew the truth of this path she was set on. No matter how many realizations she experienced, no matter how many truths she was told—she now knew the only truth that mattered. That no matter how aware she was of the Academy's alleged true nature, she couldn't deny *her own* nature. The Academy had already won—they had changed her, molded her into a fighter—into a killer—into a person whose instincts were what *they* had designed them to be.

I am what they made me to be. . .

She glanced to Elijah; he felt her stare and offered her a meek smile. She didn't reciprocate; instead she let her gaze fall back onto the road ahead. He might have been thankful that she had saved his life—*twice*—but he would never be able to look at her the same way. She had killed in front of him. She couldn't help but think of how Jared would react to witnessing her action. She wasn't precious, the way Elijah constantly made her out to be—she was dangerous, the way the Academy *made* her to be. Jared had known that long ago. Sloan could finally feel the underlying bond that she shared with Jared—a dangerous instinct . . . a darkness.

No matter how much it bothered her—it wasn't something she could change.

Sloan turned her sore hands into fists. The Academy had changed her basic nature and she could never turn back. Romani had, in a sense, won . . . Sloan had one thought, though, that made all of this bearable. The Academy had shaped her into a weapon—*that* was undeniable . . .

. . . But they no longer dictated whom she was aimed at.

With a scan of their chips, they drove on to the Academy base. They hadn't been shot yet, which meant either no one knew about Young, or they just hadn't linked it to them yet. Elijah stopped the vehicle, leaping out and crossing the garage to Donny's office. She grabbed her bag and made her way to the pod, not caring to wait for him. She took a seat and was surprised to see Elijah lunge through the closing gap of the doors.

"Happy faces, Sloan." He needed her to pretend, to lie, to act like she had spent the past three days falling in love. She *needed* people to stop telling her what to do.

"This *is* my happy face," she snarled.

The pod doors hummed open and Sloan got to her feet, stepping into Elijah's living quarters. She was startled to find General Stone standing in the living area, looking out their window. He turned to her slowly and crossed the room, stopping a foot before her.

"General," Elijah greeted him with a salute. Sloan didn't bother—she was done playing games.

He looked her up and down—he understood. "You two, my office, twenty minutes." He clapped Elijah on the shoulder affectionately, but kept his eyes on Sloan. *I'm sorry*, he mouthed. She shook her head at him, warning him off the topic. She left them standing there, moving into the bedroom to get changed into uniform.

She stripped her shirt off as Elijah walked in. He jerked his head in the direction of the bathroom and reluctantly, she followed him. He turned the shower taps on and leaned into her, their voices muffled by the pounding water. He brought his mouth to her cheek—but it wasn't the same as before. Every move he had ever made around her had been fueled by lust, with a constant *want* for her. Not since Young. Not since he had seen her true self.

"We are being watched—listened to. We only speak in here now," he whispered, gesturing to the shower area.

She nodded, intentionally expressing disinterest. He arched his brow at her. "What's wrong with you?"

Really?

She stifled a scoff. "What's wrong with me?" She raised her hand and grabbed his neck, pulling his face to her. They kissed. She navigated his mouth and held her body close to his, and he reciprocated . . . but it wasn't the same. It wasn't the same as the day on the road. She was right—he didn't see her the same way anymore. She pushed him away, eyeing him with anger. "*That's* what's wrong with me."

It took him a moment, but as his brow furrowed and his eyes softened, she saw him realize. "Look, Sloan—"

"Don't bother," she hissed, and for good measure, added, "It's not like I loved you."

She didn't know why it bothered her so much—why *being right* bothered her. She had said it from the start; he had an obsession with her, an idea of saving her and keeping her precious. He didn't love her for who she really was—and he could deny it all he wanted to, but the truth was in his eyes, it was in his kiss. She had saved his life and in doing just that, he had stopped seeing her as a delicate object of desire.

Good, she thought, turning and leaving him standing there.

Sloan pushed the doors to the training hall wide open, stepping inside, Elijah close on her heel. Although the room was fairly full, she immediately spotted 27—spotted Jared. She might still be a part of that table, but just like her long-forgotten parents in Fort Destiny, these people were no longer her family. She *had* no family.

She kept her eyes on Jared as she crossed the room, the new knowledge she had of *his* family and role in the Academy playing through her mind. And he watched her too. He narrowed his eyes on her and studied her carefully—as though he could see something had changed.

Her table slowly made their way across the room, deliberately getting in her path.

Sloan slowed to a stop, holding Jared's gaze. Elijah stood confidently beside her, knowing it was best to let her take the lead.

"How was the excursion, *whore?*" Mika's tight-voiced laugh cut through the group. Sloan, without hesitation, lashed out, backhanding the girl across the face. Mika shrieked and Will immediately took a step towards Sloan, ready to defend his partner.

She was ready—she was ready for anything. But Jared grabbed Will's shoulder, pulling him back.

Jared took a step closer to her. His one arm was still in a sling, but his face had healed up quickly. He continued to study her. *You can tell, can't you—you can tell I'm somehow different?*

He took another step towards her. "What happened?" he asked knowingly. She held on to his blue gaze and every fiber of her being wanted to close the gap between them. She wanted to kiss him, to hold him, to disclose everything to him.

Instead, she shook her head slowly. "Like you care."

She brushed past him, but he grabbed her arm. She jerked it free. He couldn't touch her—she couldn't stand to have him touch her without breaking, without giving in and forgiving him. *"Get away from me,"* she ordered, throwing his words back at him.

She turned and pushed through the group, making her way to Stone's office.

She threw Stone's door open and coolly took a seat, not bothering with formalities. Formalities inferred respect—he didn't respect her so why should she respect him? Stone watched her disregard protocol and she watched him watch her. He studied her thoughtfully, just as Jared had. He knew—she was certain of it. He knew, just like Jared had known, that she had finally become that which she had trained to be.

Stone gestured for Elijah to sit. "We can speak freely in here for now."

But they didn't, not right away. The three of them sat in silence. Sloan tapped her foot against the floor, restless. "Did you call us here for a reason?"

Stone tensed his jaw, leaning back in his chair. She was pushing it, but she didn't care. *Where had caring gotten her so far?*

Stone took a deep breath. "Yes, I need to be briefed on what Elijah has told you."

"He told me about you, *what* you are, *who* you lead," she answered tightly, each word a jab. He nodded at her, studying her attentively.

"You're on board then?"

For a moment—she expected him to laugh, or stare at her in shock. She expected him to say Elijah clearly had been deluded and that none of this was true. But he didn't.

Sloan slumped back in her seat. "Didn't give me much choice, did you?"

He inclined his head at her. "It's too late to turn back, if that's what you mean."

"Yeah, *that's* what I mean," she sneered. He arched a brow at her, but what had he expected?

He drummed his fingers on the desk. "You should know we have a plan then, an intervention before Departing Ceremonies. Our primary aim will be to evacuate the children. We can discuss details of all that later, with the Others."

Her anger couldn't shield her from this shock. She had gone along with it, she had listened to Elijah's story, but it hadn't actually registered in her mind as wholly true until this exact moment. He was *their* leader. He had a plan. He had kept greater secrets from her than she had ever imagined.

Just another betrayal.

Elijah leaned forward. "Sir, we had an issue this weekend. I . . . I killed a guard." He tripped over his words with uncertainty and she felt disgust. Killing had to be spoken about the same way it was done—with conviction. Sloan watched Stone take in Elijah's lie, but his face betrayed nothing. She didn't need him to try to take the heat off of her—she didn't need *any* favors from him.

"Don't lie for me," Sloan said, remaining relaxed in her seat. Elijah shot her a shocked glance, but she was narrowed in on Stone. "*I* killed the guard."

"I know," Stone said, leaning forward and reading her face. "Or at least I suspected—Kevin Young."

"What?" Sloan asked.

"His name was Kevin."

Kevin. *Kevin.*

"He had been on patrol," Stone continued. "I'm sorry this happened."

Sloan snorted at his apology and it seemed to be the last straw. "Daniels, wait outside for a moment." Elijah immediately stood and eyed her over before slowly exiting.

Stone leaned across his desk. "Do we have a problem, Lieutenant?"

She glared at him. "Why would we?" she pushed sarcastically.

"Because it seems like you have something you want to say to me," he pressed.

"*That's* rich, sir, truly," she laughed. Hadn't he had something to say to her all these years?

"Watch it, Radcliffe."

Sloan stood. "Or what?" she demanded.

He stood, mirroring her. "I don't need to explain my motives to you, *Lieutenant*."

"If you're asking me to commit treason then yes—you do," she snapped back.

"I'm not asking—I am *ordering* you to."

Sloan froze under his words. Despite her unbridled rage, despite her overt indifference, she still hesitated at the sound of an order.

He relaxed, taking his seat again. "I know you've been in the dark, Sloan. I know you're hurting—and I *am* sorry—but I'm finally in a position to offer you some light."

She took her seat, taking a deep breath, but she remained silent. With a quick knock on the door, Elijah popped his head in. Stone waved him back in and he returned to his seat beside Sloan.

"You two should know that, while you were gone, Jared was promoted to major—in fact, he will be the first student to ever receive that rank."

Sloan felt an odd sensation in her chest—*pride*. She was proud of Jared . . . but she didn't want to feel *that*. She narrowed her gaze on Stone and concentrated on her anger instead, willing it to consume her.

"Regardless, we can discuss this all further at a later date—I have a meeting to get to," Stone announced, standing.

Sloan and Elijah stood slowly, turning to the door. "Sloan, wait a moment," the general spoke. Elijah saluted Stone and once again left her in the room.

She watched Stone regard her slowly. Finally, he spoke. "Are you alright?"

She shook her head—she didn't want him to care; she didn't want him to be nice to her.

He carried on, seemingly insistent on doing just that. "I understand I have disappointed you," he said. "I wish things could have been different. I wish you didn't have to kill."

She jerked her head up at that. "How dare you say that to me? You *wish* I didn't have to kill? Was there ever a situation where that *wouldn't* have happened? You already got your wish—I am what *you* made me. Aren't you proud?"

"Every day."

"Excuse me?"

He nodded at her slowly. "I am proud of you every single day." His words were sincere, his eyes somber. His genuineness was an affront—she didn't want to feel anything for this man anymore. The problem was, she still did. Sloan turned from him, ready to leave

"Sloan—one more thing." She didn't bother turning around; she remained staring at the door. Noting her refusal to look at him, he finally spoke. "Everyone needs to believe you're in love with Elijah . . . Stay away from Jared."

Sloan's hands curled into fists as her familiar anger washed over her.

"*You* do *not* tell me what to do anymore."

Everywhere Sloan went she seemed to move with an aura of danger. Trainers and professors kept their distance; students backed away from her. She could move down the hall and a path would develop in the rush of cadets. Despite her antisocial demeanor, Elijah wouldn't leave her side.

Of course, Jared watched her constantly; he sat behind her in class, he trained near her in the hall, he would appear outside her other classes, or go for runs at the same time she went. The only time she didn't see him was during meals, because John, the kitchen head, still had food sent up to her living quarters and as such, she still had to train his son privately.

"Duck!" Sloan barked, swinging at Jack's head. The boy, a natural, lurched under her arm. He was small for an eleven-year-old, but he was eager and adept. He was also very green. So, as soon as he bolted upright, she gave him a light tap over the head. Hitting him hard wasn't necessary. Sloan knew the other trainers hit hard enough. The boy rubbed his temple, taking a step back. "You're a good fighter, Lieutenant."

She tilted his chin up to check she hadn't hurt him. Sure, it was training, but she didn't want to hurt him— he would find enough pain in this place without her. She smiled, reaching for their water bottles. "So are you, kid." She tossed a bottle to Jack and took a seat down on the mat. Jack mirrored her.

"So, why does your dad have you train so much?"

The boy shrugged, swigging his water back thirstily. "To be prepared." He stared at her with an atypical gaze, intensity in his young eyes, as though he were trying to tell her he knew there was something to be prepared for. Sloan shook the notion away—did it matter who else knew the truth? She thought she had been miserable when secrets had been kept from her, but now she knew it all and her life felt truly awful most days.

His childish features lit up curiously. "Why do you eat in your room?"

"Your dad told you that, huh?" Sloan sighed, leaning back on the mat. She decided on the truth—or at least some version of it. "It's so I can be alone."

"Oh. You have no friends."

She laughed pathetically at his forwardness, shrugging in agreement. She sat back up slowly.

"Have you tried asking for forgiveness?"

Sloan arched her brow at the kid's insightful question, half impressed at his perception, half offended that he assumed it was her fault she had no one left. She thought of Tandy, of Kenny, of Kevin Young—the people she needed forgiveness from . . . She couldn't ask it of them. And she couldn't explain that to an eleven-year-old. Before she could answer, the hall doors swung open loudly.

Jared walked through and, finding her quickly in the near empty room, began to walk over to her. She jumped to her feet. "Jack, get to class." The boy leaped up, eyeing up Jared as he approached.

"Go on," she insisted, patting him on the shoulder. Hesitantly he walked off, sidestepping Jared.

She immediately noticed his elbow was no longer in a sling—he must have had it taken off that morning.

His blue eyes bored into her as he approached. She still fought the urge to tell him *everything*—knowing she should, understanding she couldn't. He stopped a foot away from her.

Despite his close proximity since her return from the woods—they hadn't spoken.

She crossed her arms over her chest. "Congratulations on the promotion."

He shrugged his shoulders indifferently. "Thanks."

They stood in silence, eyeing one another up. Assessing how much they had changed since losing everything they had once shared. His eyes flicked over her body before locking in on her gaze.

"You're different." He nodded.

She shrugged, not knowing how to respond.

"You're . . . *colder*, angrier."

"You think?" she laughed, narrowing her gaze as he continued to stare. "Take a good look, Jare—you helped make me this way."

He arched a brow at her, a defensive expression crossing his face. "Don't be like that."

"*Don't* tell me how to be. You lied to me, betrayed me, kept every possible secret from me, ignored all my pleas, and in the end—when I rushed to you—*you* turned me away."

"How was I supposed to react when—"

"*When* what? When I declared my unwavering love for you, when I threw myself at your side despite the fact that you betrayed me, despite that you asked the Order for the one thing I begged you not to."

He threw his hands up. "I didn't come here to argue, Sloan!"

"Then what did you come for?"

"This is driving me insane! Seeing Daniels follow you around like a lapdog, knowing you're with him *every day* and *every night*—I need to know, I need to know that you aren't . . . that you haven't—"

She realized what he *needed* to know. He wanted to know that her body was still his. And it was . . . but she didn't need to tell him that.

"That's *none* of your business," she growled, glaring up at him.

"You belonged to me!"

"Yes. Yes, I did! And *you* threw it away. *You* destroyed us and don't you ever pretend otherwise. You're so miserable? Great—so am I! Don't think for one second that this is anyone's fault but your own. You ruined *me*," she said, a whisper and a shout rolled into one. "You ruined *us!*" She was in his face now; she could see her anger reflected in his eyes.

His face came into focus—his tensed jaw, his helplessly pursed lips, his fiery cobalt eyes boring into her. She pushed past him, storming out of the hall into the corridor. A pool of students still idled in the corridor, turning to see her as she slammed the door hard behind her. In an instant, it was flying open, nearly knocking her forward as Jared appeared.

"Sloan, I can't do *this* anymore!"

Jared never made public scenes—and now, he was doing just that. His loud voice echoed through the hallway, falling on the ears of everyone desperate to see this transpire.

"How do you think *I* feel?" she yelled back, pushing hard against his chest.

In an instant, his strong hands were holding her, gruffly pushing her back. "Tell me then!"

"Tell you what? *Nothing* can fix this so just *back* off!" she yelled.

"Don't you understand? *I can't.* If I could I would—do you think I want to feel this way? Do you think I want to still love you every waking minute of every day?"

With every word he roughly shook her, jolting her body back and forth in his shaking hands. She wriggled in his arms, too sad, too angry to be here anymore. But he didn't let her go.

"Tell me the truth—tell me it's still *just me,*" he pleaded, shaking her gruffly.

"Get off of her!" Elijah's voice surprised her. He grabbed Jared, freeing Sloan from his tight grip.

Jared seemed to return to reality—his sad eyes falling on her. "I'm sorry." He pushed past Elijah, keeping his stare trained on her. "I'm *so* sorry . . ." he whispered, and then, before his own tears could break, he ran off.

"What the hell was *that* about?" Elijah asked, following her into the pod. Sloan slumped down on the sofa, running a hand through her hair. Elijah sat opposite her, waiting for some explanation.

"Jared's coming undone . . ." She shrugged.

Elijah stared at her thoughtfully. "You two really can't live without one another."

Sloan stared back at him—*I tried to tell you just that a million times.* "We're managing," she lied.

He ran a hand over his face and then let it fall onto her knee. "We never talked about *everything* that happened when we got back here."

About how you realized you didn't want me anymore?

She sat in silence, unsure what to say. He moved to sit beside her. "Sloan, I just . . . I don't know—I've never seen something like that and I guess, I had never seen how similar you were to Jared before that moment. It took me a while to come to terms with it."

She stared at his hand on her thigh. She thought of Jared's concern about the nature of her relationship with Elijah, of Elijah's tumultuous feelings, of the state of her life.

He turned to her. "You know I still *want* you. My feelings on that never changed."

Sloan stifled a laugh at the timing of his declaration . . . as soon as Jared became paranoid she was sleeping with Elijah, Elijah reaffirmed his feelings for her.

She laid her hand on his . . .

. . . And slowly removed him from her. "Mine did."

CHAPTER 10

The sound of Kevin Young's body hitting the ground was a drum, amplified impossibly loud. Sloan's blond hair whipped slowly around her, her hands still poised to kill. Elijah's face transformed, a mask of shock and fear. His mouth closing around her name, a hand outstretched to stop her. Sloan didn't understand. She looked to her feet: Kevin Young was dressed all in white. Lying beside Kevin was Tandy Norman, in a white dress, her hand held by Kenneth Merose, his white uniform crisp and bloody. They lay in a row of white, eyes closed, small smiles across their cold faces. She pivoted around to find Elijah was gone. She fell to her knees and let her hands touch the cool skin of Tandy's cheek.

"All your fault."

She looked up—Jared, in military whites. Hands in

white gloves. She wanted to tell him it was an accident. He was backing away from her, shaking his head. He didn't see Romani standing behind him, a knife in his hand. She tried to scream; no noise. Blood blossomed across his chest, blooming death.

"SLOAN!"

"Sloan, wake up!" Elijah's hands shook her. She woke with a start, bolting upright. Her shirt was soaked with sweat, her loose hair damp. She scanned the dark room—they were in bed, Elijah propped up beside her. It had been a nightmare.

"Sorry . . . it was just a dream," she explained, running a hand over her face. Since her rejection, they had oddly grown closer. They had an intimacy that grew out of proximity instead of physicality. He slept beside her; they spent their days talking, and training together—and he woke her up when she was seized by these nightmares.

"That's the third time this week," he spoke, looking her over with tired eyes. She nodded, throwing her legs off the side of the bed. It had been nearly a month since their excursion and Sloan still couldn't sleep. She stood slowly, rummaging for her clothes.

"Where are you going?"

She found her training gear. "For a run. Go back to sleep."

She left him in the dark, dressing in the living area.

She dialed a pod and ducked inside. She groggily tied her laces as she made her way down to the outdoor field. As she walked the corridor to the outdoors, the early-morning air attacked her, whirling through her hair, clinging to her skin futilely. She didn't feel the cold. She pushed on, making her way to the grass.

She stretched her legs out, yawning. Jared was already out there—she could just make him out in the milky light. It wasn't coordinated. They hadn't planned it, but somehow, in the middle of the night, at dawn break, during supper when everyone else was eating, whenever she needed to get away, he was already there.

They always shared the field in silence. Not even their outburst in the hallway had changed that. If anything, it had solidified it.

She took off in a slow pace, jogging down the perimeter. Jared moved with an easy grace ahead of her, his shoulders bobbing rhythmically, his legs reaching out far ahead of him. Sloan continued down the field, her hands in tight fists. She took a deep swallow of air, extending her legs out further, pushing herself faster. She watched him run and she followed.

"**W**hy does Stone have to arrange these meetings on days where I just want to sleep?" Elijah complained.

Sloan glanced over the letter from the Infirmary as they walked down the hall, telling her to come in for her quarterly CI. They turned down the corridor, pushing into the training hall. Sloan made a mental note to go by the Infirmary later.

"What's the letter about?" Elijah asked, pulling open the door to Stone's office.

"Nothing." She shrugged, folding the paper up and shoving it in her pocket. They stepped into the general's office, saluting before taking a seat.

Stone took his seat and eyed her up slowly. "Kevin Young's body was found this morning."

She saw the sentry, falling dead, listlessly discarded from her hands. Sloan looked away from the general. She studied the crooked blinds of Stone's office window, refusing to close her eyes for fear that Kevin Young's face would appear.

I did what I had to do—I saved Elijah.

"He was found at the base of Green Peak and as you hoped, it has been believed that the fall snapped his neck."

She could still see the look of mortification in Elijah's face—the way he tried to revive the body.

"As such, everyone believes it was an accident."

Sloan stirred at his sentiment. They all *believed* it was an accident. "Well, at least *we* know the truth." She could taste the bitterness of her own words. Elijah and Stone stared at her darkly. Elijah turned in his seat, resting his hand on her shoulder.

"It *was* an accident." He corrected Stone's inference.

Sloan offered him a meek smile. "Falling off a cliff is

an accident—snapping someone's neck is not." At her rebuttal Elijah let his pensive gaze fall away.

"Elijah, give me a moment with Radcliffe," Stone ordered, leaning forward once more and pointing to the door. Elijah hesitated, glancing to her for some direction.

She raised her eyebrow. "What do you want? Permission to leave?"

The level of her own rudeness surprised her—but what did he expect, what did *any* of them expect? They had dragged her into this world, made her a killer, and then when she did *just that*—they treated her differently. *Elijah* treated her differently. Sure, they had grown closer, but she couldn't forget the look in his eye or the tone in his voice when he had demanded *what* exactly *was wrong with her?*

Elijah shrugged off her comment, shaking his head as he left. Closing the door on her.

Stone stared at her, his tired eyes studying her impatiently. "Talk to me, Radcliffe."

"Nice weather we're having here, General."

He narrowed his gaze. "You *know* what I mean."

Sloan readjusted in her seat, staring back at him. She wished Stone had never taken an interest in her. She wished she had never known the truth. "I have nothing to say to you."

"Sure you do. You're angry, you're disappointed, you're coming un—"

"*I'm* wondering what does any of that matter to *you?* You're the reason I'm like *this.*"

"You keep saying that—keep blaming me," he said, and his vehemence took her aback slightly. "Made you like *what*, exactly? Like an angry, petulant child? You think you're the only one who is disappointed?" He shook his head, leaning forward to carry on.

"I expected so much more from you . . . and *this* is what I have to deal with every day." His words confronted her, pushed her further back into her seat. He stood, rounding his desk.

"I thought you were stronger. I thought you had more control. Had I known that all you were was some façade, something that only existed because of Jared Dawson, then I wouldn't have bothered."

"How dare—" she began, but he towered over her, arms crossed, his heavy grey glare stilling her in her chair.

"I *do* dare. Because clearly I was wrong. He broke you beyond repair, and then, not only can I not rely on you to be the soldier I thought *I* had so aptly chosen, but then you go and *kill* someone." He shook his head. "You're a wreck, and a dangerous one at that."

Sloan stood abruptly, her chair falling back. "My life was made up by those I cared about! You—you *betrayed* me! Jared lied to me, abandoned me. Tandy—she was *taken* from me! You trained me to kill and then took away *everything* that kept me sane."

He took a step towards her and she backed away, stumbling over the chair. She fell against the wall, shaking. *How* could *he* be saying these things to her? He'd made her into something, something that required certain parts in order to function, and then he took those parts away from her and wondered *why* she was broken?

"There you go again—blaming everyone else for the horrible things you have done. Were you even thinking the day you killed Young? Honestly, Sloan, you were trained to know better, and if you didn't know better, then the least we expected was that you could do the bare minimum—kill and *move on*. Instead, you've let *it* destroy you."

"*You.*"

Sloan stepped away from the wall and pushed at the general, knocking him away from her. "*You* destroyed me! You—the Order—you ruined my life. I *loved* him and you *wrecked* him, you let me get *given* to Elijah, like some trophy, and then you bring me into this web of deceit and conspiracy. Yes, I killed someone, but it was him or Elijah and from everything you've taught me—that's not a choice at all. If I'm a killer then thank yourself because it's your *damn* fault!"

Sloan's voice broke over her tears. She pushed the general again, until he leaned against his desk, retreating from her. She hit him wildly in the chest. She pounded her fists against him and fought for breaths. She cried, breaking. He grabbed her wrists, pulling her against him, locking his large arms around her, pulling her face against his heart.

"Just let it out, Sloan."

After a moment, he spoke softly. "It *was* an accident, Radcliffe. I never wanted to hurt you—I *never* wanted to see you this way. If I could have done something about Jared and Elijah, I would have. I'm sorry you're the one who got hurt. You saved Elijah's life in the woods, you saved all of us—the ones who know—and I am so sorry you have to carry that around with you."

She hiccupped against his chest, letting him support her. He soothed her, taking back all his angry words.

"I know why you're disconnecting. The pain is too much, but you *need* to feel it. I hate to see you cry but I needed to do something to bring you *here*—this is good. You need to feel all of this suffering or you will hold on to it forever. Feel it . . . and then let it go.

"And when you do—come back to us."

She shivered in his arms, pain coursing through her. Stone held her tightly, rocking her against him gently. "I have never been more proud of anyone in my whole life. Since your first day here, you've amazed me. You have overcome everything you've ever faced—you will overcome this too. You're too strong to break."

She shook her head against his chest. She wasn't strong—any strength she once had was gone. Stone released her, tilting her head up to look at him, as though he could sense her doubt.

"You *belong* to no one, Sloan Radcliffe. We're all here for you, but what makes you different from the rest is that you are strongest when standing alone. Jared, Elijah, *me*—we get strength from you, not the other way around. You're not just a survivor, not just some prize. You're a fighter—a champion.

"Never forget that."

Sloan struggled through an apology to Elijah—she had been less than kind to him recently.

"You don't have to be sorry," he promised, holding her hand over the kitchen table. Stone had helped her *feel* something more than anger; he had brought her back—she had let her own pain get the best of her, haunted by so much death.

"Maybe you think that, but you're wrong. I shouldn't have taken so much out on you."

He took a deep breath. "Well, if we are doing this now then I guess I should apologize too. I forced you into a relationship with me . . . I thought, for a minute there, that I would be enough, that if you could just have the same time with me that you'd had with *him* . . . I don't know." He sighed.

She squeezed his hand. "It doesn't really work that way . . . but you were right in bringing me into all of this. You were the only person willing to tell me the truth."

The truth about the Order was bigger than her. No one soldier was more important than the whole army. Stone was right—she had to let go of her pain to be of use to the mission.

"I just wanted us to have what you had before—" he began, but shook his head, changing his thoughts. "You still love him, though? Don't you?"

"Yes. I still love him."

"Then that's all—" He stood, pulling away.

"Elijah—*stop*. We both know what's important

here, and you trying to compete with him for me, well, you won't win that way. You'll just be living in pain."

He nodded at her slowly. "Will you ever be able to see past what I've done? Forcing you into this union, telling you . . . what I've told you." He cupped her face, searching her eyes hopefully.

She shrugged her shoulders softly. "I can't lose anyone else." She knew it wasn't really an answer, but it was the truth. She couldn't lose him and carry on alone. She didn't want to.

And then—he kissed her. Sloan kissed him back, uncertain of her feelings really . . . She was selfish—she knew that his longing for her would keep him around. But they both knew how he saw her differently after seeing her true nature, and if letting him kiss her made her selfish, then what did actually kissing her make *him*?

He held her face and breathed her in and finally, he rested his forehead on hers. "I'm yours for as long as you want me."

"Good grouping, Radcliffe," West said, eyeing up her target. She offered him the handgun, turning away from target practice. It was a particularly hot day and she had been working with West for the past four hours. Her hands were a little shaky; it had been a while since she had been on the range. The praise helped. She wiped a bead of sweat from her brow and turned to follow West back to the safe room, where the weapons and ammunition were stored.

They found two sentries standing watch over the dial-lock door. She turned from West as he entered the code, but he didn't acknowledge her courtesy. Was this how Kenny had so easily gained access to the room—simply by watching one of the trainers idly entering the code?

Sloan followed West into the massive room. He flicked a switch and the fluorescent light fixtures flitted on, one by one, lighting up the long hall of weapons. He placed the gun on a rack for cleaning later and led her back out, securing the room shut behind him.

"How's everything with Elijah?" he questioned, leading the way back through the corridor to the pods.

"Complicated." She was close to West, but she knew that everyone needed to believe in her newly formed union.

"Well, whatever has happened, Jared's a wreck. He needs to pull it together before his ranking ceremony."

Sloan turned to him. She hadn't seen much of Jared outside of their silent, oddly timed runs. "What do you mean?"

"He mostly stays in his quarters, which is definitely unusual for him, but when he's not in there he's busy picking fights."

Sloan hadn't heard anything about this. She knew his temper, though, and she could easily imagine him raging against anyone who came too close. "Who's he hurt?"

West shot her a peculiar look. "Himself mostly. He

picks fights and then barely throws a punch. He's letting himself get beaten up over something."

Sloan thought back to the corridor—to the way he had grabbed her, to the crazed look in his eye as he shook her. Stone had pulled her through her pain; couldn't someone do the same for him? She glanced up to the major. "Have you talked to him?"

But West could only shrug his large shoulders. "I've tried. He won't open up to me."

They came to a stop at the pods. She thought of Jared, running so far ahead of her each day, letting himself lose fights. He was punishing himself . . . he was trying to feel. Apparently West had come to a similar conclusion.

"I get that you two aren't betrothed anymore," he said, "but that doesn't change much." Sloan shot him a quizzical look but he just shook his head at her thoughtfully.

"You're still his, Sloan, and he's still yours—you two are the same person. That boy will never stop loving you and you'll always be the one thing he needs."

Sloan raised her hand to stop him; she didn't want to have this conversation. She wasn't *allowed* to have this conversation. "I am betrothed to Elijah—"

West cut her off quickly. "And that's all well and good, but Jared is a loaded gun. Sure, he's always been dangerous, but you kept him sane; you kept him safe.

"He needs you, Radcliffe."

Sloan looked away. "Well, what if I don't need him?" she asked, her voice a low whisper as she voiced the absurd sentiment. West half-smiled at her, arching his brow.

"Who are you kidding, Sloan?"

In her dream, Sloan was lying in a glade with Tandy, searching the clouds for faces, laughing over one another's perception.

"I don't get it, Sloan. You swore you'd die without Jared."

Sloan sat up, her friend's question an abrupt change of pace. "I didn't have a choice."

Tandy stood, her white dress grass stained. "Sure you did. Look what Kenny did to be with me."

With her words, Kenny appeared, still in white uniform, hand outstretched to Tandy.

"It's not the same," Sloan cried at her friend's dark suggestion. "Jared's still alive."

"He won't be for much longer." And as she began to laugh maniacally, Tandy's white dress turned red with blood.

Sloan bolted up, panting. The dreams had been less frequent since her talk with Stone, but when they came they were still as vivid as ever. She crawled off the bed, leaving Elijah sleeping peacefully. She dressed and made her way into the pod. It had been a week since her conversation with West and she had suffered restless nights. She tied her running shoes as the pod twisted its way through the still-sleeping Academy.

As the doors opened up she thought of Elijah—he would wake soon. Despite keeping a friendly distance from her, she could feel his watchful eyes, his concern and his longing. He was falling back into his love for her with each day that she returned more and more to her former self . . . and she had nothing to offer him but poor companionship. She almost pitied him, because he longed for the Sloan Radcliffe who confidently dominated these halls, not the haunted girl she had become. Sure, she was recovering in a sense, but she would never be who he had first loved—who he wanted her to be.

Thanks to Stone, she was no longer running on pure rage, no longer filled with such anger, but she was no longer certain of who she was, or who she was becoming. She had nothing save the unrequited love of a boy she was pretty sure she could never love back.

Sloan made her way down the corridor and stepped out into the early-morning light. The milky violet sky was hazed with dampness and clouds, dewy grass underfoot, a stillness that marked the early hour. Still except for one thing.

There he is.

Running circuits, a hooded jumper on, arms confidently pumping at his side, legs extending in measured paces. She broke into her slow-paced jog, following after him, like she always did. He knew she was there. She knew he could feel her, running after him, chasing him the way she always had.

This was all they had been allowed to hold on to—

this measured distance. They had history enough to reach into the spaces between them. They had words, spoken and regretted, spoken and missed, unspoken and longed for, bounding back and forth between them. She pushed her feet hard into the damp grass, lunging herself further ahead, increasing her pace. Without ever glancing back, Jared knowingly sped up. His increase in pace spurred her on and she found herself running him down. She was breaking their routine.

She was gaining on him.

He was fast, though, and when he sensed her approach, he bolted. But she cut the grassy corner that he ritualistically followed, and came up on his side. He sprinted down the field when he saw she had caught up to him, and with a deep breath Sloan let herself run wild. She pushed through the tightening of her chest, she ignored the slight roll of her ankle and she blinked away the sweat that coldly pressed over her eyes. With all the speed she could muster she came up on his side once more and lunged in front of him. She immediately doubled over, taking in deep breaths, as he knelt down, wiping his face.

She crouched forward, dabbing her face against her sleeve. After a moment, they both had caught their breath, and sat there, silent, eyes on the ground. Slowly, she glanced towards him, his head bowed down under his hood. She took a moment and stared at his hunched-over form. She didn't know how to feel. She knew she was supposed to stay away from him—she had been *ordered* to stay away from him—but that

knowledge came second to the one she had known her
whole life . . . she loved him.

She could feel inside her the longing she had always
had for him . . . and she felt, on some level, as though
her mere presence here was a betrayal to Elijah. Despite all she had said to him, she knew he pursued her
still—and yet, she was here, with Jared. Her life was a
mess of contradictions: in loving the one she could not
have and being bound to the one she did not love, she
was somehow betraying them both.

She looked him over and saw his pain. She thought
of Stone and how he had ambushed her in his office,
determined to break through her anger by voicing her
greatest fears. She knew what Jared needed because it
was what she herself had needed. The only difference
was, she could give him absolution, but there was no
way she could be forgiven for failing all those she had
lost. The dead couldn't forgive.

But she could.

"It would be easier if I told you I hated you . . . If
I said I had fallen in love with him. If I told you that
you were now the monster I had always feared you
would become . . ." Her voice was clear in the chilly
air, each word crystallizing cold between them. He
kept his gaze down as she shifted her body, kneeling
before him.

"It would be easier too if I told you that what you
did—the ways you have hurt me—truly destroyed
every feeling I ever had for you." She watched his slow
rising shoulder, his twitching hands.

"It would be easier for me to hate you, and I know it would be easier for you . . . but the truth isn't easy. It's *not easy* for me to admit that I still love you, that I love you despite what you did to us. And *it's not easy* for you to know that you have someone's unconditional love—mine—because as entitled as you are you've never thought you were truly worth loving.

"None of this is *easy* . . . there are things that have happened, things I could never imagine, and the truth is, I'm broken. I'm grasping at straws of my former self and I keep looking to you to remind me of who I am, but the fact is I never should have let myself be defined by you . . . But I did—and so did you—and no, maybe we aren't our old selves anymore. Maybe, we are our own people . . ."

His shoulders heaved; his breaths were heavy, his fingers now balancing him against the ground.

"But you aren't alone, Jare . . . I can give you what I will never be able to get—and it's the *last* thing you'll want to hear.

"Look at me," she ordered. He didn't move; his strong body shuddered but he willed himself still.

"Look at me," she commanded again, inching bravely towards him. Slowly, he raised his face, and at first, she thought the hood of his sweater cast too many shadows across him. After a second, though, she saw the dark marks for what they were—bruises. She couldn't help but contemplate the state of them both. They had been the best—they had been what the Order made them to be. *Look at us now. . .*

She reached out, knocking his hood back, and cupped his mangled face in her hand. It was more than second nature, more than a reflex. Reaching for him to soothe his pain was the same response to the way she pulled her hand out of a hot flame—it was an ingrained action. Loving him was her basic instinct, protecting him, helping him.

His bruised eyes closed tightly as she slowly ran a thumb over his marks. He had healing cuts over his cheekbone and jaw. Under his eye, he had fresh welts, angry scratches, inflamed grazes. In every injury she saw his penance, his retribution for his mistakes. He brushed his swollen lips across her palm, and the mere feeling of his breath against her skin brought tears to her eyes.

"Please leave me alone," he whispered, his voice cracking. She shook her head, shuffling closer to him on her knees.

"Look at me," she urged a third time. Slowly, he blinked his eyes open and with tense apprehension, he managed to look at her. His cobalt stare bored into her; his eyes filled with fear and shame. She blinked away her own tears.

"Jared, I forgive you."

At her words he shook his head back and forth, tears now trailing down his face, sliding over her fingers. "No . . . you can't say that. *Don't* say that."

She brought her other hand up and held his face still before hers. "I forgive you. I forgive you for Fight Night, I forgive you for the lies . . . I forgive you."

He continued to shake under her touch, his tears falling freely, his mouth ajar as he fought for breath under his mounting sobs. As she watched her forgiveness overwhelm him she longed to feel that too, that sense of *being* forgiven, that chance to heal.

He buckled forward, his head falling against her shoulder, his face burrowing into her neck. His strong arms locked into an embrace and they cried.

"Please don't forgive me . . . please, please, please . . ." he cried over and over into her hair. She ran her hands over his back, she cupped his neck, and she held him tight, just whispering the same thing again and again.

"*I forgive you.*"

He turned his face, his cheek damp against hers, his breath catching in her own. She stroked his neck and held him close, and as his lips found hers, they finally stopped crying.

"**D**on't go," he urged, watching her tuck her shirt into her waistband. She glanced to where he still lay, on the bed. She *needed* to go—she needed to get to Stone.

"I have to," she answered, searching for her shoes. He sat up, grabbing her hand. He looked her over with such contentment because now he knew—he knew she was still his; he knew that she hadn't shared with Elijah what she had only ever shared with him.

"Sloan, I can try to do something—I can try to get you back?" he offered. She pulled her hand away from him.

"More than anything, I wish things could be different . . . but no—you shouldn't try to get me back."

She found her shoes and sat down, quickly pulling them on. He moved beside her, brushing her hair out of her face. *"Why?"*

"It's too difficult to explain . . ." She sighed, and decided to give him the only truth she could. "I can't be with anyone who views me as property."

He shook his head. "I don't view you as property," he protested. "I just know you belong to me." At his words she almost laughed. *Does he even hear the hypocrisy?*

"I don't *belong* to anyone."

He took a deep breath. "You can say that all you want, but you know the truth. I belong to you and I always will. My heart is yours and I *know* you're the same—your heart will always just belong to me."

She stood, ready to leave. "Jared—I am *betrothed* to Elijah now, I don't even know what the punishment is for what we have done—I don't want to know—but there is a lot more going on here than . . ." She let her voice trail off. She couldn't explain; she couldn't be candid with him. And for the first time in their shared life—Sloan was the one keeping secrets.

"You have to know I won't let anything happen to you. I tried and I just can't live without you. I won't give up."

She walked away from him, into their old living area, and dialed a pod. She took a last lingering look at him. She didn't know how to deal with this—how to love him and keep secrets from him, how to know what she now knew and not blurt it out. "You need to try to let me go, Jare."

As the doors framed his perfect marred face, she could just make out the trace of the word, dancing on his lips.

"*Never*."

Sloan knocked heavily on Stone's door and as soon as she heard him begin to answer, she stepped inside. He looked at her with confusion, obviously not expecting her.

"I need your help," she admitted, crossing the small room. He eyed her up, still obviously confused.

He's going to kill me, she thought, afraid to admit what had just happened.

"Can we speak here?" she asked, looking around, referring to whether he had a signal jammer on.

He stood, coming around his desk. "Yes."

She took a deep breath and forced herself to look into his grey eyes. "I made a mistake and I need you to get rid of recordings—or footage—or whatever it is, before someone else finds out."

His look of concern grew. "*What* did you do?"

She swallowed heavily . . . "I . . . I was *with* Jared."

His eyes widened and he leaned back against his desk. He was mad. *Of course he's mad—you defied his direct orders*.

"Where were you?" he asked, his voice low.

She wrapped her arms around herself. "We were running, and then we took a pod back . . . back to our old living quarters. And then I came straight here." She felt humiliated telling him this—so much of her private life had already been put on display for the Academy but it still cut deeply into her.

He nodded slowly. "I will fix it."

Her heart lifted and she returned her gaze to him. "Really?"

He stared at her with judgment. "I said I would."

She didn't know how to respond . . . she let her arms fall to her side. She was thankful for his help—for not dragging this out with questions and ridicule—but she was also frustrated. *He* had banned her from seeing Jared, the Order had separated them, Elijah had forced her into a union with him . . . and all along, she had said she still loved Jared. And now, when her mistakes could confirm just that, she had to ask for help.

"Um . . . thank you," she managed, unsure of what else to say or do.

He nodded, returning to his desk and reaching for his telephone. Her cue to leave. She turned and made her way for the door.

"Radcliffe," Stone called and she pivoted around quickly.

He looked her over with seriousness, and shook his head slowly. "Do *not* tell him."

She nodded slowly and turned away from him. She knew what he meant.

CHAPTER 11

Three weeks had passed and while Sloan dreamed less of her fallen friends, sleep was still mostly unattainable. She had kept her promise to Stone and remained silent about what had transpired between her and Jared. She had stopped going for early-morning runs and she hadn't spoken to him since that morning, but she couldn't avoid him in the hall; she couldn't ignore his longing glances. And it killed her as Elijah waited devotedly at her side.

He didn't ask about anything. He didn't try to initiate any contact with her. He just stayed with her, seemingly waiting for the day she could fall in love with him. She had tried talking to him, tried pointing out that he couldn't handle her basic nature, but he ignored her concerns, insisting what had happened with Young had been a mistake, that it didn't define her. His renewed sense of persistence, however docile it might have seemed, didn't help her feel any better about the secret she was keeping from him. She had become the one thing she had ridiculed all the men in her life for being—a liar.

She had slept with Jared and still not told him the truth about his family or their role in this place, the truth about their existence here. And every night, despite never having a physical relationship, she slept *next* to Elijah, and kept from him the fact that she had not only disregarded all of his pursuits but had broken every rule in her one moment of weakness.

She walked with him now, navigating the corridor to the training hall. Stone had asked to speak to them, the first time since she had begged him for his help removing any evidence of her indiscretion. Despite Stone's insistence on keeping her behavior a secret from Elijah, some irrational part of her feared him saying something that would give the secret away. She was afraid of hurting him, and if anything, that was a testament to having some semblance of feelings for him.

Elijah opened the doors to the hall and she immediately spotted 27 training with another table. Her gaze fell on Jared, who was training with Devon. He looked better—his face had healed quickly and now there were only small glossy scars where the deepest of his wounds had been. Elijah pushed her on—"Come on"—a hand on the small of her back. She carried on quickly but not before Jared had spotted her—his azure gaze holding her. He definitely seemed revitalized, having found renewed purpose: winning her back.

She dropped her gaze. It was too complicated—she

wasn't *allowed* to be with him, and even if she were, she couldn't abandon Elijah now, not when they needed her for their mission. She also knew that she couldn't just forget everything from before, everything that had helped lead to their breakup. Yet his words still rested with her, the truth evident in the fact that in a room of chaos, her eyes found him immediately—because her heart *was* his and it probably always would be.

Elijah had her presence, Jared kept her heart, but neither boy could understand that she didn't belong to either of them.

Sloan moved on quickly. She knocked on Stone's office door and with a raspy bark from the general she let herself in, Elijah following. She had half expected to meet a ridiculing glare, but instead, Stone was staring out the window, his hands held tightly behind his back. He turned slowly and the look in his eyes froze Sloan. His tight mouth twitched over whatever words he was about to say. His grey eyes narrowed in on her, a small shake of his head.

"We can't speak long," he finally said, gesturing for them to sit. Elijah slumped down in a chair but Sloan remained standing. He seemed nervous and it made her uneasy.

"What's wrong?"

"Romani has one of *us*."

Sloan backed away from the general as Elijah leaned forward. "What do you know, sir?"

Stone ran a hand over his tired face. "He announced it this morning in a meeting. He believes he's found a traitor. There will be an execution."

"*Who?* Who does he think it is?" Sloan asked, surprised at the calmness in her own voice.

"He didn't say. It could be any of us. It could be me, it could be you . . ."

At his words, Sloan felt her muscles tighten, a rush of adrenaline coursing through her veins. She didn't fear for her own life, but she wouldn't lose Elijah or Stone. *They* had a mission to achieve—a true purpose. They *needed* to survive this.

"Has this happened before?" she asked.

"Yes. Students he has suspected have been Dismissed, while members of staff are always *taken care of* in quiet," Stone explained.

Sloan thought of Tandy. "Wait—does that mean—"

Reading her thoughts, he cut her off. "No. Most of the Dismissed really were just failing to excel . . . but there have been some executed under the same guise."

She didn't know if that made her feel better.

"But Sloan ensured there would be no more Dismissed students?" Elijah reminded them.

"Unfortunately, it's not going to be like that this time."

Sloan took a step towards them. "What do you mean?"

"He's talking about making a spectacle. He says the Academy needs to eradicate this issue once and for all."

Elijah leaned forward in his chair. "What sort of *spectacle?*"

"I don't know. I don't know *anything!*" Stone said with an angry smack to his desk.

Sloan and Elijah waited in silence. He was their general; he took the lead on everything. He needed to tell them what to do.

"Have you spoken to the Others yet?" Elijah finally asked.

Stone shook his head solemnly. "Not yet. Hell, I don't even know where to begin . . ."

Sloan felt anxious. She had never seen Stone nervous, never seen him without an answer. When he spoke again, there was a distinct lack of conviction in his words.

"Just get ready for the Ranking Ceremony. If I find out more I will make contact." It wasn't a solution, but it came in the form of an order.

If only it felt like an order.

With no ideas herself, Sloan nodded to him, and Elijah stood. Abruptly, an overwhelming nausea seized her—nearly doubling her over. She grabbed the wall to steady herself and took slow breaths, steadying her stomach. Elijah was at her side in an instant.

"Sloan?" Stone asked, concerned.

She shook her head. "I'm fine . . ." She waved Elijah off. It was nerves. It was hearing this news.

"If it's you, we will run. I know the passcode to the armory—we could stock up on weapons and head out on a Skyshell . . ." His whispers stumbled out as he formed an uneasy plan. She looked up into his green eyes as they stood adjacent their shower.

"How much thought have you put into this?" she queried, impressed with learning what he knew.

"I told you—I can't let anything happen to you."

It didn't help her sense of guilt to hear him speak like this. She wanted to love him for thinking of her safety first and foremost—but she couldn't say what first came to her mind when she contemplated escaping; she didn't want to leave Jared here.

She sighed. "If we go now, we declare our guilt before it's necessarily ascertained. And if we stay—if it's not one of us—we might be able to help that person."

He shook his head at her. "Your safety is more important than whoever else it might be."

I don't deserve someone like you.

"Elijah—we can't run. We need to wait this one out," she affirmed. He nodded slowly and then pulled her into a hug, vining his strong arms around her. He kissed her temple and she closed her eyes, squeezing him tightly. She *did* love him in a way—but not the way he wanted her to. And she knew he loved her in a way—just not the way *she* needed him to.

Sloan dressed in formal white uniform, similar to Elijah's, and pulled her blond hair back in a bun. This was it. She met Elijah at the pod and they traveled in silence towards the great hall. The Ranking Ceremony would see all of the Academy dressed in their formal whites, a stage would be erected, and Jared would be honored as the first student to ever achieve the rank of major. But Sloan could barely summon feelings for that at the moment—her stomach was twisting in knots, worrying not just for the life of whomever Romani had caught but also for whatever he had *planned* for them.

What had Stone meant by *spectacle*?

Stepping into the corridor, Elijah herded her through the crowd of identically dressed students. She winked at Jack, who was filing into the room with his own age group. He waved at her, smiling wildly, and for a brief moment, she had a little joy in her life. She quickly came back to reality, though—especially when she thought about what Jack might hear or see tonight.

As she sat inside and watched the room fill, she saw Stone enter, immediately making his way onto the stage. He wore his formal whites and he no longer seemed nervous, but that was because he seemed so sickly. He kept his head bowed low, his hand resting on the back of his neck, his skin sallow and his face gaunt. On his hip was his service pistol, which took Sloan by surprise—she could not recall the last time she had seen him don the weapon.

As the lights dimmed and the students quieted, the Order entered. Romani led the way, joining Stone on stage. In the dim light Sloan could see Jared, entering the room alone and taking his place at the foot of the stage. He looked perfect, with his dark hair and meticulous uniform, and she was *so* proud of him, despite knowing the Academy for what it truly was, and who his uncle was. *He* didn't know—he had worked hard to earn his promotions. This level was something unprecedented, and it meant he had achieved greatness within this dark place.

"What are you staring at?" Elijah's quiet voice spooked her. She immediately turned her gaze to him.

"Nothing."

More lies.

Before they could speak further, Romani stepped to the front of the stage, his white gloves and ivory polished boots matching his uniform to give him an otherworldly appearance. *Like a ghost*, she thought. He scanned the room, his dark eyes traveling over them.

"Ladies and gentlemen, we are here to commend the efforts of one of our own. A young man who has excelled in the Academy with incomparable success, becoming the youngest ever to achieve the rank of major." His tight voice was hurried but clear, a violin of drawn-out notes.

"Please, welcome your newest major, Jared Jacob Dawson," he invited, extending his arm out. Jared leaped up the stairs, saluting Romani and the Order. He approached the marshal for his gold stripe. The entire room filled with the echoing claps of awestruck students, of cheers and whistles. Jared beamed as Romani added the stripe to his uniform.

Eventually, though, the clapping trickled to a halt, the cheers died out, and Jared began to shift uncomfortably on his feet—everyone waiting on Romani. Their marshal stood there in silence, a pleased smile painted across his face, his eyes honing in on the students as he looked them over. He rested one arm across his torso, the other propped up so that he could lay his chin on the back of his gloved hand. He continued to stand there, watching, seemingly enjoying the anxious tension his silence created. He glanced to Jared, whispered something, and Jared saluted before backing away and exiting the stage.

Sloan felt her muscles tense, uneasy. She knew Romani wasn't about to excuse them all—the end of the ceremony was not the end of this night. She stared at Stone until he caught her gaze, and with somber eyes, he shook his head at her. She could feel her heart drop, immediately grabbing Elijah's hand. Was this it—was *it* coming?

Romani rolled his fingers under his chin and took a step forward.

"Unfortunately, on what should just be a night of celebration, we have some regrettable news to address," he finally spoke and all her fears were confirmed. Sloan could feel the students around her shifting uncomfortably, a wave of tension and confusion. She scanned the stands for Jared, to see where he might have taken a seat, but couldn't find him.

"There is a *traitor*!"

The silence in the room thickened, overwhelming them all with uncertainty.

"A *traitor* has resided within these walls, one who has been spying on us all and reporting back to the enemy. One who has feigned loyalty and betrayed us. No—betrayed *Dei Terra*!" Romani was practically screaming, dramatically waving his hand out, pointing at the sea of students.

Sloan felt dizzy, her lungs tightening and her hand shaking in Elijah's. Around her, students stirred, all whispers and gasping speculations. She felt her stomach convulse and, worried she would be sick, bowed her head down, leaning over. She took deep breaths, trying to soothe her nerves. A scuffle of noise drew her eyes up as the doors to the hall opened and rows of sentries entered, armed. Students stood, watching, waiting. She craned her neck around the boy in front of her to see the swarm of ivory guards surround the room, some making their way to the stage.

Elijah abruptly stood. *"No . . ."*

She pulled at his hand and brought him back to his seat, hoping he hadn't drawn attention to himself. All the while, nausea was a knife in her side, and she winced in pain. After a deep breath, she whispered, "What is it?" but he said nothing. Elijah simply stared ahead. So she forced herself upright, breathing through the pain, and what she saw nearly made her double over once again.

Romani was attempting to silence the room and slowly students began to take their seats, but they struggled to remain quiet. For on the stage, kneeling, bound and gagged, was Donny—Elijah's friend from Aviation. He was covered in fresh welts, cuts and bruises, and Sloan was surprised he could even hold himself up. Guards—as well as Colonel Don Luke, the head of Aviation—flanked him. She watched as Stone approached to stand beside the colonel, wondering desperately if he had a plan.

Romani paced the stage in front of Donny.

"Donald Roberts is a traitor!" His loud voice was venomous, filled with a vitriol that spread through the Academy like a virus. Students began to shout, knocking into one another, calling out epithets and threatening Donny. Elijah jerked but Sloan held him tightly beside her.

"*Let go,*" he whispered urgently.

She gripped him tighter. "Not a chance." She wasn't going to let him die too.

Romani continued to rile up the room. "For endangering the lives of each and every one of you," he spoke, nodding at the students, "we, the Order, sentence Donald Roberts to death."

Sloan knew what was happening, yet she couldn't believe it. In her near decade and a half at the Academy, there had *never* been a public execution.

"Colonel," Romani said loudly, "if you will."

The colonel pulled his pistol. Donny thrashed out violently, screams muffled. The flanking sentries kicked him to the side, a foot in the back to hold him down.

Sloan wanted to move, to be sick, to save him. To save Elijah from the pain he was about to experience. Yet any movement would give them away.

And once more—I fail to save someone. . .

The colonel's hand shook violently as he aimed his

weapon. The older man took a deep breath but he was on the verge of tears. He was the head of Aviation; Donny was to him what West would have been to Stone. Sloan could tell the man was struggling between his duty and his conscience—but he needed to make a decision. If the Academy abhorred one thing, it was weakness, and *this* compassion would surely be seen as such.

Suddenly, Stone reached for the service pistol. He offered the colonel an understanding look. The two men held gazes, nodding. Stone trained the gun on the back of Donny's head. The general shot one last look towards Sloan, dipped his head in apology and looked away.

Sloan squeezed Elijah's hand—there was nothing she could do to save him from this horror. The body of students watched on, seemingly entranced. The room found a perfect stillness, and all was quiet barring the muffled protestations from Donny.

And then a single shot echoed through the room.

Stone stood still, his arm still outstretched, the gun still aimed. A pool of blood spread out around Donny's fiery hair. It trickled towards Romani's ivory boots. He took a small step back. Sloan could see, with perfect clarity, the body of Kevin Young, lying lifeless on the stage. She blinked away the dark vision. Turning to Elijah she found him wide-eyed and stone-faced. His glossy eyes filled with rage and devastation. She squeezed his hand tighter but it had no effect. He had joined a club; he had now suffered a loss that made him comparable to herself and Jared. A panic rushed over her at the thought of Elijah changing too.

"Let this go as a warning. We know *you're* here and we will find you." Romani's voice cut through them. With a casual wave of his hand he turned from them.

"You're dismissed."

Elijah had practically dragged her through the sea of students, pulling rank to get the first available pod. They stepped into his living quarters and she watched him pace, his hands curled in tight, shaking fists, struggling to keep his outburst in lest whoever may be listening hear Elijah's true nature. She approached him slowly, offering her hand. His sad eyes fell on her and it was more than she thought she could stand to see. He took her hand and she led him to the bathroom. Twisting the shower taps on she stumbled into the water, pulling him under with her. It was too hot and it burnt her skin through her clothes but it didn't matter. So few things mattered still.

The weight of his pain crumbled him, and they sunk to the floor in a soaked mess. He tucked his head against her and cried, holding on to her, cracking under her fingertips. She squeezed him tightly, hopeful that if she could do it just right, do for him what he had done for her, she could keep him from falling to pieces.

The three of them sat in Stone's office in silence. It had been four days since Donny's execution and while Jared had tried to talk to her every chance he got—

Elijah had barely said a word. She hadn't pressed him; his silence was much kinder than how she had handled her own sorrow.

"Romani found the jammer in his workshop," Stone finally spoke. He had aged years in a week.

"This is my fault," Elijah said. "That was the jammer I needed to speak to Sloan in the woods." His voice sounded foreign to her ears—she hadn't noticed how much she had missed hearing it.

"You're not the one who put a bullet in his head," Stone argued.

"I might as well have—"

Sloan pushed her chair back. "Stop it. This is neither of your faults . . . *Romani* is responsible for this." The two men looked to her, hopeful, seeking forgiveness for things that had been out of their control. She had become an expert at recognizing that look—having seen it so often in her own reflection.

She stood. "I'm sorry this has happened—I could just as easily blame myself—but we can't fix this. What we can do, though, is be *more* vigilant. All the jammers—barring yours, General—should be destroyed. Once that's done, we need to formulate a plan, a way to ensure this doesn't happen again."

Stone stared up at her, nodding in agreement. "Good . . . that's good, Radcliffe."

"Okay . . . then I think I have a plan," she announced. The thought had just come to her and she wasn't sure how they would respond to it. They continued to watch her with expectant gazes.

"When can you gather us—and I mean *all* of us—in one place? We need a place to talk candidly as a group . . . and it's time I meet the Others here." At her words, Elijah grabbed her hand, supporting her decision.

But Stone seemed less sure. "Gather forty-three senior students in one sitting? I don't think we can pull that off."

The number startled Sloan, and her mind started racing. She knew there were more than just the three of them—but not *that* many more.

"Excursion," Elijah blurted out.

"What?"

"Come up with a reason to lead an excursion in the woods, say you have something special in mind, or make up a reason we forty-three need to be with you, maybe need to train in something specific . . . I don't know . . ." He rambled. Sloan looked from him to the general.

"Actually, there could be one way . . ." Stone agreed, finally nodding with some excitement.

"Yes. Yes, I think I have an idea. You two finish up here. I will be in touch," Stone announced, standing. He made his way around the desk and to his door. He turned, though, and spoke once more. "Sloan?"

She turned to him.

"Well done."

She smiled and watched him leave, thankful to have finally been of some help.

Elijah stood and turned to her, eyeing her up slowly.

She waited for him to say something but he remained silent—so she spoke. "What?"

He shrugged. "Why has Jared been trying to talk to you every day this week?"

Her heart began to race . . . Elijah had been understandably seeming to pay no attention to her since Donny. But it turned out he had been. Every time Jared tapped her shoulder in class and she shook it off, when he called out to her in the hall and she ducked into a room, when he tried to join her sparring sessions and she walked out . . .

"I don't know," she lied. Well, it was a half lie. She wasn't exactly certain why he was trying to talk to her—even if she could make a few educated guesses.

"Sloan—I know how you feel about him, and *we all* know how he feels about you. Is there something I need to know?"

She took a deep breath. "He wants me back. That's no secret . . . but I told him I was betrothed to you now."

He nodded, seemingly done with this conversation. He moved past her but hesitated at the door. "Sloan?"

She turned, staring at him. "Yeah?"

"You know I'm in love with you, right? I'm *still* so in love with you."

She nodded slowly. "I know you are . . ."

There were a few faces she recognized. Some she knew by name, some whose presence surprised her. Did she surprise them as well, or had they all known she would join them eventually? It had taken four days but Stone had finally managed to come up with a reason to get all forty-three of them out on excursion. His idea was as ingenious as it was chilling. He had convinced Romani that he could put together an elite team who would essentially spy on their peers to sift out the traitors, putting forward the potential hunted as hunters.

Romani had readily agreed.

She stood on the platform of the garage as Elijah hoisted their bags into the grey terrain vehicle. She wanted to say something, to distract him from whatever thoughts came from being in such close proximity to Donny's place, but she didn't know what to say.

She instead leaned against the vehicle and watched him thoughtfully, waiting for him to need something. While she did, the large group of surrounding students were packing up vehicles and talking loudly—they were excited. The voice that made her turn didn't quite reflect that excitement.

"So I suppose we have you to thank for this little outing?"

The wry words belonged to a boy Sloan recognized from class—Samuel Chase. He was an adept fighter, but his gift was truly in academics, as he was one of the smartest of the senior students.

"No, not really." She shrugged, not quite sure what any of them had been told. She realized that although she recognized these students—she didn't *really* recognize them. She couldn't help but wonder how many boys fit into that category at the Academy, how many of them she had categorized as "not-Jared."

In Samuel's case, she saw he was tall, with a mess of dark hair and grey eyes. As if understanding their seeming disconnect after all these years sitting in the same class, he held out his hand. "Well, I'm Samuel Chase."

"I know, you're on 55—" she began, taking his hand, but he cut her off.

"Lieutenant Sloan Radcliffe. We all know who *you* are."

Sloan didn't like the way he spoke and pulled her hand free from his grip. He studied her for a moment, taking in her features, nodding slowly.

"Hopefully you're as good as they say you are." He smiled.

She shrugged off his words. "Hopefully you're as smart as they say *you* are."

He laughed, raising his hands in a defeated motion. Before he could say anymore, Elijah appeared. "Leave her be, Chase." He stood beside Sloan defensively. Chase shrugged, smiling at her, before nodding and turning away.

Sloan watched him join the others. A few of them turned, looking her over, whispering amongst themselves. She turned to Elijah. "Why do I get the feeling I am the center of attention here?"

He shrugged. "Because you are. These guys have waited a long time to meet Stone's favorite—the Academy's best."

Sloan thought over his words. She had spent years in the near exclusive company of Jared—they had bonded over the treatment, both negative and positive, they received for their status. Now, she was with the Others—the ones whom she had always felt judging her from a distance—and she wasn't sure what being in their company would entail.

CHAPTER 12

As Elijah expertly navigated the vehicle, his large hand resting comfortably on the silver disc, Sloan couldn't help but have flashbacks to their first trip together. He had told her so clearly, *"The Academy, our lives . . . it's all wrong."* She had resisted the truth wholeheartedly, like he knew she would, and then she had come round . . . like he knew she would. She watched him keenly. Elijah was brilliant and insightful, but she never gave him credit for it.

Because what would that require?

Being just his friend was hard—no, it was impossible. She knew she wasn't *just* his friend. She was technically his betrothed; she was the object of his love and affection; she was the one thing he had always lusted after. She knew everything she was to him but struggled so greatly to decipher what *he* was to *her.*

As they drove on, a black, open-top vehicle pulled

up alongside them. Sloan looked out her window to see three senior boys craning out their vehicle. She recognized the driver: Captain Joss Hendricks—he had lost a Fight Night to Jared last year. Flanking him was Samuel Chase and another boy Sloan recognized but couldn't recall a name for. Joss beeped his horn and yelled over the wind.

"Race you to the front, Daniels?"

The three boys laughed, eyeing the queue of vehicles ahead of them. Elijah smiled, the first she could remember seeing since Donny. He glanced to her, once again looking for permission. She shrugged. "Go for it." She would acquiesce to nearly anything that would keep him smiling.

"You got it!" Elijah yelled out the window past her.

Joss sped off and Elijah used his spare hand to fiddle with an array of complicated switches surrounding his steering disc. He revved the vehicle forward as Joss easily overtook the convoy. But they were now moving too, and Elijah followed, racing after them. Joss came out in front of the fleet, pulling into the middle of the road. There was only one other vehicle ahead of them—Stone's.

Elijah swerved right as if he would overtake Joss on that side, and the other driver took the bait, swerving to protect his side behind Sloan's vehicle. But Elijah quickly braked—a double tap on the disc—and then rapidly revved, clearing Joss on the left hand side. Elijah pulled up behind Stone, with Joss coming up on the side. Suddenly, aware of the game being played,

Stone swerved his vehicle, blocking Joss and allowing Elijah to take the lead. A surprised laugh escaped Sloan and it shocked her. Her life had changed so greatly since Elijah had come into it—she had lost everything she had ever clung to, had been uprooted and thrown down a treacherous path of loss and danger, but somehow, in the midst of such fear and misery, she found she still had the ability to laugh.

And she realized that in Elijah's presence she could still find the good in the world. She eyed him up, his green eyes watching the road, a half smile painted across his handsome face, the wind flicking through his dark locks. She had missed him during his silence, as he retreated into himself to heal his own wounds, and she was amazed how much she had wanted him—the *old* him—back. She had become reliant on the knowledge that he loved her . . . and in turn, she was developing some kind of feelings for him. It wasn't what she felt for Jared—not by any stretch of the imagination. It wasn't an all-consuming love—but it *was* something. She didn't want to overthink it, she didn't know what it meant, but it was there and she finally felt like she could be letting him into her heart.

An obvious result, seeing as he had been there the entire time, trying to heal it.

Sloan idled on the steps of Stone's cabin porch, running her hand down the wooden support beams.

"You did it," she said, glancing around at the students making camp.

"No, you did. You pulled Elijah and me back in; you got us going again," he answered, circling a cigar against the flame of his match. He rocked in his seat and smiled at her approvingly. She noted the jammer, idling beside him.

"I just gave you an idea." She shrugged, turning to leave.

"Sloan." He was shaking his head, blowing out a plume of thick smoke.

"Sir?"

He stood, taking a step towards her. "I wanted to tell you, before everyone else," he whispered, his grey eyes glancing down and then back up to her. "I wanted to tell you *everything*."

Her hand flickered at her side. Sloan hadn't realized how much it affected her, learning so late in the game. Hearing him say this now, even as a small gesture, meant a great deal to her. In a way, she was comforted by his words. So much had come to pass between her and the general, but ultimately, without him, she wouldn't be here. Without him, she wouldn't be regaining any sense of identity. He thanked her for pulling Elijah and him back into the fight . . . but long before that, he had pulled *her* back from the edge of her darkness.

"Thank you, sir."

She idled on his porch a moment longer, contemplating the effect so much truth and honesty had had on her life. She looked up to him knowingly.

"I need to tell him."

She couldn't live with hypocrisy—she couldn't acknowledge the power of honesty and then keep such secrets. He nodded at her slowly—he knew what she was referring to.

"Do you love him?"

She shrugged, looking upward and taking a deep breath. "He's in my heart."

She let her gaze fall back to him.

He stood, nearing her. "You should know this better than anyone by now—the truth is a dangerous thing. Think about that before you rush into anything."

The others were swimming, camp had been made, and a fire was slowly burning in the ashen pit. Stone was in his cabin and Elijah had disappeared. Sloan walked apprehensively towards the burning wood of the fire, circled it slowly and took a few paces forward. She kneeled, letting her hand hover above the soft dirt and pine and ash. This was where he had fallen dead.

Slowly, she lowered her hand to the ground and traced an outline of where he had lain. She closed her eyes and could see him: his uniform and nametag, his still body.

"I'm sorry," she whispered, once again apologizing to Kevin Young. She could only hope that he could hear her . . . that he could forgive her.

She felt a presence behind her, a hand lowering over her shoulder. "You saved my life that day," Elijah whispered, kneeling beside her.

She readjusted herself to look at him. "Two people died just so that I could find out the truth." She thought of Donny—his muffled cries still so clear in her mind.

"Countless people have died upon learning the truth," he answered and his sentiment resonated strongly with Stone's former words. The truth was dangerous.

She stood and he mirrored her. "Elijah . . . there are things you don't know, things I haven't told you."

"About you and Jared?" he asked, looking at her knowingly.

She nodded, feeling an awful anticipation.

He shook his head. "I don't want to know, Sloan."

"But—"

He cut her off too quickly, waving his hand around the campsite. "Are you with me—in all of *this*—are you with me?"

She nodded. "Yes."

"Then that's all that matters."

Easy to say when you don't know. . .

She grabbed his hand. "Then you need to know this . . . I—*wow, I don't know how to say this*—I may be starting to have feelings for you," she whispered, locking in on his green eyes.

He stared at her, as though he hadn't heard her admission. Then a small smile crept over his face. A happiness played in his eyes. He pulled her into a tight embrace and kissed her forehead, spinning her round.

"I *knew* it. I knew you were meant to be mine."

Sloan tensed under his words, knowing all too well who they reminded her of—who had first said such a thing to her. And in an instant, she couldn't help but wonder if her admission had been a mistake.

Sloan glanced around the circle. She recognized Joss, Samuel Chase and Coop, whom she had just met. Kristin Burke, her betrothed Bill Anderson, she recognized from the Calling. Lily Tana was from Masse's class, and Toni and Stephanie were twins from her math class. Aside from Elijah and Joss, the captains were Michael Lane, Jo Hart and Sava Strong. She had met the others too, but wasn't great with all their names just yet.

Stone sat front and center, a stubbed cigar in hand, peering over the fire at them all. "Look around. Get to know one another right now. Trust the person sitting next to you to never give you up. Trust them to never break under the pressure of the Order.

"Do whatever you have to on this excursion to create the army we need you to be—the one Donny sacrificed himself for."

Sloan was wedged between Elijah and a boy she had never met. She thought of Stone's order . . . Trust wasn't something that came easily to Sloan—nor was it something she seemed overly deserving of nowadays.

The general continued. "We do have a loose plan; some of you have heard the details before. Our number one priority is to evacuate the youngest children and return them to their families. This effort will require all of you. There are 204 children under the age of fourteen in the Academy. They will be the first ones to board any Skyshell out of here. As soon as we make a move, Romani will know and we will be facing the entire Academy guard as well as any students who won't see the truth." Stone leaned in, the fire flickering across his stern face.

"We'll need a distraction then—something to buy us time while we move the kids," Joss pointed out. Others nodded in agreement.

"I will take care of that," Stone answered vaguely.

"How, sir?" Michael Lane pressed.

"Just trust that you'll know when the opportunity to move arises."

The captain nodded.

Sava chimed in next. "And if we do escape—*where* are we going?"

"The Others on the warfront have a place they are prepared to collect us from once we reach the mainland, Strong."

They all sat in silence for a long moment. It was all really happening—Donny's death had sparked action. There was no time to idle, no time to second-guess.

Stone stood. "Right—get some sleep. Tomorrow you begin training together."

Elijah leaped up and helped Sloan to her feet. She followed him into their cabin, offering a few quick goodnights to the others as they passed by.

Sloan took a deep breath, letting her gaze fall over the cabin. The space where Elijah had first tied her up, where they had physically wrestled over the truth, where they had first begun to bond. She crossed her arms and watched him turn away from his newly lit fire. He smiled as he walked over to her, stopping just inches away.

Slowly, he rested his hands on her shoulders, running his thumbs over her collarbones. She looked up, watching his green gaze flick over her body. She knew she had a place for him in her heart, she knew she cared about him—but to what degree? As if reading her mind, slowly, he inclined his head to her, bringing his nose to her own, his lips just above hers.

We have kissed before, she reasoned, *and it wasn't awful*. But she could also remember their kiss after Young—the one that had told her how he saw her differently. What had changed since then? Nothing really.

Slowly, he brought his mouth down to hers, kissing her gently. His hands streaked up her neck, his fingers playing with her hair. This kiss wasn't like the others—it wasn't electric with novelty, it wasn't sad with newfound realization . . . it was loving. She kissed him back, slowly loosening her crossed arms. She let her hands fall to his chest, and she tried to clear her mind—she tried to just be in this moment, to let the happiness she recognized when she was with him lead the way.

But as his hand moved for her shirt hem, she thought of Jared—she pulled away from him. "I'm sorry—I can't."

He looked at her with confusion. "But I thought . . . ?"

"I said I had feelings for you—I didn't say I would sleep with you," she answered curtly, embarrassed by her retreat from him, angered by his confusion—and her own.

"I know that . . . I just assumed. Never mind." He sighed heavily, taking a step away from her.

She sat down heavily on the sofa. "I know it should be you, Elijah. I know I should want *everything* with you. You're bright and kind, you make me happy and it's not that I'm not attracted to you—because I am, you know I am—it's just . . ." She let her voice trail off before finishing her sentiment.

But he finished it for her. "I'm not *him*."

She could see the hurt and disappointment in his eyes.

She stood, taking a deep breath. "I just need more time."

He shook his head, stepping towards his fire. "More time to figure out if you want to have sex with me? If you love me?" His voice was angry but quiet.

"More time to figure out how I feel about you," she snapped back, tightening her fists. He wasn't entitled to her—he had seemed to understand that recently, but now . . .

He spun around, squaring off with her. "You're *my* betrothed—you're supposed to want me, to love me."

"I'm your betrothed because you *took* me, not because I *chose* you." The words sounded much meaner aloud than she had intended. She could see the way they hurt him—that wasn't what she had meant to do. But it was the truth—and the truth was indeed a dangerous thing.

"I'm sorry," she added kindly, sitting back down. He nodded, slowly sitting down beside her.

"Was it this hard for you and *him*—to want each other *this* way?" He spoke the words with stammering apprehension.

Because he already knows the answer.

She wasn't going to spell it out for him.

"Look, I just need you to be patient . . . I don't know what I want and I didn't mean to send mixed signals by telling you how I felt, but I can see how I did do *just* that. I just need more time to think."

He nodded slowly, chewing on his lip as he thought over her words. "I know I said just having time with you was enough for me . . . but I was wrong. It's not enough, Sloan. I want you. And I want you to want me too."

She shrugged helplessly at his words. She didn't know what else to say—she didn't know she felt or what she wanted when it came to Elijah. She didn't have the same certainty of love or lust with him that she had always had with Jared.

Isn't that answer enough then?

She took a slow breath, regarding his handsome face, wishing she could just see him the way he saw her. "I still love him, Elijah."

Elijah's jaw tensed, a look of frustration crossing his face. "Well—I'm not giving up that easy, Sloan. He can't just take you back."

She stood up. She was sick of having to explain this to everyone. "I am *not* an object. He cannot *take* me and you cannot *give* me. When are you going to understand that?"

She turned away from him—leaving him to think about her words.

Sloan stretched her arms out and lay back in the cool grass. They had been sparring all morning. Despite feeling ill when she woke up that morning she had helped the others train, working on their leg locks, their takedowns, their precision and execution and knife throwing. She was officially exhausted. They were all good, some better than good, and a few she was even surprised had never come up against her in a Fight Night.

She sat back up, watching Elijah move through a complicated arm lock with another boy. They hadn't spoken since last night's difficult conversation and it frustrated her. In many ways, her relationship with Elijah was indescribably calmer than it had been with Jared. He was understanding and supportive—usually. And she had felt so certain of her developing feelings for him yesterday, but when push came to shove—it was still Jared. She knew it. Elijah knew it. Everyone knew it—but she wasn't allowed to be with Jared, she wasn't even supposed to speak to Jared, and even if she did, they hadn't resolved half of their issues. Yes, in many ways, what she shared with Elijah was calmer, but her uncertainty and his perseverance made it more and more tumultuous each day.

"Joining in?" Jo called to her, flipping a knife in her hand easily.

Sloan shook her head—if sparring was tiring, training was grueling. She wanted to take five and think over her situation with Elijah. "I'm going to sit this one out." She smiled.

"Come on, Sloan. Our group has two Fight Night champs and you're really not going to get involved?" The words came from Chase.

"I'm not feeling it—I'm taking five," she answered tightly. She had already said no.

"No, you have to help out," he pressed, walking over to her. She got to her feet.

"Maybe later," she answered firmly. At her sternness Elijah walked over, crossing his arms in front of her.

"Since when did you pass up on training?" He didn't ask with any anger, but seemed genuinely concerned.

"I wasn't feeling great this morning—I just need a break," she explained.

She shrugged her shoulders, adding, "I'm just going to go for a swim."

"Alright, feel better." He nodded, offering her a small smile.

She nodded, walking past him and making her way to the lake. She didn't understand their dynamic—their arguing and their making up, their feelings or lack thereof. No wonder she was feeling ill—it was all too stressful.

The lake was abandoned. *Of course it is—they're all training.* She wanted to carry on sparring but she had woken up with knots in her stomach, on the verge of throwing up. It had taken a glass of water and sitting on the floor for ten minutes just to let the feeling pass. She *needed* a break.

She pulled off her shirt, toes just touching the water, and closed her eyes as she slowly waded in.

"Are you alright?"

The voice startled her; she spun in the water to see a young man she didn't recognize. He was striking and she was unsure how she hadn't noticed him before—with his dark skin and blue eyes. He waded into the water, splashing past her, turning in the lake and watching her.

"I'm fine." She shrugged, watching him.

"You sure?" he asked, leaning his shoulder back into the lake.

"I said so, didn't I?"

He stood, the water coming up to his stomach. "Just checking."

She waded in slowly. "What are you doing here?"

He looked around, a half smile on his face. "Swimming." He laughed off his obvious answer and waved a hand at her. "I'm Edward Kane," he smiled.

She nodded her head at him. "Sloan."

"Yeah, Sloan Radcliffe. The girl who tore Maya Woods to shreds." He smiled.

Is that what this is about? she wondered, leaning back. "She deserved it."

"No doubt," he agreed, sensing her tenseness. "I only brought it up because I liked what you had to say about the hypocrisy of it all."

Sloan thought back to that night, when everything had changed. At the time, it had felt like the crescendo of the most complicated period of her life—and then things had *actually* become complicated. "I called Maya a hypocrite because it's what she is."

And now, so am I. She wanted to be honest with Elijah—but he'd told her plain and simple, he didn't want to know. Did that mean she only wanted to tell him the truth to make herself feel better?

Edward's face became serious. "It *was* a big deal to the rest of us—still is. Your Winnings secured a lot of necks. Not everyone can fight like you, or Elijah or

Jared Dawson." He waded out of the water, making his way to the bank. She watched him move. He was a big guy, with muscles on top of muscles, and yet a fluidness that belied a certain grace. There was no way he was incapable of fighting for his own life. She wondered what this was all about . . .

"If you ever need anything, just shout, okay?" he offered, looking down at her from the bank.

Sloan was unsure what he meant, but said, "Sure, thanks." She then watched him disappear over the sloping escarpment. Their exchange had been odd, but she didn't get a bad feeling from Edward. He seemed sincere. Had her decision at Fight Night had an unexpected impact on the others? She smiled at the thought. She had been treated like a pariah since that night, and she hadn't done what she did for anyone to favor her . . . but it felt good to know some people were thankful.

It felt good to know her fighting abilities hadn't just been responsible for death and pain. They had also saved people.

Her stomach grumbled loudly, turning over in cramping pain. She lurched herself from the water, returning to the bank just in time to fall on her knees in front of a bush—throwing up violently.

"I hear you aren't feeling well," Stone spoke, leaning against the wall in her cabin. Sloan pulled her hair up into a ponytail, her skin still flushed.

"I'm fine." She shrugged, sitting on the sofa to lace up her shoes.

"Elijah says you've been sick to your stomach for the past two days."

She leaned back on the couch, looking up to him. "So? I'm still training."

Some stomach bug wouldn't slow her down—if that were even what it was. Sloan knew a lot of information had been thrown at her on this excursion. There was a lot of tension amongst the group and nerves could easily get the best of them—even someone as trained as herself.

"Alright, well I'm going to send Kane in to take a look at you," he insisted.

"Edward?"

Stone nodded, uncrossing his arms as he stepped towards the door. "He's a second year in the Infirmary—he'll have brought his equipment with him."

Sloan, ready to protest, stood up quickly—*too* quickly—and immediately grabbed the sofa to steady herself. Stone was at her side in an instant, ready to support her. She sighed heavily, lowering herself back down to the sofa.

"Sir, it's just a stomach flu—*I'm fine*," she insisted. He nodded skeptically.

"Then you shouldn't worry about having Kane confirm it."

She tensed her jaw in frustration—she didn't need to be babied. But she knew he wasn't taking no for an answer. *"Fine."*

Sloan sat on the edge of the bed, watching Edward rifle through his bag. He pulled out small metal rods, silver containers, laser pens—nothing you wouldn't find in the Infirmary. Elijah and Stone waited by the sofa, arms crossed, watching carefully. Elijah had been attentive during her sickness but they hadn't spoken about their recent argument. Edward finally stood, holding a large silver bracelet—a chip scanner, just like the ones used at the gates of the Academy. Attached to this one, though, was a small glass pane, the size of her palm.

"Alright, I'm just going to get a read on your chip and that will let us know what's going on," he explained. He hesitated before slowly turning to face Stone and Elijah. "Elijah, sir, you two can wait outside."

Elijah looked shocked—Stone taken aback. Edward didn't concede—staring at them until they moved. Sloan didn't care if they stayed or not; either way they would see that she was just fine. "No—let them stay and see that I *am* fine."

Edward turned to her, arching his brow skeptically. "That's not a good—"

She shrugged off his concern, interrupting him. "I said it's fine. Now let's just get this over with."

He pursed his lips at her insistence, but carried on. She offered him her chipped arm and after a moment of fiddling with the bracelet, he ran it over her hand, up her wrist, over her forearm and back down. Once off, she lowered her arm, waiting. Edward held the glass pane up into the light and Sloan could see lines of orange script appearing. She couldn't decipher the alphanumeric codes but she watched Edward's eyes widen. He shot her a concerned glance.

What's wrong?

Quickly, he lowered the pane, kneeling to the ground and shoving his belongings back into his bag.

"Well?" Stone asked first, taking a step towards them.

"She's fine," Edward answered curtly, standing and looking at her now. "You're fine—like you said, it's nothing."

Sloan sighed heavily—relieved and smug. She turned to Elijah and Stone. "*Told* you." She shrugged.

"Alright—good. Thanks for that, Kane." Stone nodded. Sloan stood from the bed, stretching out.

"Sorry you had to waste your time." She shrugged to Kane. He looked her over and slowly nodded.

What's wrong with him? she wondered, noting his concerned look. She ignored him, turning to Stone and Elijah.

"Let's go get some training done before we have to head out."

They had managed to get a few sparring sessions in before they had to leave—although, to her great annoyance, Stone had insisted she just advise and not partake. She had argued with him, saying Edward had told her she was fine, but he insisted she take it easy for the day until she was fully back on track. So she had spent the morning instructing and envying Elijah. Having a purpose had given him momentum—he sparred constantly, solidifying bonds with the others and creating camaraderie—just as Stone had hoped would happen. And now it was time to go back.

"Let me give you a hand with that." Edward's voice surprised her. He had been watching her from a small distance all morning. Quickly, he was bending down to grab her bags.

"It's fine, I've got it," she argued, reaching for her belongings, but he got ahold of them first, tossing them into the vehicle.

"It's cool." He shrugged. "Just trying to help."

Sloan nodded, leaning back against the vehicle. He crossed his arms and studied her thoughtfully.

"So . . . how *are* you feeling?"

She stared at him, confused. "Fine—*you* saw that I was fine."

He nodded slowly, about to speak, when Chase's voice called out. "Ah—Edward and the alleged champ."

Sloan arched her brow, watching him stride over confidently, a bag hanging over his shoulder. *Alleged?* "What's that supposed to mean?"

He dropped the bag at his feet. "You've spent most of this time *not* sparring—a Fight Champ who won't fight seems odd to me."

She rolled her eyes at him. "Consider yourself lucky I haven't been feeling well."

Chase took a step towards her. "Tell me, Sloan, if

you're feeling fine enough to order *us* around, how are you too sick to train?"

"Back off, Chase," she growled, standing up straighter.

He smiled, dramatically rolling his eyes at her. "You're supposed to be the best—Stone's favorite—the *big bad* of the Academy. You don't look all that dangerous to me."

Sloan uncrossed her arms. "Then you aren't looking hard enough."

She didn't know what his problem with her was—but she could wager a guess. She had spent her life growing accustomed to these kinds of insults; her status at the Academy had made her a target for vicious taunts and provocations. But she had put down every person to ever challenge her—she had *proven* her abilities again and again. If Chase wanted to test that, she would happily put him down too.

"Leave it, Chase," Edward interjected, stepping closer towards the other boy.

Chase laughed. "She's a Fight Champ screwing another Fight Champ."

Sloan took a quick step forward. "*What* did you just say?"

Edward quickly moved in between the two of them. "What are you getting at?"

"I don't think she needs *your* protection, Kane."

She *didn't* need protecting—she sidestepped Edward, narrowing her gaze on Chase. "What is your problem?" she demanded.

He shrugged. "Just tell me why you haven't been

sparring. Because you're Stone's favorite you think you can just stand around telling us what to do?"

She spoke through a tensed jaw. She was growing tired of this. "I told you *already*—I haven't been feeling well."

She didn't need to put up with this; she didn't need to be harangued by some guy she barely knew. She had been dealing with his attitude for days and she was sick of it.

"You know what, Chase—" she began, but he cut her off quickly.

"First Dawson, now Daniels—would you screw me too if I were a Champ?"

Sloan lunged, but Edward beat her to it—swinging so quickly Sloan was almost knocked over in the process of stepping back. Chase fell to the ground, holding his jaw.

"What the *hell*, Edward? I was just messing with her!" he said, slowly getting to his feet. Edward's fists were still tight, his broad body towering over Chase.

"It's *not* funny, Chase. Mess with her again and you'll deal with me," Edward growled.

Sloan didn't know Kane very well but she had been shocked to see him transform from this relaxed, intuitive guy into someone ready—someone *dangerous*. Chase looked from her to Kane, shaking his head. Heeding Kane's warning, he pivoted around, grabbed his bag and walked off. Edward turned to face her, and she was amazed to see his calm demeanor had already returned.

His gaze fell on her and she felt . . . *embarrassed*. She couldn't believe Chase would say those things to her—did everyone think *that* about her? That she was sleeping with Elijah, that she was attracted to whoever held a champion title?

She tried to shake off the feeling, holding Kane's stare. "I wish you hadn't done that—I can handle an ass like Chase."

He arched his brow at her. "I'm sure you could—*normally*."

Sloan studied his critical expression. "What's *that* supposed to mean?"

He shook his head at her, lowering his voice. "I *know*."

She looked around, confused by his sudden attitude. "Know *what*?"

He almost laughed, acting as though she were playing games with him. She really didn't *know* what he was talking about. She stared up at him, waiting for him to elaborate.

"I *know*, Sloan. I know you missed your CI this quarter—so I know *you* know why you've been feeling sick, and it has nothing to do with nerves or flu."

She had stopped listening at the words *CI*. She thought back to the letter she had received from the Infirmary, to making a mental note to go by there—to forgetting to ever do it at all. Her CI—her *contraceptive injection*.

She stumbled away from him, in shock, falling

against the vehicle. *No, no, no* . . . Her hand immediately flew to her stomach—she could have thrown up right then and there at this realization. Edward's face changed from knowing and accusatory to stunned.

"You didn't know?" he demanded, his voice quiet.

How could she have been *so* stupid—how could she have let *this* happen? She shook her head. "I'm . . . I'm not . . ."

"I'm so sorry—I thought you knew and were keeping it quiet . . . *How* did you miss your CI?" he rambled.

She glared up at him. How had she forgotten to go into the Infirmary? Maybe because she had been busy raging against the world, maybe because she had been angry and depressed, disconnected, reeling from losing Jared and still in shock from finding out the truth about her life. *Jared.*

She would need to tell him—*wouldn't she?* And then another name crossed her mind—*Elijah.* He was going to kill her. Her refusal to have *that sort* of relationship with him upset him enough; now he would know she had gone back to Jared that day . . .

She forcefully grabbed Edward's arm. "If you tell *anyone*—" she began, ready to threaten anything he held dear, but he shook his head earnestly.

"I wouldn't do that. Even if I wanted to, which *I don't*, I'm bound to doctor-patient confidentiality."

She nodded slowly, releasing her grip on him. "Good—*no one* can know. I mean it, Edward, do *not* tell a soul."

He nodded, looking her over with sincerity. "I won't, Sloan—but *you* should. This changes everything. And it might not be so bad—I think Elijah might even be happy."

She shook her head. "I'm certain he won't be."

CHAPTER 13

As the weeks passed by, Stone reported to Romani that his special group were keeping their ears and eyes peeled, but that any would-be defectors were lying low since Donny's execution. They weren't certain Romani bought the story, but he hadn't found anything to convince him otherwise, and for the meantime, he seemed content with the status update. Meanwhile, Sloan had kept her mouth shut about *everything*.

She had been busy avoiding Edward—who was consistently trying to get her to come into the Infirmary. He wanted to check on her—*on it*—by running tests. But she refused. Tests led to confirmation, led to documentation, led to something that could be used against her. So she busied herself with West in the shooting range. He didn't entirely understand her revitalized interest in the range, insisting she was already one of his best marksmen, but he had been happy nonetheless to spend time with her.

She had avoided sparring and any kind of fighting—just because she wasn't accepting of the news didn't make her an idiot. Once again, Elijah responded well to her newfound pacifism, believing it to be a mark of happiness and growth. She let him think that but the reality was that she was going stir crazy without her usual training. She hadn't let him touch her in weeks, not so much as a hug, but for some reason, he still persevered, certain she could be worn down.

Avoiding Jared had been the hardest part. He was insistent on seeing her or speaking to her and it took everything she had to not break and tell him the truth. She *couldn't* tell him without telling the Order—and whoever else listened in to every word uttered in these halls. She knew her body was yet to change, she still had her taut abs and slender frame—but Jared knew her shape better than she did. She was paranoid that he, being so in tune with her body, would miraculously figure it out.

The stress of it all just made her want to spar more . . . .

So, she had taken to spending all of her time with the Others, mainly Sava and Jo. Their lives distracted her from her own—and Sloan couldn't deny that they shared a bond in knowing the truth about the Academy. When they finally received word from Stone that they would be going back on excursion, there was a flurry of both excitement *and* concern amongst the group. The only reason they would be called back out was if Stone needed to tell them all something in a safe place. If that didn't worry her enough, knowing that she would need to abstain from sparring again would draw more unwanted attention from the Others.

Maybe it's time to visit Edward.

He had sworn to not document a thing—nothing would be put in her file regarding this visit. He had booked her into a room under a different name and had ensured the floor was abandoned before shuffling her into the examination area unseen. She appreciated his understanding—more than she could express.

"It will only take a few minutes. Just try to relax," Edward said, sitting opposite her. She sat on the white-sheeted bed, drumming her fingers nervously.

Unable to wait in silence, she asked, "Is Jo packing for you two?" hoping to distract herself.

"I hope not—my betrothed wouldn't take too kindly to Jo being in our living quarters," Edward laughed.

"I thought . . ." Sloan began, but realized she didn't know what to say. She had thought Jo was *with* Edward. They were always together, whispering, laughing or sharing moments.

"It's complicated." He shrugged. "Jo and I are both betrothed to people who don't want to be with us as much as *we* don't want to be with them. It happens, but that's what Nuptia decided."

She thought about her own experience with the

Betrothal Calling and couldn't help but sympathize. "I know how you feel . . . Being apart from the one you love can kill you."

She immediately regretted her candor—Edward was a good friend, but she didn't know how he would handle her inference that she still loved Jared when she was supposed to be devoted to Elijah.

He studied her thoughtfully. "Missing Dawson?"

She shrugged, shaking her head. "I'm just saying the Calling messes up people's lives," she pressed on before he had any opportunity to question her. "How much longer is this going to take?"

Edward spun on his swivel chair, flicking buttons on a chrome box until a holographic display of codes appeared against the white wall beside him. "We should be just about good to go . . . Yep, it says it right here . . ." he rambled, scanning over the words and images.

She stood up. Her heart was racing and she wished she could read the machine's output just so she could know what he was about to say. He spun back around, nodding his head. "About nine weeks in."

Sloan shook her head, backing away from the truth he had to offer her. "No." The single word—a refusal to accept *this*—fell from her mouth. Edward stood.

"Sloan, it's going to be just fine. You can tell the group; we've got your back," he offered, smiling supportively.

"No—I *cannot* tell the group. I can't fight *like this*, I can't protect myself . . ." she rambled, grabbing the bed to steady herself. A thousand thoughts raced through her mind. This was *bad*—really bad.

"The group can protect you."

Sloan's hands curled into frustrated fists. "How many times do I have to tell you *I am not* telling the group?"

He shook his head, confused at her anger. "Well, you should at least talk it over with Elijah."

"*Edward!* Just stop."

At her fury he was quiet. And he knew. She could see it in his eyes as he put the pieces together—he knew what she had done. He looked downward and back up to her. "*Oh.*"

Sloan sat on the edge of the sofa, watching Elijah make himself lunch in the cabin kitchen. She had begun to view every object in the room as a tool he could use to kill her with if she told him the truth. She wasn't stupid—she knew she couldn't hide *this* forever, but she also knew she couldn't fight without risking serious damage to herself. She envisioned scenario after scenario; she contemplated telling him in front of Edward. *Sure*, she thought, *add insult to injury by humiliating him in front of someone*. She thought about talking to Stone, but she could picture his face, she could imagine the look of disappointment in his eyes. He had gone out of his way to ensure her indiscretion had been kept a secret and now it turned out she would be the reason that secret came to light.

"What?" Elijah's voice startled her—he was watching her watch him.

"Nothing," she answered quickly, forcing herself to look away from him. She thought about the truth coming out, how it would prove she had been dishonorable in her union, and what punishment would be exacted for that. She knew she wasn't the only one— Edward and Jo were betrothed to other people—but that didn't really matter now. They weren't in a situation where the Order could prove their infidelity.

She grew frustrated with her thoughts. She hadn't ever had *that* kind of relationship with Elijah! She had only ever been with Jared and she had told everyone to not try to separate them. She had told everyone that she loved him still, that they were meant to stay together . . . despite all their issues. She sat back on the sofa. This was a mess—*her life* was a mess. She had already imagined telling Jared and while she knew he would be happy, he would also probably do something crazy. Something to ensure the Order reinstated their relationship—*what, though?* Would he challenge Elijah to another Fight Night, would he try to kill him, get rid of him somehow?

She couldn't let that happen.

What if Jared tried to keep her at the Academy? She couldn't abandon the Others now—even if she wanted to, which she *didn't*, she was certain they wouldn't allow it. She knew too much and would be too great a threat to their mission. And yet, they insisted Jared couldn't come into the fold, that in ways he didn't even know, he was too ingrained in the Academy regime.

A knock on their door pulled her from her thoughts. It swung open, revealing Joss. He peeked his head in. "Stone wants us out there in five."

"**N**one of you will make it to Departing Ceremonies." Stone's words fell over the group heavily. *What?* Sloan looked around, wondering if anyone had any insight into what their general had just announced, but the group was stirring with whispers, looking entirely perplexed.

"Romani wants the senior class to deploy in several weeks," he continued, looking over them with somber eyes. *What—why?* Sloan's mind raced. Deploy? She couldn't deploy—she couldn't even fight. Suddenly, Elijah was holding her hand. She wanted to pull away but then she heard someone crying, people behind her arguing—friends comforting one another. They were all afraid.

Stone raised his hands, willing them to settle down. "This obviously brings forward our timeline drastically—once you're gone there's no getting back to the Academy. We have one chance to make our move. Monday."

Another flurry of noise—of tears and whispers, of terror and excitement. This would be their last weekend here.

"Skyshell Aviation—that's you, Daniels, even if

you're a bit out of practice. Hook, Hart, Stevenson, Lane, Strong, Burke and Birch—you're our pilots. We will need you to man eight Odyssey Skyshells. You'll only have a few days to get comfortable with the logistics of our largest fleet.

"Kane, where are you? Oh, there. Edward, Louis, Thorpe and Ramsey, you're our medical team. You'll need to spread out amongst the Skyshells—we cannot risk losing you in case any who board are wounded. Pick a pilot and team up.

"Radcliffe." Stone said her name, jolting her eyes up to him. "You, Chase and Joss are our best shots. We need you to get to the armory, load up and take sniper positions. Corbin and Banks—you watch their backs while they keep the sentries at bay when the kids are being loaded up."

Sloan nodded—happy to know she would be manning rifles on the day, but angered to hear Chase would be at her side. *Will you even be involved in this?* she thought, having temporarily forgotten that she didn't actually have a plan to address her *situation*.

"The rest of you," Stone carried on. "There are 204 children, eight pilots, three snipers, two watch-guards and thirty of you soldiers. You will each need to get six or seven kids into the hangars. You will meet *heavy* fire and *strong* resistance. Your main priority is boarding the children—trust the snipers to keep the sentries off you."

Elijah cleared his throat, taking the floor. "What about the gate and our chips? It will incapacitate all of us, even from within a Skyshell."

Stone nodded, rubbing his own forearm. "Donny helped me with something—before . . . It's his way of still being with us. I can bring down the power for ten, *maybe* fifteen minutes."

Fifteen minutes? To get in position, grab and board 204 screaming children, and get out of here? Sloan didn't need to voice what they were all thinking—the odds were *not* in their favor.

Sava stood, crossing her arms. "Sir, where will you be?"

Stone tilted his head up, and, with a small shrug of his shoulder, answered, "I already told you—someone has to provide the distraction."

They spent the rest of the excursion coordinating, hashing out the details of their plan. Sloan was thankful for the distraction that planning gave her, but couldn't keep her mind from wandering back to its true concern every so often. If everything did go according to Stone's plan—she would be out of here soon. *What about this situation you have landed yourself in?* She knew that whether she was here or on the mainland—it wouldn't change her situation. She couldn't abandon the Others now—she had to be there when it all went down.

What about Jared? Would she abandon him—leave him in this place, with the enemy? Would he be safe here—as Romani's nephew, with his supposedly influential family? Would those factors protect him from being drilled by the Order due to his love for Sloan? Was it better if he didn't know about her *news*?

She needed answers—and she knew only one person whom she could speak to. She knocked on Stone's door, waiting for a response. It was late and the majority of the students were getting into bed, knowing they had an early start back to the Academy in the morning.

With a noisy creak, the door opened. Stone had reading glasses on and a book in one hand—she didn't think she had ever seen him look so *normal* . . .

"Sorry, sir, I didn't mean to interrupt your—*er*— downtime."

He took his glasses off, smiling softly. "No, it's fine, come in." He stepped aside, allowing her entrance. He closed the door and gestured to a chair by the fire. She took a seat and watched as he dragged another chair over from his dining table. He sat in front of her— watching her expectantly.

"I need to speak to you about something . . ." she began tentatively.

He half-smiled. "I figured as much." She tried to smile back but couldn't. This was going to be the most disappointed he had ever been in her. She had messed up—she had put her role in *his* mission at risk. She had hurt Elijah—whom Stone doted on—and all over her failure to follow his direct orders in the first place. She took a slow breath.

"I messed up, sir," she whispered, forcing herself to look into his grey eyes. He waited, a look of concern growing in his face.

"I . . ." She didn't know how to say it—how to *admit* it. She had never said the truth aloud, never uttered that *word* that described the state she was now in. She took a deep breath. Her hands were shaking.

"I'm *pregnant*."

The silence seemed to last a lifetime. He kept his eyes on her, his face giving nothing away. She *knew* it—she had ruined his image of her. She had disappointed him. Finally, he leaned forward in his seat. "Does Jared know?"

Of course he knows it's Jared's.

She shook her head. "No." Her voice sounded so small, barely reaching across the small space between them.

And then he stood, grabbing her hand and pulling her to her feet. And before she could understand why, his arms were around her, embracing her in a strong hug. He held her for the longest time and she felt, momentarily, as if everything *was* better. When he finally let her go, he squeezed her hand.

"What are you going to do?"

At his words, she fell back into her seat. "I don't know . . . I can't tell Elijah, I can't tell Jared and then just leave, and I can't *not* tell him either. I'm so—" She hesitated, for her sentiment was so foreign to her.

"I'm so *afraid*," she finally admitted.

He nodded. "Sloan, you can't stay here—your life would be in danger. Because even if I told you to back out of the mission, you know Elijah won't, and when they see he's a defector—they will come for you. In the same breath, I *cannot* risk having Jared know the truth and ruin everything."

She nodded, chewing her lip. *What were her options then?* Everything seemed utterly hopeless.

Stone ran a hand over the back of his neck, taking a deep breath. "If you can find him tomorrow, when *everything* happens, you have fifteen minutes to get him on board. Whether you spend those fifteen minutes helping us fight the sentries off or spend them finding him—that's up to you."

CHAPTER 14

Everything was about to go down, and yet Sloan felt oddly relaxed. She hadn't figured out how she was going to spend her fifteen minutes. She hadn't told Elijah. She hadn't even seen Jared. Yet, somehow, she felt very unexplainably calm. Maybe it was because, as they all readied to get to the hall, she knew what Romani was going to announce. Maybe not. She supposed it was acceptance or just the inevitable state of becoming resigned to one's fate. She felt that once it all began, she would just know what to do. She had been trained for war—this was the first battle.

Elijah held her hand as they traveled in the pod—and she let him. Who knew when that would ever happen again; who knew when he would discover her secret and let all his love transform into hate? The pod doors opened up to the corridor outside the training hall. Pools of seniors were slowly trudging into the room, some excitedly talking amongst friends, some apprehensive of the suddenness of this conference—*all* oblivious to what was about to be said, to what was about to happen.

Sloan easily spotted the Others and pulled Elijah through the throngs of people to where Edward, Jo, Sava and Wesley stood. Michael and Banks were roughhousing. Chase, Joss and Corbin were talking in low voices. It seemed that no one knew how to feel—despite all their elaborate planning, no one knew what to anticipate. But they were ready. They were Stone's chosen soldiers for a reason.

The remaining students in the corridor slowly made their way in and soon, all that was left was their small group. Edward sighed heavily and pulled a tire iron out from underneath the back of his shirt, tossing it behind the door—for later. "It's go time," he said with a smile. They hugged. They patted shoulders. They promised to find one another *after.* And then slowly, they all began to make their way in. As she began to follow, Elijah pulled her back, wanting a minute alone.

She looked up into his brilliant green eyes, wishing things had been different for them. Wishing he hadn't loved her the way he did, or that she had been able to love him the way he wanted her to. She wished a lot of things could be different. He squeezed her hand tightly.

"I just wanted to tell you—in case I can't again—I love you, Sloan." He stared down at her with longing, with a thousand more thoughts that he didn't have the time to verbalize. Quickly, though, he added, "And I'm sorry . . . I'm sorry for dragging you from the life you loved to *this* one."

She nodded up at him, realizing he had never apologized to her for all of *this*. She appreciated it—more than she had thought she would. She squeezed his hand back. "I'm sorry too. For . . . *everything*," she whispered. It was all she had to offer him now, with so little time to spare. He nodded and turned to enter.

"Elijah," she called to him. He looked over his shoulder to her.

She gave him a half smile. "I do love you too, you know. I love you in the way I know how to," she explained.

She hoped he understood. Whether he did or not, she was unsure, but he smiled back at her and led the way into the hall—the room where, once again, her life would be changed forever.

Sloan was wedged between Elijah and Chase, on a stand nearest the exit. As expected, the Order was sitting at their usual panel desk atop a stage. She locked eyes briefly with Stone, but he turned his gaze from her, engaging with Colonel Luke. To Sloan's interest, the room wasn't just filled with seniors—lining the perimeter of the room were rows of Academy sentries. She wondered if that was Romani's call, to ensure order upon making his announcement about early deployment, or Stone's, who knew that having a good majority of them in one spot would assist with *their* plans.

Finally, her eyes fell onto Romani, and slowly he stood, drawing out his long stare until the room was perfectly silent. As they stilled beneath his gaze, he smiled. "*My* senior students, I have called upon you this day to discuss a serious matter. A matter perhaps *more* serious than any we have previously addressed."

He walked out from behind the panel desk, nearing the edge of the stage. "Today, we—the *Order*—call upon you to fulfill your duty. We call upon you to leave behind the classrooms of *youth* and enter the *battlefields* of men and women."

We plan to do just that, Sloan thought wryly. She could feel the students around her begin to shift in their seats, uncertain what their leader was inferring.

"Never before have I seen such a *capable* group and I cannot ignore the crying pleas from *Dei Terra* any longer. I will *not* drag this out in colorful words and anecdotes—for you are not children, but *soldiers*. It is as simple as this," he continued, slowly raising his white-gloved hand to his chin.

"Your country *needs* you."

The room came alive with whispering speculations and Romani simply smiled on. He had an undeniable gift for riling up them up; his oratory skills made him a master manipulator, as Sloan had learned.

He nodded slowly, his chin bobbing against the back of his hand. "I would never send you to your deaths—I am only content with such plans because I have *unwavering* faith in each and every one of you, as soldiers . . . as leaders."

Sloan narrowed her gaze on the man. She imagined strangling him . . . shooting him so he could die like Donny or Kenny. Injecting him, so he could go slowly, like Tandy. Or snapping his neck—so that he could know the horror he had trained her to be capable of.

"The time is *now*. Everything you have trained for, everything your parents sent you here to achieve—it lies before you, ready for the taking," he pressed, stirring up the room with delusions of glory.

"Are you ready for deployment? Are you ready to serve?" he asked, his voice rising. Students began to clap, excited, cheering at the false hopes he provided. Sloan could see so clearly how he had once had such a tight hold on her as well. He smiled at them, allowing them to bask in their excitement. And once they quieted, he carried on. "A word from your general, *my* students." He quickly stepped aside, allowing Stone to take center stage.

Stone slowly walked out from behind the desk, crossing over the stage to where Romani had just stood. Sloan sat up straighter, certain if he were going to cue them to make their move, it would happen soon. And then, uncharacteristically, Stone clapped Romani on the back. "Well said, Marshal," he laughed. *No one ever touched Romani*. The marshal shied away from Stone.

Slowly, the general turned his attention to the room. "Your marshal is right . . . of all whom I have trained, you seniors have been my finest. You all have a unique determination, a fierce loyalty, an independence and a courage . . . a courage I didn't—*couldn't*—have taught you. A courage that grows from within. A courage that is born in the heart."

His quiet voice and beautiful words carried over them all, and even those who weren't Others felt humbled—silenced—by the magnitude of his compliment.

"You are indeed ready for war . . ." He began to pace. A man of few words, his drawn-out speech was beginning to markedly irritate Romani.

"Some of you are prepared for *more* than war. You're prepared for life, prepared to raise families, to love and truly live . . ." He stopped, glancing into the stands, finding Sloan. She held his familiar gaze.

"You are all prepared to have that which this Academy seeks to *take away* from you." At Stone's words, Romani spun, glaring at his general, sending him a warning stare. And in that moment—Sloan finally understood.

She knew what he was doing and she had no way of stopping it. If she moved, it would spark the movement.

"I've watched you all grow up and my only regret is that I couldn't have been honest with you sooner. I wish I could have done something to save you from *this place*, to save you from becoming the sort of soldiers they would have us make you," he continued, his cracking voice drawing on them all.

If there was ever a man who had earned the loyalty of every student in this room, it was General Walt Stone. He had trained them—he had raised them.

Romani stormed over. "I think that is *quite* enough!"

But Stone spun on him wildly. "I am nearly done, Marshal." He turned from Romani and once again honed in on Sloan, holding her in his grey eyes, speaking to her and her alone. "You're going to be just fine, kid. I promise."

Silent tears trailed down Sloan's face. *Please, no. . .*

Stone spun around to face the Order, his gaze falling onto the only one who stood—Colonel Christopher Don Luke. Stone took a large breath, his massive shoulders heaving. "It was you; it was always you." The colonel clapped a hand over his heart—he was crying.

Sloan craned forward, trying to will Stone into changing his mind. No rebellion was worth *this*— *nothing* was worth *this*. She would live out her life here, she would serve Romani, they all would do anything to stop him from doing *this*.

But it was too late. Stone spiraled back around. "Senior students of the Academy—*you have been fooled!* You were all abducted as children, brought here by *this* man!" he yelled, furiously pointing at Romani.

The Order looked on in shock. A handful of students stood. Romani lunged, feral, at Stone, but their general easily deflected, holding the small man in an arm lock. He continued to yell, as the sentries marched towards the stage . . .

"You have been trained here to fight *for* the enemy—

your families are searching for you! You have a choice! Do not be what we made you—get away!"

Romani fought to break free from Stone. *"Guards!"*

The sentries circled, storming the stage. In the mess of it all, she could still hear him. *"GO! Leave this place now!"*

Elijah abruptly stood. "NOW!" And at his cry, all forty-three leaped to their feet, chaos breaking out in the room. Elijah grabbed Sloan, fighting her towards the exit when, despite any plans, she struggled to get to Stone. She wriggled in his arms, forcing herself to turn back, forcing herself to get to Stone somehow. She could see him—in the mess of everything—she could see him. He was on his knees. Romani was yelling. The Order was holding someone back. A gun was trained on his head.

"NO!" Sloan screamed. Elijah whirled her around in his arms, forcing her to look away as the shot rang out.

It took six of the boys to hold the doors shut against their screaming peers, fighting to break out. Edward rammed the discarded tire iron through the handles— temporarily trapping them. It would give the Others just enough time to get to their positions, and by the time the seniors broke free, it would give *them* enough time to either stay or follow. Elijah spun. "Go, Sloan! Get to my Skyshell as soon as you can!"

She looked around her group. She scanned over the bobbing, running heads of those panicked students who had escaped—she saw him nowhere. And she knew what she had to do. Stone had given his life for the cause—how could she abandon the mission he had died for?

She spun on her heel and took off, running with Chase and Joss, Corbin and Banks in tow. It didn't take them long to reach the armory and Chase easily brought down the two sentries standing guard as Joss opened the safe room. She followed him in and they each grabbed their assault rifles, ammunition and a spare handgun. She pulled on a thigh holster, locking in the handgun, and shoved as much extra ammunition as she could into her pockets.

"Let's go!" she yelled at the boys and within an instant, they had taken off, sprinting back down the corridor for the nearest pod. It didn't take long before they were in the Infirmary. At their sudden entrance, the hospital staff fled—abandoning their tasks at hand in a flurry of fear. The entire Academy now knew something was happening. The five of them ran down the tight corridor, hefting along their weapons, following the mental blueprint Edward had mapped for them.

They ran in a single file up a flight of spiral stairs, let by Chase, who had Edward's key card. A burst of sunlight blinded Sloan as he pushed open an escape hatch, and just like that, they were on the graveled roof. She trotted over to the edge of the roof and looked down—they had an eagle-eye view from here. She could see the large Odyssey Skyshells, some of them already lowering their back trays to load the children. She could see

the guards rushing in from the gate, and to her amaze-
ment, they were being resisted by guards and students
who hadn't been Others. Which meant two things—
the seniors had escaped the hall and Stone's final words
had truly impacted them.

She knelt to the ground, setting up her rifle, securing her precision scope and mounting it on her quickly
assembled tripod. She loaded her rounds, crouched
down, found her sight—and took aim. *This is for you.*

The ivory sentries rushed the hangar and she took
a deep breath. She thought of Tandy—and she fired.
Pulling the lever, she opened the breech, ramming
it forward to reload. They only had a matter of minutes left. She took aim and, seeing Kenny's face, fired.
Reload. She thought of Kevin Young—and fired. She
could see Donny—and fired. And finally, she could see
Stone—and she fired.

Guard after guard fell, bursts of cherry burgeon-
ing from their white uniforms. It was horrifying . . .
and it was necessary. She looked into her scope and
scanned the tarmac. She saw Edward, two children in
his arms, his medical supplies hauled over his shoulder, sprinting to Jo's Odyssey. She found Elijah—he
was perched on the loading tray, pulling kids up to
him from Kristin, on the fifth Odyssey in the line. The
children were reluctant, terrified and screaming. She
saw Jack get hoisted up and she felt a wave of relief
wash through her.

"We need to get out of here!" Corbin yelled from his
spot. He was right. The masses of children were being

boarded—they didn't have long to get down there and board themselves. She didn't have long to find him.

Shots fired out wildly behind them—sentries were trying to get on the roof. Sloan spun over to see Corbin and Banks dealing with the situation. "Definitely time to get moving!" Banks called.

Sloan leaped to her feet, abandoning her assault rifle and pulling out her 9 mm. She leaped over the bodies of the sentries Joss and Corbin had taken down, and ducked into the escape hatch. Chase led the way, navigating them to the unfamiliar service pod Edward had suggested they get to. Sloan, 9 mm in hand, took the high aim, Joss the low.

Sentries appeared on every corner. Sloan fired at will, nearly deafening them all in the small corridor. They rounded the corner—two more appeared. Chase leaped on one—Joss took care of the other. Sloan leaped past them, dialing in the pod code, and as they all fell in, the doors closed around them just in time—a spray of bullets denting the thick metal.

"We need to get going," Chase reaffirmed. Sloan wiped her brow against her sleeve. She tried to push the image of Stone out of her mind. Had anyone else known that by *distraction* he had meant self-sacrifice? Had Elijah known?

The pod doors opened and the sound of the mayhem in the garage was an assault on her ears: the cries of children, the gunfire, the heavy whirring turbines. They were behind Donny's office and slowly, they each crept out into the madness. She kept close to the wall and snuck up to a sleek all-terrain vehicle. She trained her 9 mm over the hood, taking aim on the sentries, and fired. The familiar slick sound of pod doors drew her eyes—the main pod had opened up and a handful of guards poured out. She fired at will.

A rush of heavy return fire had her duck low. She glanced over her shoulder; Chase was perched at the office door, firing. Joss knelt beside him. Banks and Corbin rushed in, appearing at her side. She glanced around at all the chaos—the destruction. Small fires had erupted from engines, a child's scream ripped through her, the never-ending explosions of gunfire echoed all around, and the droning engines of the Odysseys surrounded them with a muted backdrop.

"I've got this. You advance!" Banks yelled, leaping over the hood of the vehicle. Sloan lurched up, watching him, 9 mm in his one hand, hunting blade in his other. She couldn't help but briefly wonder if he had picked that up in the armory—or taken it off one of the many bodies that had fallen before them today.

"Let's move!" Chase yelled, running to her side. She bolted forward, keeping her body low against the next row of vehicles. She checked her clip and reloaded. A muffled cry drew her eye up. An angry assault of bullets and Banks had fallen, lifeless, onto the bodies of his victims.

Raising her weapon, she fired at the guards. Bodies mounding—lifeless sentries scattered across the tarmac, many of whom she had killed. Many of the Others. They were many and motionless—lying like fallen leaves. Sloan quickly noted that there were no more children in sight. They had all boarded—and the last remaining were her, Chase, Joss and Corbin.

And Jared.

"Get to the fifth one down—it's Elijah's!" she yelled to the boys, and without hesitation they took off. She waited back, scanning the tarmac, slowly stepping out from behind the vehicle. Any calm that she had felt previously had completely dissipated. It was go time. And she didn't know—

"SLOAN!"

His familiar voice tore through her. She whirled around, until she saw him. He leaped over the piled-up bodies. He had a streak of blood across his head, his shirt was torn, and his eyes were wild. And he ran to her.

"Jared, come *on!*" she urged, reaching out her hand to him. In an instant he was in front of her.

"What's going on? What happened—Stone's *dead*," he rambled crazily.

"I know—I will tell you everything, but we have to go!"

She grabbed his hand and lurched him forward onto the tarmac. "Go where—Sloan, this crazy! They're saying you're defectors."

She turned, looking into his big blue eyes. "I will explain *later*," she promised, trying to pull him on.

"No—*no*—we can't! It's treason." He fought her, holding her back.

She spun on him. "Jared—do you trust me?"

This was it. This had been the downfall of their relationship—and after everything, here it was, coming to the forefront at the downfall of their Academy. He looked her over and she could practically see him contemplating an answer.

And finally, he spoke. "*Yes.*"

She wrenched him forward, running for the Odyssey. They ran across the tarmac and as a sentry appeared in the distance, Sloan felt a sharp tear run through her shoulder. She released Jared's hand—raised her weapon and fired.

They were so nearly there. She fought against the powerful wind coming off the Odysseys. Twenty paces left. She forced her legs forward—her arm felt on fire. Leaning out of the tray from the Odyssey was Chase, his arm outstretched for her. Ten paces. She stumbled in a slick of oil and blood. Jared hauled her to her feet. Five paces.

Three paces.

Two. And her hand was in Chase's. With a mighty heave from Jared—she was on the tray. Chase pulled and she scrambled with her legs, finally boarding. She turned around for Jared but he wasn't there.

"JARED!"

He stumbled into view, fighting a sentry who had seemingly appeared from nowhere. The guard struck at him violently. Sloan reached for weapon—but it was gone. Fallen from her when she slipped.

Elijah was beginning to move the Odyssey forward. "JARED!" she screamed.

Jared spun, landing a roundhouse kick against the sentry. The guard went down and Jared scanned for her—his eyes locking in on hers. Elijah kept the aircraft moving—gaining pace.

Jared ran and with a forceful leap, managed to land heavily against the tray—catching her wrist. His weight was too much; she could feel a burning in her shoulder and a straining in her abdomen—the baby.

"Chase—help me!"

He looked to her and hesitated. "He's one of *them*—let him go, Sloan!"

She glared at him before turning her gaze back to Jared. His eyes were panicked as he scrambled to get footing on the metal tray.

"*Never!*"

Her stomach buckled—her body warning her off the strain.

"Dammit, Chase—*I'm pregnant*. Now help me!"

She turned her gaze to him and found his shocked stare, his mouth slightly ajar, his eyes wide. And then he moved to her side. He grabbed Jared's wrist and helped, hauling him on board. Jared fell into her arms, rolling them back.

He sat up slowly as the tray began to close. He pulled her up. She felt dizzy and nauseous. She looked to her shoulder—blood was streaming from her. A gunshot wound. Her hand instinctively fell to her stomach. Her vision began to blur. Jared's face was all she could see. His voice all she could hear.

"*You're what?*"

She closed her eyes. He was on board. They were all on board—leaving this place. She hadn't left him behind. Which, really, when she thought about it, came as no surprise at all—Sloan Radcliffe had never been able to walk away from Jared Dawson.

ACKNOWLEDGMENTS

Having completed this, my first book, I have learned a great deal about the process of book writing, editing, publishing, drafting and re-drafting. Authors create stories, but it is only once they have the assistance of incredible professionals does a book get created. I would like to thank Richard Curtis, my wonderful and patient agent, who has been with me every step of the way. Without his guidance I would be lost—he has been fundamental in transforming the book from rough draft to polished manuscript. Richard took a great leap of faith with my piece; he saw past the messiness, typical of a first-time author, and envisioned what the story could become. He had my full trust from day one and I could not dream of a better mentor. Furthermore, I would like to thank David Pomerico and his entire team at Harper Voyager. David, from his first look at the book, could see what I had written and what I *wanted* to be writing, and helped me put my vision into words. David showed me how to take a step back and reconnect with the essence of the piece, and for this I am forever grateful. I would also like to thank the incredible group of editors I have had the privilege of working with during this time. Betsy Mitchell, Jena Karmali, Joan Burkeitt, and everyone else who leant their time and skill to this piece—you make writers look good. I would also like to thank my family, without whom I would never have been able to achieve this. Your patience and support—your late night reading and note making—well, I couldn't have done it without you. In particular, I would like to thank my mother, for her unwavering strength, love and guidance. Thank you for giving us your all. I would like to thank my grandparents for their incredible literary achievements and their support of my own writing pursuits. I would like to thank my godfather John, for always supporting me. Finally, I would like to thank Jamie, for telling me that if I knew what I wanted to do with my life, why would I waste my time doing anything else. From the bottom of my heart, I thank you all.

ABOUT THE AUTHOR

R. H. SCOTT, born 1991, has spent the better part of her life traveling with her mother and sisters. Having lived on three continents by the age of twenty-one, she developed a unique interest in differing societies and psychology. Scott completed a BA in sociology and socio-legal studies and is currently working on her MS in experimental psychology. The granddaughter of two published authors, Scott has had a lifelong passion for writing. Outside of her academic endeavors, Scott writes full-time and enjoys spending time with her family, traveling and reading.

Discover great authors, exclusive offers, and more at hc.com.